HORROR UNCUT

Tales of Social Insecurity
and Economic Unease

READ ORDER

2	43	9
79	99	86
215	193	110
71	204 (11)	55
125		176
166 (10)		

HORROR UNCUT

Tales of Social Insecurity and Economic Unease

Edited by

Joel Lane & Tom Johnstone

HORROR UNCUT
Tales of Social Insecurity and Economic Unease

First published in 2014 by Gray Friar Press.
9 Abbey Terrace, Whitby,
North Yorkshire, YO21 3HQ, England.
Email: gary.fry@virgin.net
www.grayfriarpress.com

Typesetting and design by Gary Fry

ISBN: 978-1-906331-46-7

TABLE OF CONTENTS

Foreword by Tom Johnsone   1

A Cry for Help by Joel Lane   *2*

The Battering Stone by Simon Bestwick   *9*

The Ballad of Boomtown by Priya Sharma   *23*

The Lucky Ones by John Llewellyn Probert   *43*

The Sun Trap by Stephen Hampton   *55*

Only Bleeding by Gary McMahon   *71*

The Lemmy / Trump Test by Anna Taborska   *79*

Falling into Stone by John Howard   *86*

Ptichka by Laura Lauro   *99*

The Devil's Only Friend by Stephen Bacon   *110*

The Procedure by David Williams   *125*

Pieces of Ourselves by Rosanne Rabinowitz   *134*

A Simple Matter of Space by John Forth   *166*

The Privilege Card by David Turnbell   *176*

The Ghost at the Feast by Alison Littlewood   *193*

The Opaque District by Andrew Hook   *204*

No History of Violence by Thana Niveau   *215*

Afterword by Tom Johnstone   222

Contacts   242

Foreword
By Tom Johnstone

The horrors in this book come from the imaginations of some of the finest writers currently working in the field, and depict a world that may be all too familiar to many: a world of poverty and deprivation, of austerity and exploitation.

Some take place in the present, and portray characters scarred by the policies of both the present and previous governments. Others project a harsh future that doesn't seem very far off.

Some of them may upset you, others may amuse even as they enrage you.

Here are ghost stories, *contes cruelles*, tales of dark fantasy, weird tales, strange stories, and some that just turn the conventions of the horror genre on their head, to challenge the present political and economic orthodoxy of 'deficit reduction'.

I believe this anthology breaks new ground, with tales of terror and the supernatural about the 'bedroom tax', food banks and the dismantling of the NHS, ushering in a new era of socially engaged but entertaining and darkly funny horror fiction, which may not change the world but will, I hope, change the way we look at it.

A Cry for Help
By Joel Lane

The train journey to Harrogate took nearly four hours, including an hour in the metal and concrete maze that was Leeds Station. It was an overcast day; the sun flashed occasionally through the leaden clouds like a police car on a city street. Between the railway line and the bare fields were various small industrial units that resembled factories without walls: engines, pipes, steel walkways suspended in mid-air. Plastic huts where people stayed.

Carl should have been looking through the conference programme, briefing himself on who to talk to and where to be. Networking didn't happen by itself. But as usual on trains, he kept shifting into and out of sleep. There'd been too many late nights recently. He needed to sharpen up his attitude. The conference would help. Janice had never understood why work was so important to him. It did more than pay the rent: it kept him sane.

The moments when he fell asleep, or almost fell asleep, while travelling were when he really missed her. His phone and laptop enabled him to contact everyone who counted - but who did he want to talk to? There was no e-hand you could reach out and touch, no e-mouth you could kiss. At least not yet. He travels fastest who travels alone. He didn't need company. What he did need, he wasn't sure.

By the time he reached Harrogate, night had fallen; the town centre had the trustworthy glow of electric light. Carl walked down through the main street, past the elaborate facades of theme bars and restaurants. The pink silhouette of a crouching woman with cat ears and a tail advertised a gentlemen's club. A camera flashed on the steps of a hotel, where a young couple were leaning into a stage-managed kiss. The air was thin and cold.

Beyond the conference centre, the streetlamps were further apart and the buildings mostly dark. Trees, stripped by autumn, trembled in the headlights of passing cars. Rain brushed Carl's face gently. His hotel was set back from the road, a small renovated building with flawless off-white pillars. As he walked up the path, carrying his briefcase and overnight bag, an early firework exploded behind the hotel and wept silver tears over its roof.

His room, on the third floor, turned out to be a twin room charged at single rate. The wall behind the beds was plasterboard; he hoped his neighbours were quiet. The TV offered terrestrial and satellite channels, plus classic films and pay-per-view porn. He wanted to lie down and catch a few minutes' sleep, but the room depressed him: it was too obviously prefabricated, like a stage set.

Hotels always made him think of Janice. How she'd make herself at home in a double bed, turning her head from side to side as if they were already making love. How utterly still she was when sleeping. One of the signs that things were coming apart was that she stopped sleeping well. Had he done the right thing to let her go? Or would it have been even worse?

Janice lived on her own, and had recently lost her job. It was a fortnight before they found her. The unanswered phone calls led her sister to contact the police. Her neighbours had put the smell down to a blocked drain. She'd opened the veins in her wrists. There'd been a note, but Carl had no idea what it said. Her family hadn't invited him to Janice's funeral - just sent him a cutting about her from the *Express & Star*.

It still chilled him to think about, nearly a year later. He tried not to. Shit happened, people broke up. People broke down. Janice had been quite irrational at times - and not only those times, though mostly then. He wasn't responsible for that. The real world was there to be lived in.

3

The rain was heavier when he left the hotel. To save getting wet, he ate at the nearest restaurant: an up-market Italian place that served pizzas with balsamic vinegar and olive oil. His beer came in a frosted glass that stuck to his hand. Despite its cost (his company expense account took the pain away), the food didn't seem to taste of anything. Through a glass pane, he could see two chefs at work in the kitchen. One of them must have spilt some oil, because a flare like a magnesium ribbon lit up the corner of his eye. He could still see it when he rubbed the eyelid, and soon he smelt the burning. His mouth felt dry.

Leaving the restaurant, Carl decided a short walk would clear his head. The rain had stopped. He ran through the essentials of his presentation as he strolled up Cheltenham Parade towards the train station. *We see private health insurance as a contract between provider and customer, a doorway to security and wellness for all. We're taking the ambitions of the discredited NHS model and rebranding them for a society freed from the shackles of state control.* The rest was PowerPoint and some free DVDs of the corporate video for potential contractees.

The dryness had spread to his throat. A bad cough was the last thing he needed for tomorrow. Carl dropped into a crowded basement bar and downed a quick vodka and tonic, then another. A few young women in business suits were gathered at the bar; their eyes and teeth gleamed as they talked, but the music soaked up their voices. He was getting too old to fancy his chances, these days. How much did the porn channel at the hotel cost? But however they disguised it on his bill (and he wouldn't claim it), Carl's manager would know what he'd done. He didn't want to pay for an escort - and it worried him that he was even considering that. At what point did you become capable of something?

Suddenly angry with himself, Carl walked out of the bar and turned back towards the hotel. Except apparently not, because – as often with alcohol – he'd swapped left and right on his inner map. A few minutes later, he was completely lost. An old man was standing under a railway bridge just ahead, smoking a thin roll-up. Maybe he'd know the way back to the station. The smoker looked up at the roof of the tunnel, then turned away. Carl ran to catch him up.

Under the bridge, rainwater was dripping through brickwork. Mercury tubes in wire cages gave off a weak unreal light. The old man had stopped to put out his cigarette underfoot. He was wearing an old check jacket of the kind Terry-Thomas would have worn. Carl stepped past him and said, "Excuse me. Do you know the way to the train station?"

The old man glanced at him. "Can you help me?" he said. There was some kind of growth over his left eye. He fumbled in his jacket pocket, took out a coil of plastic-covered wire. One end was tied crudely in a noose. "I need to fix this to something." He gestured towards one of the wire cages. "Do you think that will take my weight?"

Carl couldn't stop himself looking up. He doubted it. "I'm sorry," he said. "I can't help you." As he walked on, embarrassment stiffening his face, he wondered how long the guy had been waiting there. How many people he'd asked.

There was no-one in the street beyond the bridge. None of the houses were lit. This was clearly a less wealthy part of town: the cars were grimy, the houses narrow and run-down, the front gardens overgrown. But he couldn't face going back past the old man. There had to be other routes. Carl walked up the road, turned right. A skinny teenager in a combat jacket was waiting to cross the road as a long goods vehicle passed. Carl felt his hands tense involuntarily. He could do some damage if he had to defend himself. "Hey," he called.

The youth turned slowly. His face was stained with yellow light. "Please help us," he said. Carl stared at him, unable to answer. The boy pointed to the roadway. His left leg was distorted, the foot caught in a futile dance step.

5

"Push us under a lorry. I can't jump." Another long vehicle approached and he leaned forward, his face taut with longing. Carl backed away, then turned and ran.

He was afraid of not finding the bridge, but panic restored his sense of direction. The old man was still waiting there; Carl ran straight past him. A few minutes later, he reached the cluster of bus shelters outside the train station. A black cab was approaching; he waved it down. The driver didn't ask him for help.

A couple of large brandies in the hotel bar took the edge off his fear and let his exhaustion soak through. The amber light of Remy Martin glowed in his unsteady hand. Near midnight, he stumbled to the lift and went up to his room. He chose the left-hand bed, because he'd always slept on the left when sharing his bed with Janice. She liked to be nearer the wall.

The couple in the next room argued all night, the wall too thin to keep their business private. Fireworks went off somewhere behind the building. Carl's mattress was flimsy and too short for him; it felt like a bunk bed. He got up a few times to drink water or piss, a cycle he often fell into when tired. At last he drifted into a dull, inert blankness that passed for sleep.

The sound of ragged breathing woke him. He opened his eyes and saw two figures on the other bed. Just enough light filtered through the curtains to show him one figure was a man. The other was a blurred grey thing, terribly incomplete. They were locked in some intense congress, both a death-struggle and an act of love. He watched them for a couple of minutes, afraid to prove the vision real by moving. Then his alarm clock began to shrill. He turned it off, and when he looked back the other bed was empty. Then he switched on the light. The unused bedspread was smooth, but flakes of ash were scattered over it.

*

The conference was a long, hard day of networking - or, as they called it in these parts, chiselling. Shaking hands, exchanging business cards and corporate brand messages. Carl's presentation was well received and earned him a pocketful of contacts, at least half a dozen of which he expected would lead to business. By the end of the day, he'd filled three pages of his notebook with other people's thoughts to be digested, assimilated and passed off as his own. From a health insurance consultant: *The American model is a visionary healthcare system that lights up the way for Europe.* And from a university lecturer in marketing: *Health and safety legislation is an attempt to mimic the effect of market forces in a state-run economy.*

As he left the conference centre, the streets were getting dark. His throat was burning from the dry air and the amount of talking he'd done. But if he stopped for a drink, he wouldn't get back to Solihull before midnight. He could get a beer and a sandwich when he changed trains at Leeds. A hard day, but worth it – and not just from his company's point of view. It helped him not to think about Janice. Coming through like a bruise.

He was near the station when a violent flare drowned the street in red-gold light. No sound followed it. Was that a firework or something going up in flames? Or the night itself splitting open to reveal its fiery heart? He kept walking, but the light didn't come back. By the time its afterimage had faded, he was at the bridge. A young woman was standing in the tunnel.

This time he didn't run away. There were people who needed his help. Their voices, like the rose of fire, had been trying to reach him for a long time. Whether they knew it or not. The girl under the bridge had ash-blonde hair; she was dressed in a long fabric coat. As he came closer, he could see that her hands were severely burned. The fingers were shrunken claws. She turned to face him, holding a razor blade in the scarred palm of her left hand. "Help me," she said. "Please." She mimed putting the blade to her right

7

wrist. The sliver of metal fell to the pavement.

Carl looked at the darkness of her eyes. He crouched to pick up the razor. The light from a passing car flared in it, blue and white. He stood up and touched the girl's thin arm. "That'll be fifty pounds," he said. "I can take a card."

The Battering Stone
By Simon Bestwick

The winter of 2005 was the bitterest I can recall. It hadn't helped that my central heating had gone west and took, for one reason or another, a couple of months to fix. Christmas was shaping up to be a lonely one, but I found I almost looked forward to that. I'd got to the point where I liked my own company again.

But it wasn't going to be a quiet Christmas; peace on earth, goodwill to all men (or anyone else) didn't seem to get a look-in these days. Not that DS Dougie Poole had called me in about a murder.

"Suicide," I said flatly, shaking in the cold and trying not to sound pissed off. Unsuccessfully.

Poole shrugged. "Suicide."

"So what am I doing here?" In the past two years, I'd brushed up more than once against the just plain weird. On several occasions, Poole had been involved, and now insisted on calling me in on anything even vaguely off the wall. If I was of any help, it tended to be more by luck than judgement, but that didn't stop him. This time, though, I didn't get it.

The crime scene was a vacant lot off Salford's Chapel Street, in the shadow of two ugly 1960s tower-blocks, big blocks of stone planted round its perimeter. The body lay sprawled in the centre. A white dust of frost rimed it and the lot's thin grass.

"Take a closer look," said Poole.

"What am I supposed to see?"

"How about the big hole in the ground?" Poole's patience was thin without his nicotine fix; I guessed he was trying to quit again. I gave him another hour, max.

"OK. What about it?"

9

Poole pinched the bridge of his nose. "Cause of death to be confirmed, but the poor bastard's head's caved in."

"And he did it himself?"

"Looks like. No sign of a struggle. Never is."

"Never?" The first stirrings of something in my gut; I couldn't tell, anymore, if it was interest or apprehension. "This isn't the first?"

"Fifth in a week."

"Jesus."

Poole half-smiled. "Interested now?"

I grunted. He nodded, looked back towards the limp, sprawled body. "I can tell," he said. "I always can."

The dead man's name was Anthony Hutchins. He was seventeen, recently made redundant from an electronics firm in Irlam feeling the first pinch of a decelerating economy. No history of depression, a stable enough family background, even a girlfriend he'd been going steady with. No breakups, arguments, not even a tiff. He'd just bought her an engagement ring. Wedding date not set yet, but that was only a matter of time. Had been.

If I had to play psychic detectives, at least I got to skip the worst parts of the detective side: the families, the loved ones. God knew I had enough dark waters in my own past to deal with.

Post mortem confirmed that by all indications, Hutchins had died after ramming his head into a hard rock. Not one of the stone blocks around the vacant lot. This was sharp-edged, and a different kind of stone; tiny particles of flint had been found in the head wounds. Indications were it'd taken three or four blows to finish the job. Cause of death: cerebral haemorrhage from a fractured skull. I winced, reading the report in my cold flat, huddled by the glow of a plugged-in halogen heater, wrapped in umpteen layers of coats and sweaters and gulping coffee in an effort to defrost.

The others: Ade Mkoyo, a student from the University of Salford struggling to pay off student debts; Lucy Ackridge, who'd just broken up with her boyfriend (I know the feeling, Lucy, it hurts, but this much?); Stanley Nicholson, a security guard nearing retirement; and Donna Collier, housewife and mother, on anti-depressants.

All at low points, and god knew the suicide rate skyrocketed over the festive season. But even so; like Anthony Hutchins, they all had means of support. Ade Mkoyo had work, a bar job and some temping over the holidays; he lived frugally, kept his head above water. Lucy Ackridge had been on a couple of dates with a work colleague and her family said she'd been brightening up. Stanley Nicholson, money saved and looking at retirement to the Costa Del Sol, and Donna Collier's depression had seemed under control. It didn't fit.

And then there was the way they'd chosen to check out. All found in vacant lots, or patches of parkland, dotted between Chapel Street and the Height, all killed by apparently self-inflicted blows to the head. And all found lying beside a big raw hole in the earth, their blood dripping down into it.

Traces of flint in all the wounds.

A big sharp edge. Not a piece of rock you could hold in one hand. They'd grabbed onto something fixed in the ground and head-butted it again and again, till they collapsed and died in the winter frost. Except for Lucy Ackridge, who'd staved in her skull on the first attempt. A lucky blow. Or unlucky, depending on how you looked at it.

A rock fixed in the earth; a picture of it formed in my head. Something like a huge fang, made out of chipped rock, like one of those old flint arrow- or axe-heads you saw in museums. Rooted in the ground, and then taken away.

"Some kind of ritual killing?" I suggested to Poole. We'd met up in Mulligan's, an Irish bar in Manchester where they served a decent Bushmills. He was doing the buying. He always did when he brought me in on a case.

11

He offered me a cigarette – his abstinence never lasted long, as I'd predicted. I waved it away; I was trying to cut back myself. He lit up and looked moody.

"Know what you mean," he said. "All dying the same way, and that rock… Someone else must've been involved – put the damn thing there and taken it away. But – no sign of a struggle, remember? All the indications are, mad as it looks, they did it of their own accord."

"Drugs?" I suggested.

"Can't you keep your mind on the job for five min – Oh. See what you mean. No. We ran blood tests. The Hutchins lad'd been at the waccy baccy a bit the past few weeks, but who isn't these days?" Poole shook his head at the youth of Salford's declining morals, then went on. "But nothing that could've caused anything like that."

I knew too much weed could cause psychiatric problems – one reason I rarely smoked the stuff myself these days – but most of the other victims'd come up clean. Ade Mkoyo'd been a Jehovah's Witness, didn't even drink.

"Hypnosis, maybe?" I ventured. Sounded stupid, even as I said it. Making someone quack like a duck every time they heard Abba play *Dancing Queen* was one thing, but braining themselves on a flint spike was a different bottle of newts altogether.

Poole shook his head. "Maybe it's witchcraft, summat like that."

"Witchcraft?" I nearly choked on my whiskey.

"Wouldn't've thought you'd be the one to make mock of that, Paul, lad. Besides," Poole nodded Salford-wards, "it's Lancashire, you know. Witch country. Pendle Witches and so forth."

A bunch of old women condemned by prejudice and stupidity, I nearly said, then decided that'd get us nowhere. Something was going on, that much was obvious. And Poole expected me to have an answer, and as usual I had nothing of the kind, just the hope history would repeat itself and I'd stumble across something useful.

12

"Another?" asked Poole.

"Why not?" I glanced at his packet of Embassy. "Mind if I pick one?"

My abstinence rarely outlasted his.

We went our separate ways as the sky dimmed and streetlights blinked on. I caught the bus back towards my flat in Swinton, then got off in Chapel Street by the vacant lot where Anthony Hutchins' body had been found.

Scraps of shrivelled incident tape blew in the low wind. Floral tributes lay heaped at one corner of the lot, sheltered in the lee of one of the big stone blocks. I crouched, glanced at them. *Mum and Dad; Angie* (that'd been the girlfriend); *Daz, Gaz, Jez, Wayne and Deano*. I rose and stepped into the lot, walking to the hole. A few bare trees were black against a sky the colour of damp ash.

I didn't know what I'd expected to find, or feel, there. I didn't think I'd find it, and all I felt was a sort of generalised melancholy at the waste of it all. I vaguely remember the peaks and troughs of life at seventeen. Things which you had more of a perspective on at thirty-four loomed a lot larger. Had it been as simple as that for Anthony? Maybe, or Lucy; maybe even for Ade. But Donna Collier, or Stanley Nicholson? No.

I looked around. Chapel Street was changing. Newer buildings were springing up; offices and housing for yuppies. Slowly but surely, Salford was being gentrified. They called it regeneration, but the people who lived there were being inexorably squeezed out, by rising council tax, compulsory purchase orders or just plain rehousing if they were council tenants. They'd be dumped somewhere else, a sink estate nearby, to push the property values down somewhere else. And build a new slum for the developers to muscle in on, with the Council's enthusiastic connivance. The same old racket.

"Bloody parasites," I muttered to myself.

But they won, of course. It broke up the communities they preyed on. Groups of atomised individuals are much, much easier prey than a pack or herd.

Bastards. I could see what was happening, and I wasn't the only one, but from where I stood, there seemed no stopping it.

Not exactly happy thoughts. Much longer here, and I'd be ramming my head into a big bloody rock myself. That thought stopped me in my tracks. Was that what Anthony had felt, and Lucy, Ade, Donna, Stanley? Was I feeling some lingering after-trace of what they had?

There might be something there, I thought, but I couldn't see it. The whiskies I'd downed with Poole weren't helping in that regard. I was turning to go when I saw it.

At the edge of the vacant lot stood a row of shops. The wall of the nearest faced me; the upper half was covered by an advertising poster above a Clear Channel sign, but the bare brick below it swarmed with graffiti.

Most of them were the usual declarations of love or threats of vengeance, but there was one, a new one, that stood out. It was in plain white, painted over older messages. Fresh paint, not long dried, I reckoned. Not a scrawl, either, but neat, careful, painstakingly done block capitals, like *NO PARKING* or *PRIVATE PROPERTY.* That kind.

It said, simply, *BEWARE THE BATTERING STONE.*

It was dark when I got home, but a couple of strong black coffees later I grabbed a torch and, muffled against the cold, went back out.

First step was Lightoaks Park in the Height, where Lucy Ackridge's body had been found. The hole in the ground was behind the railings that fenced off the duck-pond, in amongst the stand of trees nearby. Her body had rolled into the water and was taken for a drowning at first; puffed up from immersion and already nibbled at by the fish. I flashed the torch around, but there was nothing here, nothing to write on.

I found what I was looking for on a wall near the war memorial. The same message as at Chapel Street. The words leapt out at me again, big and pale: *The Battering Stone*.

I climbed the railings and made my way out.

Ade Mkoyo had died in Peel Park on the University campus. The message had been daubed on half a dozen walls there. Donna Collier's body had been on another vacant lot, where a couple of tower blocks had stood, in the clutch of them behind Salford Market and Pendleton Shopping City that the locals called 'Beirut'. I saw another half dozen daubings on walls there. I also saw a knot of teenagers watching me, and starting to move my way. I headed double-quick for the next bus stop on the A6, and decided to finish my search the next day.

It was easily done, and soon checked out. Stanley Nicholson's body had been found in Lower Broughton, another vacant lot by the industrial estate. It was painted on a fence across the road: *Beware The Battering Stone*.

I rang Poole and told him what I'd found. He wasn't particularly impressed.

"Sounds like a graffiti artist to me," he said. "Don't see the fuss."

"The battering stone, Dougie," I said. "Sounds pretty specific."

"Good guess, that's all. Not exactly a state secret how they all died. Folk tales." But he was mulling. "Want me to see if we can catch whoever's up to it in the act?"

"No," I almost yelped. "You'd just scare them off. They'd've come to see you themselves if they thought you'd believe 'em."

"Believe them about what?"

"Why did you get me in on this in the first place, Dougie?" I asked pointedly, and waited.

15

He let out a long sigh. "Weird shit."

"Yup. So try leaving this one to me, eh?"

"Fair enough, Sherlock."

Sherlock Holmes had never had to deal with the likes of this, I felt like reminding him. But something occurred to me. "Actually, though…"

"What?"

"There is *something* you could do."

"What's that?"

I decided to stake out the University campus; it was the least dangerous from my point of view, but still a high risk if there was… What? Someone, something? A cult of someones? All I had were the words *the battering stone*, and the conviction that whoever'd written it knew something.

There were still plenty of students living on campus during the holidays. Easy prey in the event of a recurrence. Of whatever it was.

Wrapped in coats, and a thermos of coffee close at hand, I huddled on the cinder-path near the river, and watched.

Soon enough, I saw it; the fitful, flickering beam of a torch, dancing away at the edge of the park. I say *soon enough*, but it couldn't've been soon enough as far as I was concerned; my fingers were already numb. I got up and crept towards the torchlight as noiselessly as I could with half-frozen limbs.

At my request, Poole had got the council in to paint out the warnings. And as I'd hoped, the painter'd come back. He or she was on a mission, to pass a warning on. I saw a short, bulky figure in a hooded coat, busily painting the B in *Battering*, and didn't hear me approach. "Evening," I called.

He spun round, dropping his tin of white paint. I leapt back from the splatter. He started to run, but I moved to block his exit. "I just want to talk," I said.

He squinted back at me. He was old, early in his seventies or older, with a thick, matted beard. His coat and hands were grimy, and his eyes were bloodshot. But they were also ferrety and bright, his movements quick. "Over a pint, lad?" he suggested, finally.

I had to laugh. "Alright, then. Over a pint."

The Crescent pub stands, funnily enough, on Salford Crescent, opposite the Irwell river, and does a good line in real ale. The old man, who gave his name as Terence (he offered no surname) was happy to tell me all over a pint or two.

"So come on," I said. "What's the battering stone?"

He shook his head sadly. "Time was, folk round here all knew about it, watched for it. But now…" He sighed.

"Come on," I said.

"Ah. Well, alright, then." His accent was proper old Lancashire, the kind you'd expect to hear in one of the local folk clubs. "Don't know exactly how long it's been round these parts. Some folk say the Romans brought it with them. Some as said it were here before then. There's been people living round these parts from that time and before, you know."

I did. Nearby was Castlefield, which'd got its name from the remains of the Roman fort there: the castle in the field. As tactfully as I could, I moved the old man on.

His beard was stained by tobacco and god knew what else. I tried not to listen to the slurping sounds as he worked on his pint and gave thanks I'd cut back on the booze, last night's session with Poole notwithstanding.

"It'd pop up when times were hard," he said. "When people had troubles, when they were low. Can imagine, can't you, there'd be plenty of that round Salford way."

For the past couple of centuries perhaps, when the Industrial Revolution'd made it a city. Pickings might've been slimmer before that… but I let it go. I wanted to hear.

"It… it *called* to folk, somehow," he said. "Folk as were feeling low. Lot of them in the Depression, when I was born. It'd call them, and they'd go to it, wherever it was.

17

And then they'd-" He mimed grabbing hold of something and driving his head against it, time and time again.

"It'd feed on that," he said. "And when times got better, it'd wait. Sleep and wait, till they were hard again."

He looked down at his nearly empty glass, turning it side to side. I took the hint and went to the bar.

"It killed my father," he said when I came back.

"What?"

"He was one of them, just one. He'd had a job... Without him, times were harder still. I had six brothers. Big families folk had then. Not much else to do on those cold winter nights." He cackled, showing rotten teeth, and poked my arm. Then the laughter was gone.

"And, of course," he said, "'cos a lot've kids wouldn't live to grow up. Like my brother Hughie. The battering stone took him too. Him, me Dad..." He shook his head, eyes going somewhere else. "...So many others, too."

According to Terence, it'd come back again, in other lean times. The late seventies and the eighties, the recession in the nineties. Plenty of grim times there, places like Langworthy, Seedley, Kersal, Charlestown. Just another body, head smashed in. An under-funded and overworked police force would've barely noticed.

"It's back again," he said. "Can't think why, though. Times aren't that hard, not yet. But mebbe cos other things're changing."

"Like?"

"Well, like Salford, lad. All getting so's it's for posh folk, now. No good for a thing like the stone, that is. Mebbe it wants to go further afield. Getting its strength up for the move..."

Poole wasn't greatly impressed.

"That's all you've got?" he demanded. "An old wives' tale from some old wino?"

18

"Well, it's more than you bloody woodentops've managed so far," I snapped back. Unwise, but I'd a bitch of a hangover from one too many last night.

"Just you bloody watch who you're calling a woodentop. And for your information, you might want to pull your finger out if you do have any bright ideas. We've got another one, last night."

"Where?"

"Lightoaks Park, again. Another student. A girl. Only this one's got a daddy who's a councillor down south with a few influential ears he can bend. And he will, which makes my life a real fucking delight."

"Sorry."

"Forget it. But if you know owt, then do something about it, alright?"

"OK, OK," I muttered to the dial tone. No point telling Poole I wasn't a magician. He'd decided I was his 'weird shit man' and therefore I was.

I had no idea what to do, until the battering stone claimed its seventh victim.

Pale in death on the slab, Terence looked very different. Shrunken. He took some recognising. But in the end I nodded. "Yes. It's him."

They drew the sheet up over his face. They'd cleaned him up a bit, but the ugly dent in his forehead, the tracks of torn and broken skin like claw marks down his face, were still there. I turned back to Poole.

"I'm sorry," he said.

"Yeah." I couldn't think of much else to say.

"What now?"

I looked at him. "Leave this one to me."

I spent the night going from murder site to murder site. The sixth victim, Fiona Edgington, had been found in Lightoaks again, while Terence's body'd turned up on the site in Lower Broughton. Maybe it was because there were seven sites now. I wondered if they'd form a pattern on a map; I hadn't thought to check. Maybe the number meant something. Or maybe not. Maybe there was no meaning to any of it, except hunger.

After a while I started greying out. I was wandering and wondering, footsore and cold, and soon enough I was on automatic pilot. And I was thinking too much; thinking about a lonely Christmas, people I missed, people I'd lost… Big chunks of time disappeared in all of that.

The next thing, I knew, I was back on Chapel Street. My fingers and feet were numb, my nose and throat burned from the winter air, and the road was silent. Up above the moon glowed in a clear sky, stars a strewing of powdered glass across it.

Whatever I'd been planning on, it wasn't getting anywhere. Time to head home. I started fumbling for my mobile.

Then I stopped, pivoted on my heel and strode into the vacant lot where Anthony Hutchins's body had been found.

Something stood in the centre of the lot, just beside where Anthony had fallen, filling the hole it'd made. It was about eight feet tall, and glisteningly black. It had edges that glittered where it caught the moon. I kept going towards it; what surprised me was how similar the thing was to what I'd imagined. Like a giant tooth, made of flint. It looked just like it'd been chipped into shape by another, equally big chunk of flint, held in an equally big hand.

The edges and the hollows fascinated me. Light gleamed and caught, dancing and cascading like water, sliding down it. It seemed so natural to put my hands *there* and *there*. The stone seemed to welcome them, moulded to fit them. And my forehead… my forehead rested against that sharp edge of flint.

One good head-butt and… Go on, Paul. Try it.

Are you mad? It'll kill me.

What if it does? You're not gonna be missed, are you? And it's not as if you're really going anywhere.

I thought of my job.

But no-one to share your life, eh, Paul? Now come on, admit it, you know you're never gonna have that again, don't you? Sonia was a one-off. Blokes like you only get one chance like that, and you blew yours. So come on. Do it. It'll be an *experience*. Give it a go. What else've you got to look forward to?

The worst part was the lure of the curiosity, to find out what it was like to smash my head into the flint. I almost did it, too. I'm not sure where it came from, the resistance to it; the other victims hadn't been much worse off than me. They'd just had a chink in their armour, a flaw to be exploited. Same as anyone else. All I was, was forewarned. Not that it'd helped Terence. But he'd been older, with the losses he'd already sustained to bring him down; maybe that was it. That, and I was also forearmed.

The ball-pein hammer came out of my pocket and I swung hard, felt the stone crack, chip and split. As fragments nicked my face, there was a noise in the air, a screeching. I swung the hammer again. Faster and faster. I can remember shouting something like "How do you like it, you bastard?" and feeling the shock of impact up my arm like one continuous jolt. The screech was deafening, and the next I knew it was done and they were loading me in back of the ambulance. The haft of the ball-pein hammer was locked in my hand. They found the iron head in the hole where the battering stone had been.

That was three days before Christmas; they let me out on Christmas Eve, treated for hypothermia and with a shed-load of last minute shopping to do.

Poole came to pick me up from the hospital. "There haven't been any more," he said awkwardly.

"Probably won't be," I said. "Not for now, anyway."

"Not for now? You didn't –"

"Kill it? How do you kill stone? But I don't think we'll see it round here again, if that's any consolation."

"Well, that's good. You did a good job, then."

"Did I?"

I'd spoken to my dad while I was in hospital; he lived up on the coast now. He'd invited me up for the holiday. I'd said yes. I'd pick up a bottle of decent whisky on my way.

I'd come to love Salford as my adoptive home, but for once I was glad to see the city lights recede behind me as the train pulled out. The battering stone wasn't gone; it'd only moved in search of a new hunting ground. Well fed, it would make its move, settle and sleep and wait. For the wheel to turn, the cycle like a season: boom and bust, let the hard times roll, when the pickings are rich and the folk are poor and run-down and so, so easy to draw in. To another sink estate, the dispossessed swirling round the plughole, drowning; to return to haunt us, to hunt the afflicted, in another place, in another, darker time.

The Ballad of Boomtown
By Priya Sharma

*I*t's estimated that in 2011 there were 2,881 semi or unoccupied housing developments in Ireland.

There was a time when we put our faith in Euros, shares and the sanctity of brick. A time when we bought our books from stores as big as barns and ate strawberries from Andalusia, when only a generation before they'd been grown on farms up the road.

The wide avenues of Boomtown were named for trees when there was grand optimism for growth. Now nothing booms in Boomtown. It's bust and broken.

I miss you. You were a lick of cream. I can still taste you.

I walk to the village on Mondays. I pull my shopping trolley the three miles there and back along the lanes. I used to drive to the supermarket, just for a pint of milk, without a thought to the cost of fuel. It doesn't matter now. I like to walk.

Sheila-na-gigs look down on me from the church walls as I pass by. These stone carvings are of women with bulging eyes and gaping mouths, displaying their private parts. These wantons are a warning against lust. Or a medieval stone mason's dirty joke.

The shop's beside the church. Deceased, desiccated flies lie between the sun faded signs. There's a queue inside. I've heard all their grumbling about prices and supplies. They decry the current government, the one before, the banks and then apportion blame abroad. Despite the orderly line and polite chatter, I can imagine these women battling it out with their meaty fists if the last bag of flour in Ireland was at stake.

23

We're not so poor as yet that we can't afford a veneer of civilised behaviour.

I put my face to the glass as the shop owner takes the last slab of beef from the chilled counter and wraps it. I wish I'd got up earlier. I would've spent half my week's grocery allowance to smell the marbled flesh sizzling in a pan.

The bell jangles as I push the door open. A few heads turn. A woman leans towards her companion and whispers in his ear. I catch the words *blow in*. I'm a Boomtown interloper, buffeted by changing fortune. There's a pause before the man looks at me. His salacious glance suggests he's heard scandalous stories.

I've no doubt a few of them recall me from before, when I first came here to talk to them about my book. There was a certain glamour in talking to me.

I take my time considering the shelves' contents while the others pay and leave. There are budget brands with unappetising photos on the cans. Boxes of cheap smelling soap powder and white bread in plastic bags. I tip what I need into my basket.

"I want freshly ground coffee."

I can't help myself. I'm the Boomtown Bitch. It's cruel. The shop owner's never done me any harm. She always offers me a slow, sweet smile. It's fading now.

"We only have instant."

"Olives then." I want my city living, here in the country. I want delicatessens and coffee bars. Fresh pastries and artisan loaves.

She shakes her head.

"Anchovies, balsamic vinegar. Risotto rice." The world was once a cauldron of plenty.

"I only have what's on the shelves."

She's struggling to contain herself in the face of my ridiculous demands. I sling the basket on the counter where it lands with a metallic thud and slide. There's a dogged precision in how she enters the price of each item into the till. She doesn't speak but turns the display to show me the

24

total, waiting as I load my shopping into the trolley. Her refusal to look at me isn't anger. There's a glimmer of unshed tears. It's not her fault. It's yours. It's mine.

I feel sick. Yet another thing that can't be undone. I try and catch her eye as I hand her a note but she's having none of it. I want to tell her that I'm sorry. It's shameful that I don't even know her name and now she'll believe the worst she's heard and won't ever smile at me again. She slides my change over the counter rather than putting it into my hand.

The bell above the door jangles as I leave.

The chieftain stood before the three sisters, flanked by men bearing swords and spears, and said, "This is my land now."

"We lived here long before you came," they replied.

"By what right do you claim it? Where's your army?"

"You can't own the land, it owns you." That was the eldest sister. "Rid yourself of such foolish desires."

"No. Everything you see belongs to me."

"Do you own that patch of sky?" the middle born said.

The chieftain was silent.

"Is that water yours?" That was the youngest. "See how it runs away from you."

"I want this land." The chieftain stamped his feet. "Look at my torque. Even metal submits to my will."

"You'll be choked by that gold around your throat." The eldest stepped forward. "You're master of ores and oxen, wheat and men alike, but not us. We're like the grass. We only bow our heads to the wind."

The chieftain looked at them, pale witches in rags with swathes of dark hair and there were the stirrings of a different sort of desire.

The chieftain and his men raped the sisters, one by one.

"See," he said, "I possess everything."

"We are ancient. We are one and we are three." The youngest covered herself with the tatters of her clothes. "We

25

were there at the world's birth. We are wedded to the earth. We don't submit. We endure."

A cold wind came in carrying rain even though it was a summer's day.

"We curse you and your greed." The middle sibling swallowed her sobs and raised her chin. "It'll grow so large that it'll devour you and your kind."

Thunderbolts cracked the sky.

"We'll dog your children's steps from womb to tomb." The eldest had the final word. "When their fortune's in decline we'll rise again. No one will be spared our wrath. Then we'll return to heal what you've rent."

The eldest gathered up the other two and retreated to a place where the hills were at their backs and enfolded themselves in stone.

The Three Sisters are a group of three stones that occupy a small plateau on the eastern side of the _____ hills in County Meath. Their history has been retold for generations in the local village of _____. There are several variations of the tale. The one I've included here is the most detailed.

— *Songs of Stones: Collected Oral Traditions of Ireland's Standing Stones* by Grainne Kennedy

I drove us from Dublin. You directed. You kept glancing at my legs as they worked the pedals, which excited me. It felt like you were touching me. Sliding your hand between my knees.

"Turn right."

The indicator winked. We were on Oak Avenue.

"Does this all belong to Boom Developments?"

"Yes."

I whistled, wanting you to know I was impressed.

"Left here." Then, "This is Acacia Drive."

26

There were diggers, trucks, the cries and calls of men. We bumped along the unfinished road. Stones crunched under the tyres and ochre dust rose around us.

"Pull over here." You buzzed, happy amongst the evidence of your success. "I asked the lads to complete some of the houses up here first."

You ran up the road towards a group of men in jeans and T-shirts. The men looked at me when you'd turned away and I could tell they'd said something smutty from the way they sniggered.

You returned, carrying hard hats and keys. "Put this on."

I refused to be embarrassed by our audience. I piled up my hair and put my hat on, back arched in mock burlesque. You took my elbow with a light touch, as if unsure of yourself. I liked that you weren't adept with women when you seemed so proficient at the rest of life. You guided me towards a house.

"Here." You unlocked the door.

Our feet rang out on the bare boards. Fresh plaster dried in shades of pink and brown.

"This model's the best of the lot. It'll be done to the highest spec."

I followed you upstairs.

"Huge master bedroom. Nice en-suite too."

It was the view that I admired most. The hills, the open sky was spread out for us. I couldn't tell you that I'd been here before your burgeoning success scarred the land. That I'd trekked for miles under rotten skies that threatened rain, across open fields carrying my notebook, cameras and a tripod. I didn't want to spoil the moment by making it anything but yours.

You should've known though. If you'd looked at the copy of the book I'd given you, my own modest enterprise, you'd have seen. You weren't interested in history, not the ones of Ireland's standing stones, not even mine. I was a woman of the past. You were a man of the future.

"We could lie in bed together and look at this view." Your tone had changed from business to tenderness and I was beguiled by the use of *we*. "Don't feel pressured. Just think on it. You said you wanted to move somewhere quiet to write."

"I can't afford this."

"You're looking to buy outright. This would be yours at cost price."

"Can you do that?"

"I'm the MD," you laughed, "of course I can."

"I couldn't accept it."

"Grainne, you'd be helping me. Selling the first few will help to sell more. Things snowball. This property will treble in value over the next ten years, I promise."

I didn't enjoy this talk of values and assets. I did like the prospect of us sharing a bed that was ours.

"I'll think about a smaller one, at full price."

I'd always been careful not to take anything from you. Need's not erotic.

"It's cost price or nothing. Please, Grainne, it's the least that I can do for you."

The estate looks normal from this approach. There are cars on drives and curtains at windows. I can see a woman inside one of the houses. She bends down and comes back into a view with an infant on her hip. The portrait makes me wince. *Madonna with child*. She turns her back when she sees me.

I stop at Nancy's on Oak Avenue, the main artery of the estate.

"Have a drink with me." She ushers me in and shuffles along behind me.

Water rushes into the metallic belly of the kettle. I unload her groceries. UHT milk. Teabags. Canned sardines.

"Pay me next time."

Nancy snorts and forces money into my palm. "I'll come with you next week, if you don't mind taking it slow."

28

"It's a long walk."

"Don't cheek me." Her spark belies her age. She must've been a corker in her time.

"I need to take the car out for a run. I'll drive us somewhere as a treat."

I wonder how long it'll take the village shopkeeper to forget my tantrum. Longer than a week.

Steaming water arcs into one mug, then the other.

"Grainne…" Her tone changes. "Lads are loitering about up here. Be careful."

When Nancy bends to add milk to the tea I can see her pink scalp through the fine white curls.

"I'm just going to come out and say this." She touches my hand. Her finger joints are large, hard knots. "You're neglecting yourself. You're losing weight. And your lovely hair…"

I can't recall when I last brushed it.

"You're not sleeping either. I've seen you, walking past at night."

"You're not sleeping either."

"That's my age."

Nancy sips her tea. I gulp mine down. It's my first drink of the day.

"You're all alone up at that end of the estate."

I can't answer. I've been too lonely to realise that I'm alone.

"Life's too sweet to throw away."

Then why does it taste so bitter?

She tries again, exasperated by my silence.

"What happened up there isn't my business but I can't bear to watch you punishing yourself."

I should be pilloried for my past. I should be stricken with shame but I can't tell Nancy that it's not remorse that's destroying me. It's pining for you.

"You're full of opinions." It comes out as a growl but there's no bite.

29

"You can stay here anytime. God knows I've room enough to spare."

She opens a pack of biscuits and makes me eat one.

"Be careful out there on the hills, Grainne. You could turn your ankle and die up there and no one would know."

I kept a well made bed, dressed with cotton sheets. Worthy of the time we spent upon it. Sunlight moved across our bare bodies, which moved across one another. Hands and mouths roamed over necks, chest, breasts, stomachs, genitals and thighs, stoking a deep ache that only you could sate.

Afterward we lay like pashas on piles of pillows.

"I loved you from the first moment I saw you."

"That's a cliché." I meant to tease you but it sounded bitter.

"You don't believe me. You don't believe anything I say."

"I do."

I did believe you because I felt it too. From that first moment I wanted to open my arms to you. I wanted to open my legs to you. I promise it wasn't just lust because I wanted to open my heart to you too.

"I'm just someone you sleep with."

"Dan, don't play games to make yourself feel better."

"You don't need me, not the way I need you."

"Of course I do."

You thought yourself the more in love of the two of us. Not true. I hated sharing you. I hated not knowing when I'd see you or when you'd call.

"You've never asked me to leave her."

"Do you want me to?"

"Yes." You paused. "No." Then: "I don't know. I don't love her. I did once. I can't leave her now. Ben's still so young. But wait for me, Grainne. Our time will come. I promise."

"Don't make promises."

"I wish I'd met you first."

I wish it all the time, for so many reasons.

The short cut to Acacia Drive goes through Boomtown's underbelly. There's a square that would've been a green but now it's the brown of churned mud. It should've been flanked by shops. Some are only foundations, others have been abandoned at hip height. A few have made it to the state of squatting skeletons. Piles of rotted timbers and broken breeze blocks litter the verges. An upturned hard hat is full of dirty rainwater. A portable toilet lies on its side and I get a whiff of its spilled contents.

I flip over a tin sign lying in the road and it lands with a clatter. I clean it with the hem of my shirt. BOOM DEVELOPMENTS, it exclaims. The symbol's a crouched tiger, its stripes orange, green and white.

I go straight to bed when I get home, leaving my shopping in the hall. The once pristine sheets are creased and grey. I push my nose against the pillowcase but can't smell you there, only my own unwashed hair. Frustrated, I strip the bed and lie down again. I touch myself in a ferocity of wanting but it's a hollow sham that ends in a dry spasm. I'll not be moved. Not without you.

I put my walking boots and coat back on. I feel the reassuring weight of my torch in my pocket. My premium property backs onto open country. I open the gate at the bottom of my garden and walk out to where the land undulates and settles into long summer grasses that lean towards the hills.

Out here, away from the estate, nothing's inert. Buzzing insects stir the grass. The wind lifts my hair and drops it. A chill settles in and I wish I'd worn another layer. I cross the stream, sliding on wet stones and splashing water up my jeans. The stream's unconcerned. It has places to go.

The sun's sinking fast. The sky is broken by a string of emerging stars as night arrives.

The ground rises and I have to work harder until I'm climbing on all fours onto the plateau. The hills crowd around to protect the Three Sisters. This trio of stones are eternal, bathed in sun and rain, steeped in the ashes of our ancestors. They're more substantial than our bricks and mortar. They'll sing long after our sagas are exhausted. They outshine our light.

The Sisters cluster together. They're not angular, phallic slabs. Their Neolithic design looks daringly modernist, each shaped to suggest womanhood. The smallest, which I think of as the youngest, has a slender neck and sloping shoulders. The middle one has a jutting chin and a swell that marks breasts. The eldest has a narrow waist and flaring hips. I touch each in turn. They're rugged and covered in lichen. I put my ear against them, wanting to hear the sibilant whispers of their myths. I kiss their unyielding faces but they don't want my apologies for ancestral wrongs. There's only silence. They wait, of course, for us to abate.

I walk back home, not looking down, playing dare with the uneven ground. My torch stays in my pocket. *You could turn your ankle and die up there and no one would know.*

Death comes for me. It's a white, soundless shape on the wing. A moon faced barn owl, dome headed and flat faced. I'm transfixed. It swoops, a sudden, sharp trajectory led by outstretched claws. How small have I become that it thinks it can carry me away?

I've read that owls regurgitate their prey's remains as bone and gristle. I laugh, imagining myself a mouse sized casket devoid of life.

The owl swoops low over the grass and heads for Boomtown. I press my sleeve to my cheek. Dizziness makes me lie down. The long grass surrounds me, reducing the sky to a circle. I don't know how long I'm there but cold inflames my bones. Eventually I get up and walk home, coming up Acacia Drive from the far end where the houses are unfinished. The street lamps can't help, having never seen the light. I'm convinced it's whispering, not the wind

32

that's walking through the bare bones of the houses. Now that I've survived the menace of the hills and fields, I allow myself my torch. What should be windows are soulless holes in my swinging yellow beam. The door frames are gaping mouths that will devour me.

I don't look at *the house* but I feel it trying to catch my eye.

There's something akin to relief when the road curves and I see the porch light of my home. It looks like the last house at the end of the world.

You were in the shower sluicing away all evidence of our afternoon. Your clothes were laid out on the back of a chair. You were careful to avoid a scramble that might crumple your shirt or crease your trousers.

The gush of water stopped and you came in, bare, damp, the hair of your chest and stomach darkened swirls. You'd left a trail of wet footprints on the carpet. You weren't shy. I enjoyed this view of you. The asymmetry of your collarbones and the soft, sparse hair on the small of your back. My fascination for you endured, as if I'd never seen a man before.

"When will they start work again?"

By *they* I'd meant the builders. The estate had fallen silent. No more stuttering engines, no more drills or shouting.

You'd been drying your chest. The towel paused, as if I'd struck you in the heart. I cursed my clumsiness.

"Soon. There's been a bit of a hiatus in our cash flow. People are just a bit nervous, that's all. Everything moves in cycles. Money will start flowing again."

"Of course it will." My optimism had a brittle ring.

You wrapped the towel around your waist in a sudden need to protect yourself, even from me.

I wake in the afternoon, having lost the natural demarcations of my day. My cheek smarts when I yawn. I pick at the parallel scabs.

My mobile's by my bed. I've stopped carrying it around. You never call. It's flashing a warning that its battery is low. I ignore its pleas for power and turn it off.

I did get through to your number once. There was the sound of breathing at the other end. It wasn't you.

"Kate," I said.

The breathing stopped and she hung up before I could say *I'm sorry.*

You haunt me. I see your footprints on the carpet where you once stood, shower fresh and dripping. I catch glimpses of you in the mirror and through the narrow angles of partially closed doors. These echoes are the essentials of my happiness. For that fraction of a second I can pretend you're here.

It's rained while I slept. Everything drips. The ground's too saturated to take all the water in. It's not cleansed Boomtown, just added another layer of grime.

From the spare bedroom I can see the street. I put my forehead against the window, savouring the coolness of the glass. I tilt my forehead so I can see Helen's house, further along the opposite side of Acacia Drive. The other house, the one where it happened, is out of sight, at the incomplete end of the road. It's defeated me so far.

I slip on my boots and snatch up my coat. I shut my front door and freeze, the key still in the lock. Something's behind me, eyes boring into my back. It waits, daring me to turn. I can feel it coming closer. I make a fist, my door key wedged between my ring and forefinger so that its point and ragged teeth are protruding. It's a poor weapon, especially as I've never thrown a punch in my life. I turn quickly to shock my assailant, only to find it's a cat shuddering in an ecstatic arch against the sharp corner of the garage wall. It's not like other strays. The uncollared, unneutered, incestuous brood that roam around Boomtown are shy. This ginger monster's not scared of anything. It fixes me with yellow eyes and hisses. It bares it fangs and postures. I hiss back but it stands its ground, leaving me to back away down the drive.

I find myself at Helen's, which is stupid because Helen doesn't live there anymore. The FOR SALE sign's been ripped down and trampled on.

I walk around the house, looking through windows. It's just a shell without Helen and her family but evidence that it was once a home remains. The lounge's wallpaper, a daring mix of black and gold. Tangled wind chimes hang from a hook by the kitchen door. There's a cloth by the sink, as though Helen's last act was to wipe down the worktops.

We used to stand and chat as her brood played in the road. When they got too boisterous she'd turn and shout, "Quit your squalling and yomping, you bunch of hooligans! Just wait until your dad gets back." Then she'd wink at me and say something like, "He's in Dubai this time. Not that they're scared of him, soft sod that he is."

I used to get the girls, Rosie and Anna, mixed up. Tom squealed as he chased his sisters. Patrick rode around us on his bike in circles that got tighter and tighter.

Patrick.

I'm sick of thinking about that day.

I'm sick of not thinking about it.

Today, I decide, *today I'll go inside the house where it happened.*

It's about twenty doors down from Helen's. The chain link fence that was set up around it has long since fallen down and been mounted by ivy intent on having its way. The Three Sisters are reclaiming what's theirs by attrition. There are lines of grass in the guttering of Boomtown, wasps' and birds' nests are uncontested in the eaves. Lilies flourish in ditches and foxes trot about like lonely monarchs. The Sisters will reclaim us too, our flesh, blood and bones.

I stand on the threshold of the past. A breeze moves through the house carrying a top note of mould and piss, then the threatening musk lingering beneath.

The house is gutless. One wall is bare plasterboard, the rest partition frames so I can see all the way through, even up into the gloom above. There used to be ladders but they've been removed.

From the doorway I can see the stain on the concrete floor. It's a darkness that won't be moved. The blackest part gnashes its teeth at me.

I put a foot inside and then the other. I realise my mistake too late. I've already inhaled the shadows. They fill up my nose and clog my throat. I can't move. I can't breathe. My lungs seize up. Something's there. The darkness is moving.

The shadow rushes at me and takes my legs from under me. The ginger cat. It watches with yellow eyes as I land on my back. Everything goes black.

I roll onto my side and retch. Acidic vomit burns my nose and throat. When I put a hand to the back of my head I find a boggy swelling. My hair's matted and stuck to my scalp.

I stand, test my legs and find them sound. I get away from the house, to the middle of the road, but looking around I see I'm not alone. Company's coming up the street. A trio of creatures that are neither men nor boys. One throws his empty beer can away and fingers his crotch when he sees me.

"You," he says.

He's skinny, grown into his height but yet to fill out. It occurs to me that he expects me to run. His face is hard. He's gone past being abused into abusing.

"You're the Boomtown Bitch."

I turn my back and walk away at a deliberate pace.

"I'm talking to you." I know without looking that he's lengthening his stride to catch me. "Pull down your knickers and show us what all the fuss is about."

36

My heart's a flailing hammer. He's done this before and is looking to initiate his friends, who seem less certain of themselves. I can see him reach out to grasp my shoulder in the far corner of my vision.

I strike before he can touch me. I jab at his eyes and rake at his face with dirty claws. I'm a moon faced owl. I'll regurgitate his carcass. I'm the feral feline who'll jab his corpse with my paws. The boy's screaming now but I don't stop. Even a chink of fear will let the others in and I can't fend off all three. My would-be rapist retreats. I must put him down before he gathers his wits and tries to save face. I advance, hissing and spitting like the ginger cat.

I *am* crazy, scarred and unkempt, a bloodied scalp and big eyes in the dark hollows of my face. I pick up a brick and run at him and to my relief, he sprints away.

They shout from a safe distance, taunts that I'm happy to ignore. I don't look back as I walk away in case they realise I'm weak.

I saw your outline through the glass of my front door. You were wearing your suit, even though it was a Saturday.

You weren't alone. A boy stood before you. Even though you had your hands on his shoulders it took me a moment to realise it was your son. Ben. You were there in the shape of his mouth and chin. The other parts must've been your wife. I resented this child, this scrap of you and her made flesh.

"Miss Kennedy – " you mouthed *sorry* at me over Ben's head " – I've come to see you about your complaint over the house."

I wanted to laugh. You were a terrible actor.

"That's good of you."

"Apologies, I had to bring my son. Say hello, Ben."

"Hello." He squirmed in your grasp.

"I had to let you know I'd not forgotten you. Shall we make an appointment for next week?"

37

"Would you both like a drink?" I knelt before Ben, hating him because he was getting in our way. "Would you like to play outside? It's a lovely day."

I stood up and raised a hand, a plan already formed. "Patrick, over here."

Helen's brood were on their drive. Patrick cycled over. The bike was too small for him and his knees stuck out at angles.

"Meet Ben. Can he play with you?"

"Sure." Patrick sat back on the saddle. He'd no need for deference, being older than Ben and on home turf. The other children stood on the far pavement, waiting to take their cue from their brother.

"As long it's okay with your father, of course." I couldn't look at you. *Please say yes.* My longing was indecent. Even the children would see it.

You hesitated.

Please say yes.

"Ben – " you put a hand on his head " – stay with the other children on this road. Don't stray."

I could tell that you were proud of Ben and wanted me to see him but a dull, creeping jealousy stole over me because of the trinity of *Dan, Kate and Ben.*

"This way," Patrick beckoned and Ben followed, glancing back at you.

"I can't stay long," you said as I closed the door.

We raced upstairs.

"Won't your neighbours wonder when they see Ben? Won't they guess?"

"Who cares?"

I didn't. I was too busy with your belt. There was a sudden shriek of laughter and I stopped you from going to the window by snatching at your tie and pulling you into the bedroom.

"Leave them. They're enjoying themselves. So are we."

You hesitated again and then undressed, your ardour cooled by the tug of parental love. I shoved you, ineffectual considering your size. Your carefully folded clothes enraged me. You'd brought your son to my door. You'd been honest about your life when you could've lied but you'd been a coward and made the decision mine.

I shoved you again.

You picked me up and threw me on the bed. We grappled and when you understood I meant to hurt you, you held my wrists so I couldn't mark you with my nails. You didn't kiss me for fear I'd bite. I wish I'd known it was the final time. I wish we'd taken it slow. I'd have savoured the slip and slide, then the sudden sensation of you inside.

You dozed. I watched. Your breathing changed to slower, deeper tones. I treasured the minutiae of you, the banal details that made you real, like how you took your coffee, brushed your teeth, the slackness of your face in sleep.

The doorbell rang, a sudden sequence of chimes that struggled to keep up with the finger on the bell. A fist hammered at the door, followed by shouts. It went through my mind that it was your wife, that she'd followed you here spoiling for a fight. Then I recognised Helen's voice. Its urgency boomed through the hall and up the stairs.

Silence. There'd been silence during our post-coital nap. No squeals or calls.

I snatched up my blouse, fingers stumbling over the buttons.

"Dan." I reached for my skirt. "Dan, wake up."

You sat up, dazed. "What is it?"

Helen, even in panic, saw the flagrant signs. The buttons of my blouse were done up wrong and I was bra-less beneath the sheer fabric. You'd followed me down the stairs with your tousled hair and bare feet.

"You'd better come. I've called an ambulance."

You pulled on the shoes that you'd discarded by the door. You and Helen were faster than I as she led us to the empty houses. Three of the children were outside one of them. Rosie and Anna were red faced from crying. Tom sat on the step beside them, staring at the ground.

"Stay here", Helen ordered them even though it was clear they weren't about to move.

I followed you from light into the shade of the house. It took a few moments for my eyes to readjust. The coolness inside felt pleasant for a second, as did the smell of cut timber.

You and Helen squatted by the shattered body on the floor. Ben's silhouette didn't make sense and I had to rearrange the pieces in my mind. His arms had been flung out on impact but it was his leg that confused me. It was folded under him at an impossible angle that revealed bone, so white that it looked unnatural against the torn red flesh. Ben was a small vessel, his integrity easily breached.

"He must've fallen from up there."

We looked up towards the eyrie that was the unfinished loft where Patrick perched astride a joist. A ladder spanned the full height of both floors which is how they must've climbed so high. Helen's husband was at the top, reaching for the whimpering boy.

A dark stain crept out from beneath Ben's head. His eyes stared at nothing. There was an appalling sound. A dog's howl, the scream of an abandoned child. The keening of something bereft and inconsolable. It grew until it filled the room. I realised it was you. I put a hand on your shoulder and said your name.

You shook me off.

I wake up on the sofa. It's early and the grey light of dawn creeps through the parted curtains. Sleep's not healed me. I smell of spoiling meat. There's a dull throb in my head but I can't locate whether it's in my eye, my teeth, or somewhere in between. I'm cold and clammy, as if in the aftermath of a drenching sweat.

I go to the mantel mirror. There's enough light now to see that the marks on my cheek are raised, the scabs lifted by lines of pus. I touch one and it gives under gentle pressure, bringing relief and yellow ooze. The back of my head feels like it belongs to someone else.

I eat a dry cracker, drink a pint of water and then vomit in the kitchen sink. There's a pounding now, at a different rate and rhythm to my headache. A drumming that escalates.

It's outside the house.

Hooves thunder on the earth. Something's racing through the grass, running towards the rising sun as if about to engage it in battle.

I go out to the road. Someone, perhaps my failed assailants from yesterday, has spray painted filthy graffiti across the front of my house. It doesn't matter. The wind's changed and is bringing something much fouler with it. Things left too long without light or laughter. Things nursing grudges and dwelling on outrages for too long. My heart pauses and restarts. The horse's gallop makes me gasp. Its cadence changes as it hits the tarmac.

This nightmare is gleaming black. Its rolling black eyes are wild. It tosses its head about and snorts. I can't look away. The mare slows to a canter as it approaches, circling me in rings that get tighter and tighter. It's big, a seventeen hander, heavily muscled. It hits my shoulder on its next pass. When it turns and comes again I have to dodge it to avoid being knocked down.

Adh Seidh. A bad spirit. I'd be safe from its malice if I'd led an upright life.

It flattens its ears and flares its nostrils, then rears up before me and paws at the air as if losing patience. I try to edge to the safety of my open door but it kicks out again, forcing me to retreat. It follows at a trot. Each step jolts my head but I turn and run. When I shout for help my voice is faint from lack of use. There's no one to hear it anyway.

I try and dart up Helen's driveway but the horse isn't confused by my sudden change in direction. It comes

41

around me, right, then left. Lunging at me, kicking out if I stray. Herding me.

I'm panting. My chest's tight and the stitch in my side's a sharp knife. I want to lie down and die. To let it dance on me until I'm dust beneath its hooves.

I'm at *the house* now. The horse waits beyond the fallen chain link fence in case I try to bolt. I've been brought here to atone for my crimes. The only place I can go is that cold, dark hole.

Broken beer bottles and rubble crunches underfoot. Kids have been in here since my last visit. I feel hot again. Sweat stings my forehead. The past is too heavy. I can't carry it anymore. The stain accuses me. It rises from the floor and spreads itself across the wall. It's absolute, sucking all the light from the room. It smells my guilt and swells, emboldened. Its waiting is over. It's Ben. It's Kate. It's you. It's all the people I can't face. It's the Sisters, taken to the wing. They have hooves and paws studded with claws. They're done with waiting. They've risen up to smother us.

They're not out there on the hills. They're not walking through the dying summer grass. They're not lingering by the streams, fingers stirring the water.

They're not out there. They're in here.

The Lucky Ones
By John Llewellyn Probert

The nineteen year old girl on the screen was completely naked.

The money in which she was rolling was helping to maintain her modesty, of course. Brand new ten pound notes clasped to pert breasts, crisp twenties against her taut buttocks, and strategically placed fifties for anyone whose eyes might be tempted to stray to somewhere more intimate

The girl was quite literally rolling in money, and as she threw sheafs of it into the air, as she bathed in the fluttering paper, rubbing the notes that she caught in tiny, exquisitely manicured fingers against her flawless, milk-white skin, she breathed, seductively, repeatedly and relentlessly, the same words, over and over.

"Oh, love, love, love. I love it. I love it so much."

Before her moans could be justifiably complained about (the network was allowed a maximum of five seconds of such behaviour before it could be legally considered as pornographic) a cheerful, slick, well-greased male voice cut in.

"And so remember, folks," it said, "that for you to be in with a chance to win the Daily Messenger's jackpot prize, make sure you pick up a copy of your favourite newspaper every day this week! Remember – every day, so you can collect the special tokens and – "

"Cut!"

Martin Johnston waved his arms in the air, which just made the sweat stains soaked into his red pinstripe shirt all the more obvious. Smoke from the cigarette jammed into the corner of his mouth filled the air in the preview room.

"Cut! Cut! Cut!"

43

From the projection booth the promotional film was halted, freezing the frame on an especially intimate image.

"You can see a fucking nipple!" said Martin, withdrawing a silver telescopic pointer from the pocket of his waistcoat. It was hanging open, much like the mouths of his assembled production team right at that moment. He extended the pointer to its full length and prodded at a minute but nevertheless discernible area of pink areola on the screen.

"What the fuck did I tell you fucking lot about the fucking nipples?" he screamed at his silent audience. "Do you know what percentage of our market demographic is going to complain if that shot stays in? And what's more important, the percentage that will switch over to watch something else?" He threw the crumpled script at a startled continuity girl and left the screening room.

On his way out he was accosted by a brylcreemed young man whose hands never left the confines of the trouser pockets of his finely tailored suit as they spoke.

"Trouble?"

Martin shook his head. "No, Steve, no trouble. They just don't always do as they're told."

Steve Watson, vice-president of BrightGrace Productions, shrugged. "If they don't know how to do their job properly, they know where the door is. Or we can show it to them."

Martin nodded. "I've made that clear," he said. "But it should only take a minute in the editing room and they'll have it sorted."

"Good." There was a pause as Steve looked Martin up and down. "I'd smarten myself up if I were you. The Old Man's requested a meeting."

Martin shuddered and refastened his top button, pulling his red silk tie into place. "How many of us?" he asked.

Steve gave him a lizard's smile. "Just you. Now."

Martin was running down the gleaming white corridor almost before Steve had finished speaking. He took the lift at the end, pausing on the building's fourth floor to grab his suit jacket from his office and splash on some Hugo Boss from the cabinet in the adjoining private bathroom. Then he returned to the elevator, punched in his private pass code, and pressed the top button.

The one that would take him to the Old Man.

Everyone in the building thought of him in capitals. Everyone knew his real name was Royston Furlong. No-one called him anything but Sir. At least, not in front of him.

Martin could feel his throat drying out as he ascended, his palms moistening as he lost the ability to speak. As a bell rang to signify his arrival he coughed, swallowed, and hoped that would suffice to allow him to be intelligible as the doors slid apart.

The Old Man's office took up the entire top floor of the BrightGrace Productions building, affording the company's owner a spectacular view across London's Docklands. The view included a number of buildings similar to the BrightGrace one - all made of polished glass and steel that right now was glinting in the unforgiving glare of a harsh mid-morning October sun. Monoliths to ruthlessness and ambition, they dominated the skyline. The Old Man had always said he chose the position of the BrightGrace building so he could keep an eye on all of them. What had probably been intended as a joke still didn't seem funny to anyone who worked there, except perhaps the Old Man himself.

"You're almost late." Christina Matthews, the latest in a line of twenty-something secretaries employed by Furlong on the basis of youth, good looks, talent, ruthless ambition and unquestioning loyalty, checked her Cartier watch. The tiny diamond-studded hands showed eleven o'clock.

Martin shrugged. "But I'm not late, am I?" he said, trying to keep the disdain out of his tone. Despite her appearance, he knew any girl employed by Furlong was always just one month's pay cheque away from being on the street. "Unless of course you keep me waiting, in which case it will be your fault. Not mine."

There was little love lost between the two as Christina tapped a button on her iPad.

"You can go through," she said five seconds later, after which she pointedly ignored him.

Martin took a deep breath and approached the ornate panelled double doors that led to the Old Man's inner domain. They swung open noiselessly on perfectly balanced hinges at his touch. Martin slipped through and was careful to close them before turning round.

The Old Man wasn't actually old at all. In fact he couldn't have been more than fifty. But it wasn't so much his biological age as the length of time he had managed to spend at the top of a business renowned for its cut-throat, back-stabbing, here-today-gone-tomorrow attitude that had earned him the title. Royston Furlong had been making successful television since the nineteen eighties, and he made sure everyone knew it.

He didn't dress like Martin's idea of TV top management. The waistcoat of his three piece black suit held a pocket watch, a watch Furlong was checking as Martin stepped through the door.

"Right on time, Martin." Furlong shut the gold timepiece with a more melodramatic snap that was strictly necessary. "I do appreciate punctuality."

"Thank you, sir." Martin tried not to look nervous but it was difficult.

Furlong gestured to a drinks cabinet on which bottles of exquisitely expensive spirits jostled for attention. "Would you like anything?"

Martin shook his head. "Not just now, sir, if that's all right."

"All right?" Furlong's face broke into a smile. "My dear boy it's absolutely fine! Please, take a seat."

Martin sat in a narrow chair that was as uncomfortable as it looked.

"How is the Daily Messenger advert going?"

"Fine, fine," Martin tried hard not to fidget but it was difficult. "A tiny bit of editing and it should be ready to go."

"Good! Steve said you'd be making good progress with it. Well, actually he didn't." Furlong leaned forward. "In fact he did his best to rubbish your efforts behind your back, but it was just the last act of a desperate man on his way out of the business. I'm giving him the final series of *A Prayer, A Priest, and A Picnic*. He thinks he can turn it around but in reality it's just going to give me enough ammunition to get rid of him."

Martin raised his eyebrows. Everyone knew that show was doomed, didn't they?

"You, on the other hand, I have different plans for." Furlong got to his feet and walked to the window. He was still taking in the view as he spoke. "Tell me, Martin," he said, "what's wrong with this country at the moment?"

"All kinds of things." Martin was unsure as to what was required of him here so he thought it best to be non-specific. "Immigration, unemployment, the health service, and all the other things everyone uses to sell papers."

"The class system!" Furlong's eyes were bright as he turned to face him. "That's what's wrong with this country." Martin tried to agree but Furlong wasn't finished. "In the old days everyone knew their place, and Britain was better off for it. If you were working class, that's where you stayed. If you were rich, you understood how to behave. The only interactions were between those who gave the orders, and those who did what they were told. Otherwise, everyone kept to themselves, everyone fulfilled their roles in the pecking order. And Britain became Great.

"But now those boundaries have become blurred. The stigma of being considered working class has led to the creation of many more university places so everyone can get a degree and think they're educated. Never mind that most of the subjects these people get degrees in are so pathetic they don't prepare you to cross the street let alone do an honest day's work. And the result of that has been?"

Martin was about to answer but Furlong wouldn't let him.

"Britain now has a vast, poorly, and inappropriately educated middle class. People who a generation ago would have been factory workers, now take up worthless middle management roles, inspecting the drainpipes to make sure they're the correct shade of grey, creating reams of paperwork that can be discussed at endless meetings that only exist to create more meetings to give these useless people something to do." He threw his hands in the air. "How can they possibly escape from their dreary, pointless, dissatisfying little lives? Lives where they no longer do an honest day's work for an honest day's pay, but instead scuttle around making sure that the 'Warning - Wet Floor' signs are at the right height that disabled people can see them even though they're in wheelchairs and have as much chance of falling over as a Sherman Tank."

Martin could see where he was going now. "But we can help them escape?"

Furlong waved an index finger at him. "Exactly! Through the medium of television we can help them escape." The Old Man returned to his desk and sat down.

"I have a job for you Martin. I want you to come up with a concept for a new game show. A game show that is going to reel in the target audience I have just described to you. Not so much the great unwashed as the great lathered-in-whatever-cheap-shower-gel-we're-getting-them-to-buy-at-the-moment. The concept must involve little in the way of knowledge or skill. I want this to be something that any clod thinks they might be in with a chance of winning. Make sure there's a major luck element. There's a reason the National Lottery's been so successful. Now don't let me down. You can use whatever resources the company has to offer. Within reason."

The meeting was at an end, Martin could tell. Rather than say anything that might lose him this plum assignment, he got up, backed his way to the door, fumbled for the handle and slipped out.

"You're not crying." Christina looked surprised.

"I've been asked to create a show." Martin was still staring blankly off into his potential future, one filled with money, excess, and inevitable downfall, but he always made a point of never thinking that far ahead.

"Have you?" Furlong's secretary was looking at him differently now, the way a crocodile eyes an unsuspecting deer that has come to drink deep at a dangerous watering hole. "What are you going to do?"

Martin looked at her at last and saw nothing other than her exceptional beauty. "I don't know," he said. "I'll need to think."

"Would you like some help? Thinking, I mean."

Martin was sure that if Christina was in the room he wouldn't be able to think about anything other than getting her into bed. "That would be great," he said, because to give any other answer would, in his mind, have been idiotic.

"Good," she said. "Let's get some lunch. Enrico's does the most fabulous lobster, and then we can go back to your place and hammer things out."

The lunch was fine but Christina was finer. Martin hadn't expected her to be quite so into the rough stuff but here she was, at her request, sat naked in his desk chair with one of Martin's silk ties acting as a blindfold. Similar strips of material had been employed to secure her wrists and ankles to the chair's arms and legs.

"Hit me," she breathed.

Martin wasn't much of a sadist, and while the urge to touch that soft skin yet again was almost overwhelming, he didn't really want to strike her. And then he thought of a way he could be properly sadistic towards her.

He took a deep breath. "No."

The girl tried to squirm but Martin had tied the silk very tightly indeed.

"Please."

"No." He took off the blindfold and she regarded him with eyes pleading for punishment.

"Why not?"

"Because I've got a better idea."

Martin was gone for a couple of minutes. When he returned, he was carrying a meat skewer and a black envelope.

"I didn't think you'd actually inspire me," he said, "but let's try this." He held up the envelope. "In here is a white piece of paper. On it is written either that I slap you, which is what you want, or..." and now he held up the shining steel spike "...I pierce your arm with this. If you prefer I can throw the envelope away. It's entirely up to you if you want to take the gamble."

Christina's eyes widened in horror at this new game. But that was not the only thing Martin could see there. There was also anticipation, and fear.

And excitement.

He looked at his Hugo Boss watch. "You have a minute to decide," he said. "And then I will burn the envelope and you can go home."

It only took twenty three seconds for her to say "Open it."

Martin raised his eyebrows. "You're sure?"

The girl nodded impatiently. "Open it. I want to know what it says."

Martin tore the envelope open slowly, relishing how Christina squirmed with anticipation. Just like ten million viewers might. He slid the folded paper from its confines and stared at it.

Christina was almost in tears. "What does it say?"

Martin said nothing. He merely strode forward, and slapped so her hard across her right cheek that she coughed.

"Congratulations," he said. "You win."

The expression on Christina's face bordered on orgasm.

"Again," she panted. "Do it again."

"You mean, hit you again?" Martin needed to know.

"The same," she breathed. "I want the same again. Please, please do the same again."

Martin made a second trip to the adjoining room, and returned with another envelope.

"Same as last time," he said. "Slap or spike. But you can walk away if you want to."

Christina shook her head. "Show me," she said.

"You get a minute to decide."

"Just fucking show me!"

Despite her impatience, or rather because of it, this time Martin took even longer to open the envelope and peruse its contents. Then he gave her a grim look.

"Well?" Christina looked at him with such anguish that he was surprised she hadn't wet herself. Perhaps he should aim for that before he allowed her to leave.

Martin approached her with his right hand held high. She was flinching as he brought the skewer down, puncturing the soft skin of the inside of her forearm. As it went in she gave a squeal that was loud enough for him to consider switching on his music system. When he took out the spike bright red blood trickled from the wound across the delicate paleness of her skin. Christina gave a sob and Martin looked up to see she was crying.

"I'm sorry," he said, suddenly wondering what the hell he was doing. "Oh God I'm really sorry."

"Again," she said, looking at him with a mixture of hatred and lust.

"I think that's enough." This was getting out of hand. "I think I'd better let you go, now."

"Do it again!" Christina screamed, "or so help me I'll tell Furlong you're a closet communist. You'll be out on your ear and selling The Big Issue before you know it!"

If she had wanted to raise Martin's ire she could not have picked a better subject. The bitch! How dare she!

Some pissing little secretary wasn't going to spoil Martin's chances of success! Why, he'd see her dead before... before...

"All right," he replied, his face a mask, his voice cold. "We'll carry on."

When he returned this time he was carrying a thin strip of white material in one hand. The other was behind his back.

"This time," he said, "you get the choice between a bandage for your arm which, you will notice, is still bleeding." He brought his hand round to reveal the secateurs. "Or, you lose your left earlobe."

"But I can still walk away?"

Martin nodded. "Of course. That's the whole point of the game."

"In which case I could walk away and put a bandage on myself?"

Martin frowned. "Good point," he said. "I hadn't thought of that." He thought for a minute. "Ok," he said eventually, "let's make it really interesting."

He threw away the bandage and took out his Mont Blanc pen. "This time it's either £10 000 from my own personal bank account. Or..." he looked her up and down before brandishing the secateurs once more. "...you lose the little finger off your right hand."

Christina shook her head. "You wouldn't dare."

"Wouldn't I? Only one way to find out. Mr Furlong did say I could use any resources the company had and in any way I liked. I'm sure he has lawyers who would be able to ensure the blame for whatever loss you might incur would sit squarely on those pretty shoulders of yours. Or what's left of them by the time we're through. You can still walk away – any time."

Christina nodded her acceptance. Just as Martin had thought – the Cartier watch, the aloof attitude, it was all part of her act. Obviously she needed the money just as much as all the others. And quite possibly the thrill as well.

This time she was lucky.

The next time she wasn't.

"I have to say I like it. I like it very much."

Just over a month later, Royston Furlong was leafing through Martin's preparatory document outlining his new game show. "I'm guessing your preliminary research led you to be a little more excessive than that, though?"

Martin nodded. "You said I could use the company's resources in any way I liked."

Furlong looked pleased at that. "Oh indeed I did! Don't get me wrong, I'm glad you used what was at your disposal to get the format right. It did result in Christina's typing leaving a little to be desired, however, so I've had to dismiss her."

"I understand." Martin felt a tiny pang of regret but it soon passed. "She wouldn't have presented a good image for the company."

"Not after the state you left her in, dear boy, goodness me no." Furlong was chuckling - always a good sign. "Now let me get this straight. We get contestants on and offer them a straight fifty-fifty chance between a cash prize or a forfeit?"

"Exactly." Martin smiled and relaxed. He was in. It was just a case of ironing out the details now. "And the greater the prize the greater the forfeit. But the contestant can walk away at any time."

Furlong considered what Martin had said. "So we can go all the way from either winning a small sum or having to take their shirt off..."

"...Right the way up to big money and they could put their house on the line." Martin finished the pitch for him. "And we would ensure that the younger female contestants start with the shirt taking off thing."

"Brilliant!" Furlong smiled. "In the current financial climate there should be no shortage of individuals willing to gamble with all they've got. And no shortage of people willing to watch them do it as well." He got to his feet. "I think everyone's going to be very impressed with your line of thinking, my dear chap."

Martin's eyes narrowed. Everyone?

"Tell me," said Furlong, coming round to Martin's side of the desk and placing a hand on his shoulder, "have you ever thought of a career in politics?"

No. Never. "Now that you mention it, sir..."

"Good, good. We can discuss it over lunch. I see a very bright future for you, my dear boy. A very bright future indeed."

"Thank you, Mr Furlong."

"Call me Royston."

As they left the building Martin was tempted to toss a coin into the filthy Starbucks cup the beggar was holding out. Then he thought better of it. After all, what would Royston think?

He was so busy thinking about his future that he didn't even notice the hand holding out the crumpled polystyrene receptacle belonged to a woman, nor that it was missing two fingers.

The Sun Trap
By Stephen Hampton

There was a hole in the wall around his backyard and sometimes, after heavy rainfall, water would get in from the fields beyond the housing complex.

Stella had been nagging Joe for years to get it fixed, but like the tradesman of urban myth, he'd never got round to it. He had time now, however; his retirement last week had been a tremendous relief – the building game had become demanding for a man of his advanced years – and he still felt a buzz.

Joe stepped into his flagged rear yard, looking forward to the summer. The yard was small and surrounded by a head-high wall, but this kept it private from his over-familiar neighbours. East-facing, it was a real sun trap in the morning, and Joe relished the prospect of sitting outside with his daily newspaper and letting the busy world pass by. He'd certainly put in enough years to earn that, investing all he could in sensible ventures. He was 'sorted', as lads in his profession might have termed it.

But first he had to fix the wall.

Earlier this week, he'd had a stack of sand delivered by an old contact who worked for cash. This now lay against the wall, next to the hole from which water stole in. A bag of cement was slumped beside a small potted palm tree, which had been his wife's retirement gift to him, a tempting hint at their continental prospects. Inspired by those prospects, Joe thought he could rebuild the wall in just a few hours, but today he didn't feel like tackling it. He was sure Stella would understand when she got back from the supermarket. Besides, the family would visit later, and Joe didn't want to get dirty before greeting his grandchildren.

He returned to the kitchen and, from the pantry, collected one of the deckchairs they used during barbecues. He had a battery operated radio, which he tuned in to a station broadcasting flamenco music. That put him in the mood for a beer, and he soon took a San Miguel from the fridge, before heading back to the yard and sitting near the door. Late May heat beamed down, sending a shiver of pleasure through his body. He momentarily thought he heard a scratching sound nearby, deep beneath the music, like a discordant rhythm, but then he dismissed that.

The yard was definitely a sun trap, and before long, alcohol doing its usual thing in his blood, Joe was sound asleep.

He was rudely awakened from a dream in which he'd been reclining on a foreign beach. When Joe snapped open his eyes, it took him a moment to adjust to his humdrum surroundings, to the pile of sand near the wall where water got in. The miniature palm tree looked measly compared to the giant one he'd imagined, and now the quick, exotic music was replaced by some popular din.

Then he noticed his wife looming over him, shaking one of his shoulders with firm insistence.

"Joe. *Joe.* Come on, wake up."

"Stella? What is it?" he replied, shaping the words through the stubborn contours of a yawn. For one moment, he felt the way he had after first hearing about the 'credit crunch.' That had occurred only a few months prior to his retirement and his investments had taken a hit. But he'd been wise enough to sink his cash into recession-proof 'blue chip' companies and the impact hadn't lasted long. So what on earth was his wife fretting about now?

After he'd sat up in the deckchair, she said, "Lee, Gwyneth and the kids will be here any minute, and I see you've spent the morning lounging around."

Some might say he deserved a rest, but he didn't push his luck. Although Stella was naïve in the ways of finance and the working world, she was domestically imperious, and Joe knew when to attend to his duties.

At least she didn't mention the wall he'd again failed to rebuild. Perhaps she hadn't expected this job to be completed so soon. Last night in bed, they'd had fun planning their next holiday – one of many they'd take each year now they had time and funds to do so – and that seemed to have sustained her positive mood. But when the family was due to arrive, little else mattered; it was the most important aspect of her life and Joe loved her for it.

While Stella prepared lunch, Joe tidied the small terraced house, and when a car – their son's hire-purchased Mercedes – pulled up in front of the property about an hour later, they were ready.

Lee ran his own printing business and Gwyneth was his trophy wife, all stylish clothing and pricey jewellery. The boys were five and six years old, and a pleasing terror to their granddad, whose limbs were weary after a lifetime laying bricks. Joe liked to think he and Stella had given their only child a good start in life, making sure he got to college and realised what his options were. The family now lived in a fine detached on the other side of town, and Joe was proud to talk about them to friends in his local pub.

Nevertheless, when Lee entered the house, Joe sensed tension in his body. Gwyneth followed, looking as cheerfully impervious to problems as ever. The boys were riotous, bouncing off the furniture, and after a short lunch, Joe and his son retreated to the backyard; the women and children, all spirited affection, remained in the house. As his son had barely spoken during the meal, Joe suspected that serious matters were afoot and that only privacy would overcome Lee's reticence.

"What's the matter, son?" asked Joe, drawing on more experience than a lifetime spent bricklaying; he was sixty-five, had seen a lot, and had had much time to think.

At first, Lee didn't look like replying, his sharp clothing and designer haircut suggesting he'd laugh off his difficulties, subject them to his usual cocky confidence. But then, sunshine beaming down like an interrogatory spotlight, his bullish nature collapsed in a heap.

"I'm in trouble, Dad," he said, his tone flat. He was thirty-seven years old, but presently looked about a third of that age. Then, with similar reserve, he added, "Most of my investments have gone up in smoke."

Joe looked at him, confused. *How could this be*, he wondered? His own portfolio was fine. Finally, trying to suppress a brief recurrence of that light scratching sound he'd heard recently, he found his voice.

"Please tell me you acted on my advice," he said, hardly believing his clued-up son might have done otherwise; it had all been so sensible, after all. "You invested in pharmaceuticals, didn't you? You put your money in telecommunications and utilities? Like I said you should?"

These industries, dull yet predictable, guarantee solid returns, regardless of boom and bust. Joe had once heard the stock market described as a device for transferring wealth from the impatient to the patient, and that was all he'd needed to know. For forty years, he'd drip-fed a fifth of his salary into a Trust Fund, and the results were impressive: he had £130,000 in his portfolio, from which he drew a modest income. Combined with his State Pension, he and Stella could now travel back and forth to Spain at their leisure, at least until they were too old to do so.

Joe observed his son's furtive face. Lee looked like a child who'd been slapped, his eyes averted and lips pursed as he gulped from a beer bottle. He resembled a boy in a man's world, keen to demonstrate competence or even more than that. But the truth wouldn't allow him to do so. That was when he spoke again.

"I put all my money in cyclicals, Dad. Mining, retail, property. And during this fucking recession, they've all gone down the tube."

Lee's reference to property – the way Joe had made a modest fortune, laying bricks for decades – made Joe feel defensive, as if his son was a young buck trying to get one up on an old hand. But then he realised that such concerns were irrelevant, that masculine pride was negligible compared to the tasks of supporting loved ones, of being a father, of ensuring that his son and family survived this obvious crisis.

Joe said, "How much have you lost?"

"I was hit hard," Lee replied, sipping more from his San Miguel as sunshine beat down. "I had sixty K invested, but it's now worth about… ten."

"Jesus. Did you go for capital growth or income?"

"Growth, of course, I'm young, I have a family to consider."

"I had all that, son, and chose the regular income of dividends every time." Joe hesitated, marshalling impatience, but then went quickly on. "Compound interest is the most powerful force in the universe. I think it was Einstein who said that. And yes, that's me, a thick brickie speaking."

"But you got lucky, Dad," Lee said, peeling off the label of his bottle, as if he held the contents responsible for his financial demise. "You invested at a good time, before the credit bubble, along with a million other baby boomers. My generation has suffered since. None of us know what will happen in the markets. They're global, outside our control."

"Okay, okay," Joe replied, detecting Lee's escalating distress. A father didn't like seeing a son's tears; they were an admission of paternal failure. "Why are you telling me this? What do you want me to do?"

Lee glanced back at Joe, his doleful eyes little older than five or six years old. Joe thought their glistening sheen could move mountains, reduce oceans to a trickle. But that was when Lee revealed the goal of his uncharacteristic confession.

"I need forty grand, Dad. Our whole lives – the house, the car, the kids' schooling – are based on credit. Bankruptcy will destroy my business – I mean, my reputation would stand for nothing. I don't know where else to turn."

Joe looked around his backyard, sensing its walls closing slowly in upon him. The sun pressed down like some debt-collecting financier. Then he realised that, like an unhappy ending that felt inevitable, his lifelong dreams were about to be compromised.

Nearby, something was scratching.

A father did what he must do for offspring; that was a rule of nature, as inviolable as a mother's nurture and a child's dependence. On Monday following his family's weekend visit, Joe was in his local bank, requesting a significant withdrawal.

He wasn't obliged to provide a reason for removing such a huge sum, but as the manager authorised the transfer of forty thousand pounds from his Investment ISA, Joe felt a subservient need to justify the decision.

"It's a family matter. Bit of a disaster, I'm afraid. But that's why we save, isn't it?"

The fifty-something guy smiled, his strained expression implying that he also had dependent others to support, maybe even bullish sons who'd taken on more than they could handle. "Rainy days are frequent in the current climate, alas."

The comment put Joe in mind of his refuge, the small sun trap at the back of his modest home. All at once, he wanted to be there. But he must remain and complete the formal duties.

Later, once he'd walked home with an incongruously small cheque that represented a nearly third of his working life, Joe reflected on his and Stella's conversation in bed the previous evening. Joe had tried to convey to his wife the nature of his fiscal achievement. He'd told her, for the first time, that he'd forgone the usual strategy of a company pension and decided to invest alone. In his mid-thirties, he'd read an article in a newspaper dealing with the potential of long-term investment. This had involved the stock market, a mechanism unknown to the likes of Joe and his peers, but the central message had been clear: invest regularly, remain patient, and modest comfort will follow.

This had been far from a challenge for Joe. To his generation, born in the Sixties, austerity had come naturally, a post-war characteristic as normal as drinking water or eating bread. In truth, he felt guilty about how his son had grown up, even though Joe had been unable to combat the horizontal effect of culture, the powerful impact of the '80s and '90s, which vertical tradition had been moot to temper. Joe had tried immunizing his son against contemporary *mores*, against instant credit and needful identities. But it was all no use. Lee's wife and children had also been drawn into the rotten game.

That was why Joe felt he must compensate them. If this meant that he and Stella, his devoted, family-oriented wife, had to sacrifice a few lifelong aspirations, so be it. They still had plenty of funds left to enjoy, around £90,000, and with their State Pensions and modest government allowances, they'd be fine.

This was what Joe told himself as he sat in his backyard, soaking up the little sunlight that reached it this afternoon. Lee had promised to come round later, to receive what his mother had called to tell him was 'a lifesaver'. But now Joe could only lament his compromised plans – holidaying in Spain at least four times a year – by sitting in his deckchair, enjoying the unseasonable warmth and sipping foreign beer. He looked at the pile of sand, the shrunken palm tree and a puddle of water that the broken wall had let in. At that moment, the twitching nose of a rat appeared in the shadows of that hole, but was soon gone, frightened perhaps by the sound of the radio playing, more flamenco music, heady and quixotic.

A few weeks after Joe had 'bailed out' Lee and his family, the global economy got worse. The first rumbles of unrest had been heard in the States, several leading financial institutions collapsing under a weight of toxic debt. But when aftershocks followed, contagion had spread throughout the world. Many banks were part-nationalised by governments and economies placed on life-support systems, involving quantitative easing and Lord knew what other desperate mechanisms.

Joe, reading about these events in his backyard, felt satisfaction about avoiding most failing stock, but was also worried about whether his son would survive. The younger man's business, an independent printing company, was part of an industry susceptible to the ebb and flow of trade. Joe hoped Lee had paid off enough debt to remain afloat until commerce picked up soon.

But as days drifted by, and then weeks, and then months, it grew apparent that Lee was still struggling. Joe and Stella visited their family as often as possible, ostensibly to see the grand children, but also to keep an eye on what their son and his wife were up to. The evidence hardly inspired confidence. They'd changed their car, for one thing, the Merc now a Jaguar. They'd also bought new furniture for their showpiece lounge, a great leather suite the kids had already knocked chunks out of. But amid all this frivolous stuff, Lee had looked more forlorn than ever.

One night, in bed together, Joe asked Stella whether she thought Gwyneth, Lee's wife, realised how close her family had come to financial oblivion, let alone the role her parents-in-law had played in preventing it.

"I have no idea," Stella replied, handing Joe the tablets he took to deal with high blood pressure and bad cholesterol, along with a glass of water. "Maybe she's as in the dark as I always was. I mean, you only told me about our finances recently. You've been dealing with them all our lives."

"That's possible," Joe replied, swallowing the pills and then embracing his wife beneath the sheets. "But Gwyneth always struck me as a bit more money-oriented. All those credit cards she keeps. Surely she'd have noticed the sudden appearance of forty thousand pounds."

"But that was for Lee's business, wasn't it? He'll have put it in a company account, which Gwyneth has nothing to do with."

"I hope you're right," said Joe, marvelling at all the subterfuge involved in financial systems, including even micro ones in a family. It was hardly surprising that the world had suffered a meltdown. Then he smiled. "I think men should encourage women to have more involvement in such issues. I'm sure we could avoid a lot of this mess with a less bullish approach."

"Oh, I don't know." Stella hugged him back, one arm draped over his large belly. "From what you told me, I'd say you've done pretty well for us."

"Thanks, love," Joe replied, snuggling down in darkness. "It's nice to feel appreciated."

"You deserve it."

He smiled again, feeling drowsy. "We'll take that holiday soon, eh? A few weeks in Spain, away from…well, you know, away from it all?"

"Sounds great to me."

"That's all I've ever wanted, you know. You can keep your flash cars and big houses. I just crave a bit of the sunshine on a beach, the sound of sea nearby, a cold beer beside me, and…and…"

As sleep wrapped its tenebrous limbs around him, all the low-grade stress he'd suffered lately pitched him into a nightmare. He was sitting in his backyard, enjoying warm weather, when that broken wall collapsed under pressure from a thousand furtive rats. These toothy vermin, all fur and whipping tails, came charging towards him in his deckchair, quickly reducing him to the bone.

Joe's son stood watching, but it was impossible to tell whether he was laughing or crying. There was certainly no sign of Gwyneth or the children.

It wasn't long before Lee visited again and asked for more money.

Several months ago, he explained with less shame than Joe might expect, he'd sunk most of the forty thousand pounds he'd borrowed into depressed bank stock, believing the likes of RBS and Lloyds Banking Group were oversold and would return to profit in a matter of months. But he'd underestimated the trouble in which these institutions were, and his huge investment was now worth half its original sum.

"But, Dad, these shares are no-brainers for the long-term. If I can buy, say, another twenty-thousand quid's worth, I can pay you back the sixty in no time and make a little bit for myself."

"For *yourself*?"

"Well, for Gwyneth and the kids, I mean. You should take that as read."

Joe felt his blood stir; he was being manipulated, Lee using Joe's and Stella's grandchildren as emotional bait to attract more of Joe's hard-earned savings. It was so cruel. Although he believed his son's desires had been instilled by a corrosive society, he found it difficult not to think that his latest act was that of an arrogant fool. Even he, Joe Bale, the most cautious of men, had known when to make concessions to experts, paying a fund manager a hefty fee to look after his portfolio. Indeed, what did he understand about price-to-earnings ratios and dividend growth? He was just an ex-brickie.

But for all his flash suits and trendy lifestyle, his son clearly knew even less.

His surroundings pitching and swaying, Joe stood from his deckchair and thrust aside his newspaper. He knocked over a bottle of beer beside the small palm tree, sending frothy ale across the flagged floor of his yard, striking the pile of sand like a toxic tide. Realising he still hadn't rebuilt the wall for his wife and feeling tearful about that, he turned to face his impetuous son.

"This is the last time!" he said, agony mounting inside him, pressing against his brain. His aspirations to travel to Spain whenever he pleased had never looked more remote. "If you take another twenty, that leaves us with just over half of our original sum, and your mother and me can survive on that. I made sure I saved more than we needed, because that's what responsible men do. Do you hear me, Lee?"

"Yes, Dad, that's loud and clear."

Even though the younger man sounded submissive and slightly ashamed, Joe found it difficult not to see a self-satisfied gleam in his eyes, a pernicious glint of unquenchable greed.

"I must be mad," Joe went on, despite knowing that, in less time than he could imagine, he'd be back at the bank and arranging another withdrawal. He'd discuss this with his wife tonight, and Stella would persuade him, as she always had, that family was more important than any luxury. She was right, of course, even though Joe's heart grieved over the truth.

As he was about to sit back down, he heard Lee say, "Trust me, Dad. And just give me some credit…"

At that moment, as a scratching sound started up nearby, this time almost intolerably loud, a bolt struck Joe in his skull and he felt the world tip sideways. Then his face struck something hard, harder than the soft sand he could see up ahead and a glittering sea at a distance. He blacked out.

He'd had a stroke, a mild one to judge by his quick recovery. His wife visited him in hospital every day – he stayed for five – and supported him as he seemed to undergo every medical test ever developed. One expert in brain traumas looked troubled when Joe struggled to recall a list of items after being asked to count backwards from a hundred in sevens. But this was also a difficult task for Stella and she told him so and neither of them worried about it.

Then he was discharged, and when he got home, his family – Lee, Gwyneth and the two boys – had a surprise for him. No, none of them had paid anyone to fix that hole in his backyard wall. But, with the imminent summer in mind, they'd bought him a sturdy lounger, so that he could lay back and take it easy during this recovery period.

Joe expressed his gratitude, but kept his eyes firmly on his son. Lee surely knew that, following the latest instalment of his 'bail out' funds and in light of Joe's uncertain health, neither of his parents would be travelling anywhere in the foreseeable future. The thought aggrieved Joe, because it felt more representative of the men's attitudes to responsibility than it should. But that was just the impact of the stroke, lending his thoughts an almost radioactive aura.

Lee and Stella had arranged to have Joe sign all relevant documents from his hospital bed, but Joe hadn't protested. He'd already agreed to lend the additional funds, even though his recollection of doing so remained hazy. But something about the injury he'd sustained had left him feeling bolder, more willing to make demands. The truth was that he was frightened, and as the weeks rolled by and he saw no sign of the global economy making a long march for recovery, Joe grew increasingly dismayed.

But at least he had his backyard – or his *sun trap* as he preferred to call it. He loved lying on his new lounger and absorbing the intense heat. The British weather was a pale substitute for Spain's climate, but even so, when he squeezed shut his eyes and then reopened them, he could imagine himself somewhere more exotic. The mini palm tree beside him would grow and become a mighty one; the pile of sand would flatten out to form an idyllic beach; and the water running in beyond the broken wall mimicked the susurration of the majestic Mediterranean. There was no scratching sound, either.

On his third week of convalescence, his wife bought him a CD to play on his portable radio. It was full of New Age sounds, clear recordings of distant seas and squawking birdlife. Joe lapped it all up, letting his ailing mind travel far and wide as he dutifully read his daily newspaper.

Still the world's economies showed little evidence of improvement.

Then, on a warm August afternoon, Lee returned with another plaintive request.

"We've almost turned the corner, Dad," he said, clinging onto spreadsheets, pie-charts and box graphs. "The bank shares are *definitely* about to head north."

"Buy when there's blood in the streets?" Joe replied, his compromised mind tugging wisdom from long-term memory, in things he'd once absorbed and had stayed there. "Be fearful when others are greedy and greedy when others are fearful."

"Er...yeah," his son said, perhaps imagining that his dad's mind was more damaged than so-called specialists had said. But what did experts know, anyway? After all, most had claimed that post-recession banks were un-investable, but here was Lee, about to make a real killing. "I need another ten thousand, Dad."

Joe reacted before he could monitor his words. "Oh, leave me alone!" he yelled, now drawing Stella from the house, who'd clearly been watching at an uncompromising distance as foolish men went about their business. "Just go away! Get out of here!"

"Joe, what's wrong?" his wife called back, shoving Lee inside the small property until she worked out what had led to such an outburst. Maybe the neighbours were now listening, but that wasn't important. This was a family issue and nothing mattered more.

"I want...to go...to Spain!" Joe demanded, tears breaking up these simple words. He'd got up from his

67

lounger and was now stood at the heart of his pitiful backyard. "But there's…not enough money…left for us…my love."

"Oh Joe, we have so much more than that," Stella replied, stepping across and taking his hands. "There's the grandchildren, isn't there? And we have no mortgage. And there's plenty of food whenever we want it. And… Well, we have *everything*, really. What more does anyone need?"

How could he explain? How could he tell her that the one thing that had sustained his work over so many years – when his hands had felt frozen and his eyes smarted with dry sores; as his heart weakened and his mind atrophied; as precious time had slipped by, leaving him old and infirm – was the thought of enjoying a place in the sun?

But all he said was, "Just get rid of that greedy *fool*," and although his wife didn't understand – could *never* understand – she obeyed him, moving away to tell her beloved boy that things would be okay, that she and his father just needed time and space to think. Lee left, looking aggrieved.

It was only later, when Joe was unable to overhear, that Stella arranged for him to return to hospital for further tests. After all, she reasoned, there had to be something seriously wrong if he'd turned against family.

Months passed, and then years, and the world's economies, like Joe's son, flattered to deceive. A recovery looked likely until the Arab Spring occurred, and then the Japanese tsunami, and then the near-collapse of the Eurozone, and then a borderline Chinese 'hard landing', and then the US 'fiscal cliff', and then a deflationary environment. All the while, Lee's banking shares, all purchased with his dad's hard-earned money, betrayed little sign of elevation.

But Joe was getting along well. Despite a medical diagnosis he'd been unable to understand – something to do with 'vast colours' and 'dentures', he thought – he enjoyed his daily routine, sitting outside, reading his newspaper, and taking lengthy strolls. Folk came to visit, but he rarely bothered with them; they muttered things he couldn't decode. His wife fussed and fretted, as she always had, and he loved her for that; she was perhaps the only member of his family he retained positive feelings about. Even the noisy grandchildren had begun to irritate him, stoking his irascible mood whenever they refused to demonstrate evidence of growing up as decent people. And was that really too much to ask for?

Joe didn't think so; after all, he'd been that way all his life. And as Stella and his daughter-in-law – fashion-mad Gwyneth – remained in the house and discussed chattels, Joe took the opportunity to pace around his wonderful sun trap. After returning from hospital a second time, he'd thought this private refuge had grown bigger, but had suspected this was just an effect of his medical problems and the strong medications he'd been prescribed. But now...he wasn't so sure.

The air was filled with rich sounds, each CD-quality; Joe heard chattering birds soaring over cliffs, a sea breaking on rocks, the almost audible *thrum* of relentless sunshine. He drank beer, because none of his doctors had said he mustn't, and after rising from his lounger and pacing surprisingly quickly across a stretch of sand, past an astonishingly tall palm tree, he felt water running around his bare feet, a cool breeze caress his body, and alcohol dance in his fragile psyche.

Then, glancing back at the place from which he'd strayed, he saw innumerable footprints snaking across a golden beach. Intense light, like failing eyesight, rendered the perspective strange, but there, far away, was his family, all five of them, standing beside Joe's lounger and waving with noticeably thin expressions, especially the only man in the group. What was their problem? Couldn't they appreciate what they had in life, this beautiful world with the sun shining high above?

In stubborn protest, Joe refused to wave back and simply remained where he stood, content with his thoughts, just an ex-working man enjoying a well-earned rest, at the end of a long and admirably cautious life.

Only Bleeding
By Gary McMahon

There was fire in the sky.

I looked out of the window, across the fields at the back of my house, and saw the red glow hanging above the distant warehouses. I hoped it wasn't a sign of another riot, or criminal damage. I was sick of hearing about people destroying the areas where they lived. This wasn't protest, it was self-harm.

Turning away from the window, I glanced at the bed, and at Sarah lying there under the thin duvet. Her blonde hair was a tangled mess. She was sweating. Her small, pale hands were resting on top of the cover.

I walked across to the bed, knelt down at her side, and kissed her on the damp forehead. She moaned in her sleep and I backed away, shuffling on my knees, not wanting to wake her. Standing, I left the room. When I closed the door, I paused there, out on the landing, wishing that she would be well again.

Downstairs, I felt restless. Television could not hold my attention, I was cautious of using alcohol as a crutch, and the house seemed simultaneously too small and too large. I put on my overcoat and went outside. The street was dark. The streetlight closest to our house was broken – it had stopped working weeks ago and still the council had not sent anyone to carry out the repairs.

I started to walk in the opposite direction to the fire I'd seen reflected against the sky. No destination in mind: I simply wanted to keep moving until my restless energy was all used up. I passed the derelict pub with its steel-shuttered doors and windows, the three repossessed houses at the end of the street, and turned the corner.

To my left there was a line of trees, their thin branches scratching against the sky. They seemed restless in the chilly night, as if trying to uproot and join me on my walk. The darkness above them was big and dark and almost starless. On my right there was a row of shops, each one closed for the night. One or two of them had gone out of business and were protected by steel anti-vandal devices that resembled oversized shark cages.

Up ahead of me I could make out someone sitting in the road. This seemed unusual, even in the rough neighbourhood where I lived, so I slowed my pace and became wary. I thought it must be a vagrant, or perhaps a drunk who had stopped for a rest.

A pizza delivery moped approached from behind the figure, and when it got close the driver simply steered around the person in the road, not even sparing a glance as his vehicle wobbled slightly. The moped gained speed and was gone within seconds; I could hear its monotone engine receding into the night.

Jesus, I thought. *Is this what we've become? Are we so uncaring that we'd leave someone sitting in the road like that?*

As I neared the figure, I realised it was a child – a small boy. He was sitting in the middle of the road, staring down at the ground. Unlike the moped driver, I could not just steer around him. I had to try and help.

About twenty yards from the boy, I stopped walking. He was wearing a baseball cap that was too big for his head and a waterproof sports jacket. But underneath the modern outer layer he had on some kind of costume, perhaps Victorian in style. Something that looked like the kind of thing a Dickensian street urchin might wear. The long brown coat was too tight for even his emaciated frame and its hem hung down below his waterproof jacket. His chunky little boots with their thick soles looked like a primitive type of corrective footwear.

"Are you okay?"

He didn't answer; didn't move.

"Hello… Are you hurt?"

Still there was nothing.

"Listen, I don't mean you any harm. I'm friendly – yeah?"

Suddenly he looked up. His face was small and pale but he looked angry.

"Hi." I held out my hands in a placatory gesture. "Look…I won't hurt you. I just want to know if you're okay."

He nodded.

"You sure?"

He nodded again.

"Can I help you? I mean, do you need me to call someone?" I started to reach into my pocket for my mobile phone.

"Stop," he whispered. I could barely hear him. But for some reason I did what he said without even thinking about it. "Are you hungry?"

Puzzled, I took a step forward. "I don't….sorry? What did you say?" I looked around. There was nobody else in the vicinity. It crossed my mind that this might be some weird, convoluted prelude to a mugging.

"Are you hungry?" He smiled, and the anger faded from his features.

"I haven't thought about it… Probably, yes." I'd decided to humour him. He might not be right in the head. Perhaps he'd gone AWOL from a local hospital.

"Here." He stood in one smooth motion, as if pulled upright by strings. Raising his arms at either side of his body, he opened his hands. A straight razor dropped onto the road. Even in the darkness, I could see that he was bleeding. "Everybody's hungry. You're all so fucking hungry, all the time."

"Shit…" I ran to him, grabbed him without thinking. "What happened?"

73

"Hush," he said, softly, and his voice was nothing like that of a child. "Feed." In a movement that was too quick for me to stop, he pressed one of his bloody wrists against my face, my cheek, my open lips. I tried to pull away, but his other hand was gripping my neck and he was strong, so very strong. I went down onto my knees, forced there by his sheer strength, and the syrupy blood crawled down my throat.

It tasted good. The blood. To my absolute horror, it tasted wonderful. Like warm honey, or an ice-cold drink on a hot day; like fish and chips eaten straight out of the newspaper wrapping, or a tall glass of beer.

When I opened my eyes the boy was gone. My lips were warm with blood. I wiped them and got to my feet, stumbled back along the street to my house and locked the door behind me.

Sarah was in a bad way that night and all the next day. I was unable to leave the house. She slept most of the time, but whenever she woke up she coughed up a horrible slimy substance into the bucket I kept beside the bed and suffered painful bouts of diarrhoea. I had to keep changing the sheets. She was ashamed, but I tried my best to reassure her. To love her.

"Just leave me, Mike," she said, more than once. "Walk away and leave me. Or dump me at the hospital gates. They'll have to take me in."

Fighting back the tears, I held her against me, appalled by her frailness and the way her bones felt like sticks wrapped in old damp sheets. She was dying and there was nothing I could do. There was nothing anyone could do. We'd brought her back home to fade out. None of the treatments had worked. She was slipping away.

That night, as I sat downstairs in the dark drinking whisky and wishing that I could do something to take away her pain, I found myself thinking about the boy I'd found in the road the night before. I'd been too busy that day to give him any serious thought, but now I had no choice. I remembered how cold his hands had been, and how easily he'd overpowered me; the long Victorian coat under his jacket; his strange commanding voice.

Was he a ghost? I didn't even know what that meant; didn't believe in the supernatural. But the boy had been something other than entirely human. I knew that. I could not deny the evidence of my senses.

I finished my drink and left the house, retracing my route from the previous night. The boy was not there. The road was empty. As I turned away, feeling oddly bereft, I caught sight of something at the edge of the trees. He was standing there, hands in the pockets of his dirty brown trousers, and watching me.

"Are you still hungry?"

I nodded.

"Then come," he said, turning away and strolling into the trees. "Come and take some more."

I followed him between the trees and to a small hollow down by the narrow river. He sat down on the ground, took out the straight razor, and slashed the blade across the palms of his hands. This time the moon and the streetlights made it easy to see; his blood was not red but black. It ran slowly and thickly, like crude oil.

"Feed," he said, and his eyes were black, too. His mouth was a toothless hole in that tiny white face beneath the too-large baseball cap. For a moment, I thought he looked half-finished, like a badly-constructed doll.

I sat down opposite him and bent to his open palm, lapping at the blood like a cat or a dog. It tasted good, but not quite as wonderful as before. This time the effect was not as intense. Like a drug, it was always better the first time and you could spend a lifetime chasing down but never repeating that first experience.

Afterwards, I sat with my eyes shut. He sang to me; a soft, slow lament, something like a sailor's shanty but in a language I did not recognise. Yet I knew exactly what he was singing about: loss, forced austerity; the slow decay of

75

a society that had once been rich and dissolute but was now poverty-stricken and falling apart at the edges. Somehow the act of drinking from him made it hurt less. With his dark blood in my mouth, I could break free.

We could be free.

"Can you help me?"

He kept singing.

"Please…help me. I don't want her to die."

The singing stopped. "I can always help you, but at a price. Nothing lasts forever. All I can offer you is a little more time."

I grabbed his ice-cold hand. "That's enough. It has to be."

He nodded. We stood and walked back to my house. At the door, he paused and waited for me to do or say something.

"What's wrong?"

He laughed; a small, dry sound at the back of his throat. "Don't you know?"

"I'm sorry…"

"You have to invite me in."

"Please," I said. "Come inside."

We went upstairs, moving slowly, with a sense of ritual that only became apparent to me after the fact. At the bedroom door, I turned to him and he smiled. His face looked like a tiny skull in the gloom of the landing.

Sarah was sleeping so deeply that she was barely even breathing. The room stank of shit and vomit. The bucket at the bedside was half full and some of the contents had slopped over the side and onto the carpet.

"Sorry about the mess," I said.

The boy took my hand. A chill passed through me. I could feel his emptiness like a cold breeze.

"Where are you from? Who are you?" My voice was raw.

He turned to me, his face a blank, an open-ended statement. "I'm from all over. I don't have a name, or if I do it's long forgotten."

He went to the bed and climbed up onto the mattress, straddling Sarah. He removed his sports jacket and rolled up the sleeves of his curious little frock coat. Then he took out the straight razor and cut into the thin, white meat of his forearms. Thick black blood bubbled to the surface, hung in rubbery strings, and then dripped onto Sarah's face. In her sleep, she began to lick the blood from her lips. After several minutes of this, the boy seemed to lose strength and climbed down off the bed.

"It's done," he said, and then he went over to the corner, sat down, and lowered his head between his knees.

I went to Sarah. She was still sleeping, but her breathing was easier. Some of the colour had returned to her face. Whatever the boy had done, it had worked. She looked better – healthier – than she had done in God knew how long. But I wanted more; I needed her to gain more strength.

I went over to the boy but he was sleeping, too. I shook him but he didn't wake up. Without thinking about what I was doing, I dragged him across the floor to the bed. He seemed weaker now, as if the bloodletting had drained some of his strength. I went through his pockets and emptied them. A battered pocket watch, a small, dusty diary with nothing written inside, an ivory-handled straight razor.

To my eternal shame, I opened the razor and started to cut. I cut into his arms, his face, his throat, and pushed him onto Sarah. She reached out and embraced him, clutching his body tightly against her. The boy began to twitch, then to convulse. He bucked against her, but Sarah held on, drinking him dry.

I turned away, unable to look at what I had done. The sounds were enough. Those horrible sounds of her feeding.

When she was finished, I carried what was left of the boy downstairs and set him tenderly, almost reverentially down on the sofa. He was nothing but an empty skin. No bones, no internal organs; just a sack of flesh, emptied.

Nothing lasts forever, the boy had said. But maybe forever is too much; perhaps all we ever need is a tiny bit longer, a fraction more time to try and set things straight. But the problem is, we want that little bit more time and time again, until it becomes to seem like a form of forever.

Sarah's newfound strength lasted two weeks, and then she once again began to dim. The colour left her cheeks, her skin turned sallow, and her eyes took on a dullness that scared me so much I could not look directly into them.

There was not much to say, but we talked long into the night. I wanted her to feel close to me.

"We took too much in one go," I said, holding her hand as I lay down beside her on the bed. My nose was filled with the hot stench of her sickness but my stomach no longer turned at the smell. "We should have rationed it, made it last longer."

"I know. But don't we always? It's our greatest weakness as a species. We always take too much; destroy the very things that can sustain us." She squeezed my hand, but weakly. "Why should this be any different?"

I began to weep.

"Don't cry for me," she said. "Not any more."

Wiping my eyes on the pillow, I turned and grabbed the straight razor from the bedside table. The blade shone, catching stray light through the window from a passing car.

"What are you doing?"

"It's worth a try," I said, and pressed the sharp edge of the blade against my wrist.

Through the window, I saw the dull red haze of fire in the sky. I had no idea if it were real or simply the beginning of some kind of vision. Over in the corner of the room, something stirred. A dark patch, a shadow: the sad, cold ghost of a ghost who had once bled for us.

The Lemmy/Trump Test
By Anna Taborska

"It is difficult to know which came first, the
supply or the demand. ...Food from a food
bank – the supply – is a free good, and by
definition there is an almost infinite demand
for a free good."

> Lord David Freud,
> House of Lords debate,
> 2nd July 2013

Aim for the head – that's the only way to make sure
they stay down. Don't get their blood on you and,
whatever you do, don't let them bite you!

Oh, for Christ's sake, man, don't look so worried. We're
not going anywhere near them. Why'd you think I brought
this? ... Pretty, isn't it? Nothing like a family heirloom. My
great grandfather used it to hunt elephant in India. Just
imagine what it'll do to those stinking bastards.

They hang around the food bank during the day. Food
bank's been closed for weeks, but the dumb fucks just
won't leave. It's like they're totally brain dead – just keep
repeating what they used to do before. Shuffling around,
going through the motions... It's not need; it's greed! ...
LOL! ... At night they scavenge around the bins. Look –
over there! Here they come... They're coming to get you!

*Stacey follows the others round the back of the row of
restaurants, one hand clutching her daughter's little hand,
the other resting on her own swollen belly. She still can't
fathom how quickly her life has turned to hell.*

A tear rolls down Stacey's cheek as she recalls coming home to find police on her doorstep, waiting to give her the devastating news that the man she'd shared her life with since university had jumped off the balcony of their fifth floor council flat. The council flat they were being evicted from after losing their benefits. The note said that he was sorry, that there was nothing else he could do to keep them off the streets, and he couldn't live with that; that he loved them. Stacey had considered taking her daughter in her arms and following her husband – like the young woman she'd read about in the papers, but she didn't.

Stacey and Phoebe now lived under Hammersmith Bridge, part of a small community of homeless people who had taken in the heavily pregnant woman and her daughter. They'd lived on the one meal a day they'd been getting from the over-stretched food bank, but when that was forced to close, the hunger became unbearable.

Stacey begged outside the Riverside Studios or Hammersmith Mall during the day. Some people spat at her, accused her of having 'borrowed a child' to gain sympathy, and lectured her to get a job. Others looked at her with pity and threw her a few pence, sometimes a pound coin. One elderly gent had taken her and Phoebe to McDonald's, but the manager had soon thrown them out – their smell and general appearance was putting the other customers off their food.

On days when she didn't get enough from begging to buy food, she'd wait till dark and go through the bins, hoping that no one would see her. It seemed that many people had the same idea. They were a motley crew: many of them elderly, some disabled, some mentally ill, and some like Stacey: middle class, well educated, well adjusted, for whom what should have been a temporary setback – her husband's redundancy – had turned into a life-altering tragedy as societal safety nets had ripped open and Stacey and her family had fallen through.

Stacey tells Phoebe to wait quietly while she lifts a dustbin lid. That's when the shots ring out. Not far from Stacey an elderly man collapses, crying out in pain. Then people are screaming and running all around her. Stacey grabs her daughter by the hand, and they run too.

The hissing sound of compressed air behind her, and something strikes the back of Stacey's head. She is thrown forward onto her belly, pulling her daughter over with her. The last thing Stacey sees is her child wailing in terror and pain.

What's wrong? You're not upset, are you? They're only bloody Scroungers. You heard what the Welfare Minister said: in order to save the economy, we must get rid of 4 million useless mouths. Well, you didn't think he meant: buy them plane tickets to Timbuktu, did you? ... Come on, let's get to Rupert's. His soirée must be in full swing by now.

They're easy to pick off – Scroungers. And you're doing the country a favour. But you can't really have much fun with them. You never know what disease they might be carrying – most of them living rough now, like animals. It's best just to get a clean kill and get out. If you want to have some fun first, you should keep your old man covered, if you know what I mean. Best to sow your wild oats in the slightly 'better' areas.

We'll be sporting in Notting Hill tomorrow; if Rupert and the chaps like you, you can tag along. An initiation, if you like. We'll all be doing it together. The trick is to get a girl alone, maybe two girls. You can even do a couple – shag the girl and make the guy watch. Or shag them both. It's best not to leave any witnesses.

The Club awards points for a kill – the better the kill, the more points. And the more points, the higher you advance in the Club. Imagination is rewarded, but we value tradition above all. If you have to go in for a quick kill, try to crush the nose and gouge out the eyes at the same time – it takes some skill, but manage that and you'll get automatic membership. 'Tipping the lion', it used to be called; we just call it 'Fuckface'. But if you manage a 'Blood Eagle', you'll automatically advance to the level of Adept. It takes time so you can only do it in a secluded place. You get the prey on its front and cut the ribs by the backbone, breaking them outwards and spreading them, and pull out the lungs, one to each side. None of the other Clubs do it – it's our trademark. It has a demoralising effect on the natives, and warns other Clubs to stay off our sports ground. And it has a grand sense of the theatrical, which I must confess rather appeals to me. Have you ever thought of treading the boards?

Here we are. Rupert's is the last house on the right. Go ahead, don't be shy. I'm sure the chaps will like you.

Emily's eyes widen as the blade opens her vein. Wagner's 'Ride of the Valkyries' blares from the sound system in the corner. The girl tries to scream, but succeeds only in choking on the gag that's been shoved into her mouth. Blood pours out of her lacerated wrist, almost missing the silver cocktail shaker that's waiting to collect it. The tall young man with blonde hair and chiselled features – the one who'd offered Emily a hundred pounds to help serve drinks and canapés at his friend's party – giggles as he catches the blood. He holds down the lid on the metal container, doing a little dance as he shakes up the contents. "Shaken, not stirred!" he shouts over the opera. "Who's got the glasses?" Someone holds out a tray with tall glasses; each one has a piece of celery sticking out of it. The blonde 007 wannabe opens the cocktail shaker and distributes the contents.

I love the smell of vodka in the morning! Well, it's gone midnight – that technically makes it morning, does it not? What's wrong? Never had a proper Bloody Mary? ... Who *is* she? What do *you* care? She's a student Matthew picked

82

up. They'll do anything now that their loans have been called in. Don't worry about it. Drink up, man! To the Club!

You know, you're pretty lucky to be here. We don't usually allow non-members. But I knew from the moment I saw you that I was going to like you. You know how I knew? I call it the Lemmy/Trump test. You look puzzled. Well, when I meet someone for the first time, I try to work out whether, given the choice, they'd rather hang out with Lemmy or with Donald Trump. If I figure they'd rather hang out with Donald, then I know I'm going to like them. Don't get me wrong, I don't like new money; I wouldn't hang out with Trump myself, but I like the sensibilities of the self-made men and the city wide boys. Ruthless, like sharks. I have a certain sentiment for predators. They have a healthy attitude to life. It's the hippies I can't stand. The hippies and the rock'n'rollers, the wasters, the johnny-do-rights, the tree-huggers, the lefties, the whiners, the darkies, the single mothers and all the other scum. Too old, too sick or too lazy to be of any use to anyone. The Benefits Brigade. The Scroungers. Whether they're bleeding the country dry or helping others do so, they all have the same mentality. They're weak. They're victims. And there's nothing I hate more than a victim. Give me the Donald Trumps every time. Now you – as soon as I saw you, I knew you were a Donald Trump type.

But look at me, rambling on, while the chaps have got some entertainment lined up at the pool.

Marie whimpers as her chair is jolted roughly from behind. The wooden plank looms closer as Marie is pushed towards the deep end of the swimming-pool. She tries to cry out for help, but the multiple sclerosis took her voice a long time ago. She tries to struggle, but her muscles are no longer hers to control. The only thing she can do is grab hold of the wheels of her chair and try to block the forward motion generated by whoever is pushing it. The unseen assailant

*behind her back shoves the chair harder, and Marie flinches
as the rubber of the wheels burns her palms and fingers.*

*When the doorbell rang, Marie figured that her daughter
must have forgotten her keys when she went to the
supermarket. She'd wheeled herself to the front door and
opened the latch that had been lowered specially to be
within her reach. But it hadn't been Sylvie at the door; it
had been two smartly dressed youths, who'd taken hold of
her chair and wheeled her out into the street.*

*Marie tries to push the youths off as they strap her to her
wheelchair, and the chair to the large plank of wood. Fear
constricts her throat; she gasps like a beached fish, trying
to get air into her lungs. Another youth joins the group and,
as they push her end of the plank over the pool, Marie
urinates on herself. Then the wheelchair is over the water,
the weight of it bending the plank so that Marie is in the
pool. She tries to scream as the water closes over her head.*

*The youths attempt to pull the plank up and away from
the pool, planning to emulate the trial by water used in
medieval witchcraft trials. For a moment Marie's head is
above water again, and she pants desperately for air. But
the weight of the wheelchair is too great, and the plank
snaps, the metal of the chair dragging the terrified woman
to the bottom of the pool.*

Oh dear, she drowned. I guess she wasn't a benefit cheat
after all! … Didn't you see that cartoon on Facebook?
Assessing disability benefit claimants by ducking? If they
drown, they're eligible for benefits? Hilarious! When
Rupert saw it, he suggested it to the bird from the
Assessment Services that he's been shagging. He said she
paused way too long before laughing it off. Can you
imagine? Natural selection through benefits assessment…
LOL! … We'd soon have the country back on its feet! …
Anyway, Rupert's bit of fluff has proved a gem. She has
files full of info on Scroungers – home addresses and all.
Sometimes it's fun to choose your quarry to order. See the

look of surprise on their little faces when you ring their doorbell and address them by name.

But there I go, rambling again... Let's go back inside. I think Rupert likes you. That's a good sign. If you fare well at the sports tomorrow, you could be in.

Falling into Stone
By John Howard

Our name was my idea. The rest of it, all we did, was Josh's.

"We're living in hard times," Josh says. "Almost everyone's in trouble. But some aren't." He grins at me. He knows I'll go along with him – I always have done, ever since school. I can't help myself. "You and me, Luke," he says. "We'll get through all this. If you can't beat them, join them. We'll cause a bit of trouble of our own, make people think. But only those people who can take it. You know the types I mean. They've got enough already."

Josh has that way of drawing you in, making you go along with him, saying we're doing this together. Not anymore. Whenever I like I can leave him behind.

Josh and me, we couldn't be more different. I mean in how we ended up. We grew up on the same estate and were interested in the same subjects at school. We both really enjoyed the art class and were good students. We both drew and made models, mainly of real and imaginary buildings.

Somehow things changed, or maybe it was in me all along. Josh decided he wanted to be an architect – but all I wanted was to be with Josh. I knew it could never happen – he wasn't interested, or maybe never realised how I felt. Josh's parents supported him, while mine didn't seem very bothered what I wanted to do. Maybe I wasn't bright enough, although I'm not stupid. Anyway Josh went to university and got the qualifications. We lost touch, but I never forgot him.

Next time we meet I'm working on a restoration job on these flats as a semi-skilled hand and he's in a suit telling the foreman what to tell us to do. Friday evenings in the pub he tries to be one of the lads again and almost makes it, but not quite. There's something gets between him and us now. But he tries hard – he's genuine about it.

Josh asks me round to his place for a few drinks and to watch a film – a lads' night in, he says. He's got an apartment. He calls it an apartment, not a flat. It's in one of the new blocks near the river. These blocks look like they've got tin roofs which would come off with a gust of wind, and they're all frames with a bit of brick stuck on. Josh's place is nice inside. The rooms are all shiny wood and smooth plaster. They're small, but look bigger because they're just about empty. But the stuff Josh has must've cost him.

We drink this dark beer from the bottle. It tastes like smoky bacon crisps, and I almost fall off the sofa when Josh tells me the price. He's got the latest entertainment system and he streams a foreign film, but there are subtitles and I like it. There are these kids who break into rich people's houses when they're out and leave messages to scare the rich people. They don't do any harm or damage or anything but they want to scare the rich people.

There's a great view from his balcony but after the film and a few bottles of that beer I won't go anywhere near it. That makes Josh laugh, which I still like – but he doesn't go near the balcony either.

"It's a brilliant restoration job we're working on," he says. "It's a classic apartment block. One of those streamlined facades where the line of the windows and balconies make it resemble an ocean liner. Everything is smooth and sleek. Nothing is wasted or unnecessary. The effect depends on massing and volumes and placement – no decoration or anything that doesn't follow its function. Less is more, Luke. Those apartments give austerity a good name. You don't need anything outside of yourself. I'm going to try to get an apartment in that block. I know some of the people behind the contract and I'll have a chance if they put in a word for me. It's who you know, eh Luke?"

Josh goes on like that for a bit. I don't mind. He can talk well when it's something he knows and likes. I remember from school. I'm glad he's doing OK. Lots of people aren't. After a while he says his girlfriend's coming round later otherwise I could stay the night. I don't see where but the floor would've been fine. Josh says, "We'll do this again, soon, Luke, all right?" Somehow I get home no problem.

On Monday I'm at the site but I don't see Josh. His boss is there though. He says something to the foreman and calls us all together. "Bad news," he says. He looks like he's been crying. "Our client is bankrupt. He's pulled out of the job. It's up to his lawyers now. We probably won't get paid what we're owed. You might have to wait. I'm very sorry."

The foreman sends us home. "Sorry lads," he says. "I'll do my best with the management so you get some money to be going on with, at least." We're all on our phones calling girlfriends and wives and parents to tell them, and friends and contacts looking for new work. I wonder where Josh is.

A few days later I'm at home when Josh calls. I haven't found another job. I don't remember giving Josh my number but I must have. He invites me round his place. "Might as well finish the last of this," he says, giving me a bottle of the weird beer. "I'm out of here." I look at him. He looks as smooth as ever, but there's something about his eyes. He grins. "Yes, Luke, I've lost my job too," he says. "I've been made redundant. The firm can't keep everyone on now the jobs we were doing for Mr Bankrupt have packed in. I can't believe it – we never got the money up front." He looks around the room. It looks emptier. "I've got to sell all my stuff, everything that isn't being repossessed. I can't rent here anymore. Sarah's not coming round – ever again. Not now."

I say the usual things. I'm about to say less is more and all that, but don't. Josh grins again but it's a show. "We were going through a rough patch, to be honest," he says. "We would've split up anyway, sooner or later. It's just happened sooner. Now I really need to know who my friends are, Luke."

I put in a word for Josh and he gets a room in the big old house I share. It's small but OK. He's sold or given away most of his stuff. "It hadn't been paid for anyway," he says. "They're welcome to it." Josh's on his laptop all the time but none of his old mates from university or the firms he knows get him anything. I get a bit of casual stuff, enough to pay the rent and buy a few tins of beer at the weekend. Nothing's much different from before – there's just less of it. Josh gets more and more angry. I can tell. "This isn't where I'd planned to move to," he says. Mainly he keeps it bottled-up inside, but I can tell. One night he knocks on my door and we go to his room for a beer. Tins of lager, but they're OK. His room is as bare as his old apartment was, but there's no balcony and the view from the window isn't as nice.

"You remember that film we watched when you came round to my last place?" Josh asks. "I've been doing a bit of thinking. There are lots of houses, big, posh houses, empty some if not all of the time. And you and me, we're in a dump like this. They say we're in hard times, but not everyone is. Luke, you and me, we can make it a bit softer for ourselves. And have a bit of fun, harmless fun. Are you up for it? Just until things get better."

I still don't know why I say it. I have no idea where it came from. "You mean like austerity outlaws?" I say. "You and me – we'll be austerity outlaws?"

Josh grins and laughs. It's the first time for a while. I'm happy about that. "You're a genius, Luke!" he says. He throws me another can of beer. "Let's drink to us – the Austerity Outlaws!"

Josh makes up a logo we can draw on pieces of paper or card and leave behind us. I tell him I recognize the A for Austerity but not the other letter. He says it's still an O, but from the Greek alphabet. The whole thing can mean from the beginning to the end. I don't really get that, but it's a nice logo, easy to remember and draw. I practice it a few times to get it right. It takes me back to art class – the best part of being at school.

It's fun being an Austerity Outlaw. Josh knows about a lot of very nice places that are empty or where the people are away. I suppose it's through his old contacts. We're careful. There have to be no alarms or security, but sometimes they're so easy to dodge or fix it's like there's no security at all. Josh sorted out some electrics once or twice – I don't know where he learned to do that. If we do have a problem we run like hell. We never get caught, not me and Josh.

So we go into these houses. We move the furniture around, leave pictures at an angle, that sort of thing – harmless but scary to come home to. Sometimes we take food or something to drink, but we don't steal anything. We don't damage anything either. Josh says austerity should be creative, not destructive. He says everyone else can do the destroying. Sometimes we work hard and move furniture and valuable objects into another room to make it look like there's been a robbery. He likes it when we've made a room bare. He says that's how it was meant to be – just space to live in, which should be enough. We leave our message and go. "Let them find out how less really is more," Josh says.

Josh looks in his book a lot. It's a sort of guidebook to modern buildings and houses. There are little photos of each one, and plans. He says it's the only book he's got left. "These are some of the finest modern houses in the country," he says. "I studied them at university. The apartment block we were restoring is in here. Actually those sorts of places aren't very modern by age. Most of them were built between the two World Wars. It was a classic era." He closes the book and turns to me. "You know, Luke, back then it was like now. No – probably even worse, actually. The Great Depression. There was high unemployment, cutbacks, poverty. They taught people to be suspicious, to hate. If you had money you were fine. If not, you weren't. You could do anything if you had the money. Keep in with the right people, live like a king. Money always talks. And if you lost it, you were lost, too."

I like it when Josh talks that way, even about bad things. I can listen to him. I don't always know what he's on about, but I can tune in and out and feel different for a while afterwards. "Your life, Luke, you fell off the scaffolding," he says. "You dropped, fell into liquid concrete, went down and down and ended up buried alive with all the others. It would've been a better end to hit something solid. Luke, neither is going to happen to me." Then he says quickly, "Or us, right?"

We get some warm days and Josh looks in his book. There are quite a few of these big classic modern houses in suburbs around the city or just outside. Josh says some of the owners have lost their money or are cutting back. Their places will be empty or closed-up or both – nice for us.

We hitch our way out to one of these houses. It's white and low and only just shows above the trees. The garden's gone wild and hedges and trees grow up all around it, in front of the windows and doors. The windows are huge, and are covered by metal grills or heavy plastic panels. The house is empty. We get in easily enough. It looks as if it's been empty for months.

When we're inside Josh gets out his book and we have a tour. This place is completely bare, but Josh says it was supposed to be all austere and minimalist anyway. "Less is more," he keeps on saying. He says there was hardly any furniture and all the cupboards and things were built into the walls. As far as I can tell you have to be very rich to afford to have so few things. Josh says he wishes we could see the rooms by full daylight as that's the best way. "It's the human scale." Then he says, over and over, "It's simply beautiful."

I feel something too. Maybe not like Josh, but I'm not him. There's lots of space, and the distances between the walls feel right, somehow. How they should be. The light comes in where it should and falls where it needs to. Everything seems to fit together. I think I could get used to living in a house like this. Josh talks about the workmanship, the craftsmanship, the quality of the materials, their cost. The walls are finished perfectly – Josh says most of them are concrete. But they don't look it – they seem too smooth, like fabric stretched out tightly. I push the palm of my hand against a wall, but it doesn't bend inwards like it looks as if it should. It's solid – firm and doesn't give. The floors are stone – travertine and marble, Josh says.

There's only the one storey, but it's not just a big posh bungalow. There are steps and ramps to the different levels in other parts of the house. There's also a spiral staircase leading to the roof, but we don't try to go up there and onto it in case anyone spots us. One room is a huge curved window all on one side, but it's covered by the thick plastic panels so the light is dim and distorted, like wearing smeared sunglasses indoors. Josh goes to the wall opposite the curving window. "This is really special," he says. "The wall's panelled with British marble, really rare. Look at the colours and patterns, Luke, the flecks of silver and gold. It's like they're floating above the colours but below the surface. It's cool to the touch, even in this weather." I have a look too. I'm floating above crumpled mountains and rivers are veins in the marble. The surface is still polished and smooth as glass. I could slip over and fall in. Josh laughs when I tell him. "I'll rescue you," Josh says.

His voice trails off and he turns to me and smiles. He's let his hair grow and he brushes a strand away from his face. I keep my hair as short as ever. Before I know it I begin to stretch my arm out, but Josh grabs it like we're going to shake hands and we do. No more than that, though. Josh never hugs. We go back to the big main room. It's all shadowy but we settle down in a corner and unpack the stuff we've brought for the night.

In the morning we leave our AO message. I have to remind Josh before we move on. He doesn't seem bothered if anyone's going to know whether we've been here or not.

We do this for a while. Then one time Josh asks me if I remember the house. When he shows it me in his book I do for sure. "It's been bought by our old boss," he says. "Well, maybe he wasn't exactly that, but he's the man who declared bankruptcy and made us lose our jobs. How could he afford to buy a house like that now?"

"He's on the way up," I say. "Money talks."

I ask Josh how he found out. "On my phone," he says. "It's easy. I had to check these sorts of records a lot when I was in the office." Then he gets out this phone and does a search. He shows me. I didn't know Josh still has his phone – it's one of the latest ones, very expensive. We're supposed to be getting rid of all our extra things. We can't carry stuff about when we're the Austerity Outlaws. Josh doesn't seem to notice how I feel.

He starts getting all angry again thinking about the house and its new owner. "He's got the money," Josh says. "Somehow he has. Or the right people reckon he's got it. Listen, Luke, we've got to go back there." He smiles, but it's a different type this time. Not one I like.

The grass is cut and some of the hedges trimmed back. The grills and panels on the windows have gone. There was a wire fence and notices about guards and a patrol with dogs but we didn't see anything.

There's no problem getting in again. These people haven't got a clue. We walk around the house. It's a different place with the light coming in. It's still empty but there's lots of builders' stuff piled in one room. We can see there's a layer of dust over everything, even on the walls. But the house seems sound.

Josh walks around and looks at everything, touching and sizing-up like he's buying it himself with his own money. He doesn't care how dirty he gets. I sit down and watch.

Josh runs his hands over the walls and kneels down to touch the floors. He opens and closes doors and cupboards, stroking the wood like he's in love with it.

Seeing that doesn't make me feel good.

But what does is the way the sunlight comes in at angles. I can see it because of the dust. The light looks solid. The rooms breathe the light in, and the walls and floors suck it in like they're thirsty. They let me do that too. Shadows are waiting their turn.

"Everything is so right about this place," Josh says. "You see that, Luke?" He looks around, scanning the walls. "I should be on the way to getting somewhere like this, if it wasn't for the firm not getting its money."

I tell him I know what he's saying about the house. I mean it. Josh laughs. "Maybe you should've trained as an architect with me," he says. He sits down next to me. "You have the feel for places like this, I can tell from before." Josh is close. There's something different about him. If we'd had a few drinks I reckon I might say something. Man to man, good mates.

Josh goes quiet. I can tell when he's thinking, when something's getting to him. After a while he gets up and walks over to some sliding doors hiding some shelves. Josh says the wood is solid beech and the fittings are unique, designed only for this house. "I don't know why these doors weren't taken out for safekeeping," he says. "They should've stored all the ironmongery, too." Then he pulls a knife out of his pocket, one of the ones you slide open to cut plastic and boxes, and gouges our AO sign, big, into each door. He grunts with the effort. I jump up.

"Don't say anything, Luke," Josh says in this odd voice. We had a teacher spoke like that when he couldn't explain something properly so you couldn't quite get what he was on about. He scratches all the fittings as well. He moves so he's standing against the light. Josh is a shadow walking out of the sun, but solid, like a statue. Then he comes back over to where I'm still standing.

"You said we don't damage places," I say.

"The Austerity Outlaws don't damage places," he repeats, imitating my voice in a stupid way. "Luke, I haven't started."

I tell him no but he pushes me away. "You really do appreciate this house, don't you, Luke? Modernist masterpieces like this? You could've made the effort, made a proper career for yourself, maybe a bit of money, one day you could have owned one. You might've had better luck than me. I might've been working for you by now! Do you want to borrow my book?" He pulls it out of his pocket and rips out some pages. He holds them out to me then takes them back again. Josh has this big shiny lighter, old fashioned. Something else he shouldn't have. He sets fire to the book and drops it on the floor. He pushes me away when I try to kick the fire out. It doesn't catch anyway, but the book's damaged and there's ash and bits of torn paper on the floor. Josh rubs it across the tiles with his foot, smearing it there.

"The Austerity Outlaws have had enough," Josh shouts. "I've lost my job, my place to live. All I've got is a crappy room in a crappy house and no-one wants to know me anymore." I want to tell him that he couldn't say that, and I do still want to know him. But we had a deal. The AO had a deal together. And we're supposed to be best friends.

"Austerity Outlaws is a laugh but this time I'm not laughing," Josh says. "Not in this house. That bastard doesn't deserve it. He's not going to have it. I'm really going to leave my mark. I'm not being buried alive like you. If I'm falling it's going to be onto a floor made of marble. I'll leave my mark all right." Josh goes into the room where all the builders' stuff is and comes out with a masonry hammer. He runs over to one of the walls and smashes the hammer against it two or three times. Plaster falls off and big cracks show. I'm standing some way away but in the room it's like explosions going off next to my head. My head's ringing like someone shouted right into my ear. I run towards Josh, but trip on a step where the room's level changes. I fall over, hitting the floor and scraping skin off my hands.

I can't believe it but Josh starts to laugh. I don't know what's got into him. He lets the hammer go so it drops on the floor, and the heavy thud of it hitting goes right through me. I put my hands to my head and there's blood where I scraped them. My hands are sticky and covered with bits of grit and plaster and tiny sharp bits from where Josh dropped the hammer on the floor. And there's some of my blood on the floor but it soaks in and disappears even as I look at it.

"Look what you've done," I shout at Josh. I hold my hands out. Maybe I hope he would hold them, take me to where we left our rucksacks so he would get out one of our bottles of water and wash my hands and clean ourselves up. Josh picks up the hammer. "Less is more," he says. "He's going to have less." He looks at my hands. "Why don't you rub them on the walls? Make yourself useful, Luke. He wants blood, he can have it."

Not for the first time since I've known Josh I want to cry. But I can't show him.

Josh kneels down, smashing the hammer down on the floor. "Less – is – more!" he shouts, as it hits the floor, cracking the stone. I thought he loved that stone. He shouts each word as he brings the hammer down, smash, crash. He does it again and again. I go and lean against the wall. I rub my eyes but it's painful but now it looks like they're hurt and not that I'm trying not to cry. There's a bit of my blood on the wall but it soaks in like it was never there. I lick my hands, and taste the blood and bits of plaster and tiny chips of marble.

"Luke!" Josh shouts from another room and I go to find him. I'm back to obeying him. He's in the room with the curving window. He's standing by the wall made from polished marble. My head starts to ring with echoes. For a moment I have the feeling of falling sideways, slipping into it, like before. Josh is covered in sweat, glinting on his skin in the sunlight filling up the room. He's gripping the hammer and there are cracks and gouges in the marble. There's blood on his forehead. He wipes it off with his free hand and looks around. Josh is about to wipe his hand on his shirt when he grins, the horrible grin, not the grin he uses for me, and rubs his hand against the marble. His blood stays there like someone's flicked red paint.

"What?" I shout. Josh just wants to make me see the damage he's doing. We had a deal – the Austerity Outlaws, no damage – but he's ruining it. He strikes the wall again with the hammer, sending more slivers of marble flying. Some of them cut him as I watch. I stand away so they can't cut me. Now he's trying to hammer our AO design into the marble. He's not getting very far, even though he's really damaging the wall. Josh drops the hammer and gets out his knife and starts scratching it against the polished stone.

"Look!" He screams as he tries to carve the logo. The knife slips all over the place. "I'm having it! This is going to be my house now!" I rush over to him to grab the knife but he swings it at me and I only just dodge out of the way. "You said no damage!" I shout, trying to make him listen to me. "We agreed, together. Not this!"

"All deals are off!" Josh shouts back. He stumbles into a slanting block of yellow light that was hiding in the room all the time. Now I see it, sliding in through the window, all the way down from the sun. It's a door opening. Josh goes in as if there's a new room and comes out again like from behind a curtain. He still looks like Josh but I don't know how much he is.

Then dust and bits of marble and concrete and chippings start rising up like fog and hiding the light. Everything swirls around in a sort of dirty blizzard. I hear hammers and engines and concrete pouring and blurry voices and laughing. I collide with Josh and try to pull him out of the room but he pushes me away and I slip over and I can't tell where to get out, then the marble wall is there to meet me. I start coughing and fall over again as I twist backwards. I

97

know I'm shouting Josh's name but it's become a separate thing and anyway he can't hear me and I can't see him anymore. I never felt the wall, but the dust and fog follows me wherever I am. I roll down a step, cutting my hands and arms. The dust and fog follows me. I crawl around in the stony hard shadows and see my blood smearing on the floor. This time it stays there. "I'm out, I'm out!" I keep shouting. But marble is all there is to push against – its patterns of veins and forms.

Then I'm sitting in the sunshine with my back against a wall. It's clean and white, warm from the sun.

Sometime later I think about looking for Josh so we can get away together. I hear a noise, and he's coming out of the house. He looks a mess.

"Josh!" I shout. "Josh!" I try talking to him, all gently, like I've always really wanted to. "Josh," I whisper. He must be able to hear me – he turns his head. There's a beginning. But he stands there and doesn't say anything. I get closer, touch his hair and push it back a little. I lean in and gently brush away a splinter of marble from his cheek. Then I look into his eyes. All I see is me and the gleaming empty light. The light could be draining out of his eyes or already be outside wrapping us up. But inside it's completely bare. Behind Josh's eyes there's nothing left to value – everything's gone. They're as smooth and shiny and solid as the polished marble wall. The flecks in the marble are those in his eyes, too – just the same, embedded where there can be no depth. And now there's no help, nothing at all.

Ptichka
By Laura Mauro

The night Marta finds out she's pregnant, she cries.

In the yellowish light of an old desk lamp, Marta rifles through an NHS pamphlet "*Information for migrants giving birth in the UK*", as if they're a different species. She adds up the cost of the many and varied tests recommended by the antenatal clinic: *urinalysis, nuchal scan, rhesus factor*, strange words in a strange alphabet. She scribbles it all down on a notepad, coming up with a figure that far exceeds her wage. For Marta, free medical care seems like a distant dream, a long-ago rumour, though it's barely been two years since the law changed.

She stares down at the pregnancy test in her hands, as if sheer force of will can spirit the money into being. And then she cries. She cries so hard, and for so long that the Sri Lankan woman in the downstairs flat starts banging on the ceiling, calling up the stairs for her to *please, shut up*, or she'll call their landlord. When her baby starts crying, a barrage of florid, bilingual curses echo in the corridor, seeping in beneath her front door, and Marta has never felt so alone in all her life.

At 5 AM, Marta goes to work. She sits alone at the back of the bus, trying to ignore the fermented piss stink leftover from the late night crowd. It's still dark outside, and she dozes, face pressed up against the cold window. She dreams fitfully of the nice English boy who disappeared into thin air; who, for one night, held her close and told her she was beautiful, and left her pregnant and scared in a country she's trying very hard to think of as home.

Marta has a minimum wage job and a roof over her head; she might have had those things in Russia too, but she still believes she can have a better future here, if she works hard enough. She spends nine hours serving up chicken nuggets and chips to uninterested customers and their unbearable offspring, and tells herself this isn't forever.

She stops by an internet cafe on the way home, partly for the warmth. On a forum for Russian ex-pats she reads about clinics: illegal setups offering check-ups for migrants, undercutting NHS prices. The doctors are questionably qualified, or long retired, but in the absence of an EU passport or a lottery win, she's out of better options.

There are other places – places that *end* pregnancies – but she's not sure she wants that. Not yet.

Marta scribbles the phone number down on a scrap of paper, hides it in her inside pocket. She deletes her search history before she leaves. It's impossible to know who's watching, and it's better to be paranoid than stupid. People like her have been arrested for much less.

The obstetric clinic is tucked away above a launderette in Mile End. It's someone's flat, she realises, as she comes in through the door. A scattering of post lies unopened on the doormat, bearing the grubby shoeprints of a day's worth of patients.

An unsmiling woman instructs her to wait, so she takes a seat in the narrow hallway, feet tucked beneath her chair, feeling like a nervous child outside the headmaster's office.

At the foot of the stairs, an old birdcage hangs from a hook nailed into the wall. Inside, a cockatiel huddles on its perch, plumage ragged, watching Marta with baleful black eyes. The perches are crusted white with old shit; the ammoniac stink of it makes her faintly nauseous.

She knows the fluttering in her abdomen is just nerves, but it frightens her all the same.

"Miss…Berezhnaya?"

Marta looks up. The unsmiling woman stands at the clinic door, clipboard in hand. They're alone in the hallway, and the mangling of her surname seems redundant, but the illusion of propriety must be important to her. She leads Marta into the clinic, which overlooks the street; she can see the blurred motion of cars through the gaps in the dusty Venetian blinds. There's a worn-out examination couch pushed up against the wall, and a table stacked high with plastic storage boxes filled with drugs. Marta wonders how long ago they expired.

The doctor is an elderly English man, hair stained nicotine yellow. He has her sit on the couch while the unsmiling woman – evidently a nurse of some kind – wraps a blood pressure cuff around her arm. "You speak English?" she asks, brusque. The space beneath her eyes is bruise-blue and hollow, like she hasn't slept in days.

The machine thrums as the cuff contracts, squeezing her arm tight. "Yes," Marta says, grimacing. The nurse grunts an acknowledgement, glancing at the reading on the screen, noting it down on her clipboard. She asks an array of questions: last menstrual period, family history of diabetes, any unusual bleeding. Marta answers politely and concisely, and although her curdled-milk expression never changes, the nurse seems somewhat pacified.

"We get so many Polish girls in here," the nurse says. "They get themselves knocked up by British men – got wives already, dirty bastards – they come in snivelling because they thought they'd get a passport. Don't speak a lick of English either."

"I'm not Polish," Marta says.

"Not much difference," the nurse says, without malice.

The examination is the kind of mundane, tick-box experience Marta expected. The doctor coats her bare abdomen in clear gel. The ultrasound machine is as old and worn as the doctor himself, and although it looks barely functional, the screen is clear enough: a white blur, abstract and meaningless, forms the centre of the picture. It seems impossible to Marta that this bright smudge is a baby.

The doctor frowns, adjusts the angle of the wand, pushing it so hard into Marta's belly that she wants to

101

smack the wand right out of his hands. Outside, the cockatiel kicks into a chorus of squawking. The nurse storms over to the door and slams it shut.

Finally, gravely, the doctor looks up and says, "there's something wrong with the foetus."

The doctor suspects anencephaly. He prints her off a page from the internet, and all she's able to glean is that her baby – that formless white smudge on a grubby screen – is somehow developing wrong. There's an anatomical diagram printed blurrily at the foot of the page; the baby's face ceases entirely just above the eyes. It makes her skin crawl just to look at it.

The doctor told her that, deformed as it was, the baby would almost certainly be stillborn. And she stared numbly at the long-outdated posters tacked to the clinic walls and said "do what you think is best."

On the tube home, Marta rubs at the sore spot where he injected her. "Expect cramps and heavy bleeding," he told her, wiping away a bead of blood welling from the wound like a tiny red eye. "If you don't stop bleeding in a couple of days, or the pain becomes unbearable, go to A&E."

Which surely had to be a joke, Marta thinks; he must know the law. If she can't afford proper prenatal care, how can she possibly afford A&E?

There's a sharp, sudden twinge in her stomach.

In the clinic, she counted out the notes carefully, pressing a wad of grubby twenties into the doctor's nicotine-stained palm. He refused payment for the injection. "Think of it as a favour," he said. "Go home. Get it over with. You were unlucky this time. Next time will be better."

Marta's mother – a tall, plump woman, forever in an apron – once told her that she'd been born under unlucky stars.

She grits her teeth against the cramps, ignoring the questioning gaze of the woman sitting opposite.

If her mother were still alive, Marta would ask her why she couldn't have held on until morning.

The blood never comes.

The cramps subside before midnight, and she sleeps that night with a bath towel spread out beneath her, anticipating a terrible mess. But when she wakes, there is no blood, not even a drop. Her stomach aches a little, but even that is gone by the time she gets to work. She crams a clutch of maxi-pads into her handbag just in case.

Three days pass, and still no blood, no cramps; she digs the paper-scrap from her coat pocket and calls the clinic, but it just goes through to voicemail. She goes to work, because there's nothing else she can do, ambling blindly through another shift. It's late by the time she gets home, and the Sri Lankan woman – Ayesha, Marta has signed for her post more than once – is leaning out of the living room window, smoking a cigarette, child propped up on the sill and staring placidly at Marta. Marta says good evening, and is rewarded with a curt nod.

Upstairs, the flat is freezing; she switches on the archaic space heater and peels off her uniform, leaving it puddled on the floor. She makes to crawl into bed but stops, catching sight of herself reflected in the window.

Her belly has grown. She turns slowly, marvelling at the way her skin is stretched tight like a drum. She has been dazed, lately, paying little attention to her body except for the increasingly distant promise of blood. She stares at her reflection, at her too-long limbs and fine, dark hair. Her swollen stomach is awkward on her thin frame.

Marta presses a hand out to the window, tracing her belly in the faint condensation.

There's a sudden thump, and the rattle of loose glass as something hits the window hard. The impact reverberates up her arm. She yelps, leaping back from the window. Her feet tangle in the mess of clothes; Marta yanks the shirt from around her ankles, heart thudding hard in her chest, and peers up at the window.

The sky is clotted with black cloud, swallowing the moon entirely. Imprinted against the outside of the window, almost obscured by condensation, is the pale ghost of outstretched feathers; a chalk-outline smear detailing the impact of a bird against the glass.

Marta pulls on her trousers and coat and scurries downstairs. Ayesha's front window is closed now, curtains drawn, the remains of a cigarette smouldering on the sill outside. She tiptoes barefoot around to the back of the house, down an alley filled with two weeks' worth of uncollected black bags – even in this cold weather, the stink is eye watering – and there, lying still beneath Ayesha's kitchen window, is the bird. Its neck lists at an unnatural angle, but its eyes are open still, gazing up at her with what she imagines to be reproach.

In Russia, when a bird hits the window, a death is on the way.

She ducks low, breathing white into the dark, and scoops the bird up in both hands; its heart beats against her palms, frantic at first, growing ever slower as she sits, shivering, running a gentle thumb down its plumage. *Skvorets*. She doesn't know the English name.

Behind her, the kitchen window creaks open.

"It's dead," Ayesha says, appraising the broken little thing in Marta's hands. Her mouth is curled into a familiar frown. Ayesha never smiles. "Throw it over the fence, let the foxes have it."

"It's still alive," Marta says. "I can feel its heart beating."

Ayesha shrugs. There's a flare of bright light as she strikes a match, lights another cigarette. "It'll be dead soon," she says. A grey plume billows out from between her parted lips. Marta doesn't know how she can afford to smoke as much as she does.

104

They sit like that for a time; Ayesha silently smoking, Marta cradling the dying bird, her bare toes slowly turning numb. For ten minutes, the bird perseveres. Why? Marta wonders. Doesn't it know the battle it's fighting is hopeless?

Eventually, Ayesha's baby starts crying, and she departs without a word, pulling the window shut behind her. The child's insistent wail continues, muted now behind glass.

Abruptly, the bird's heart stops.

Marta gets to her feet and lays the bird beneath an overgrown bush at the back of the garden. Maybe the foxes will find it, she thinks. Or maybe it'll lie there, too frozen to rot, preserved and perfect until spring comes.

She looks out of the window the next morning: the bird is a small black shape just visible beneath the frost-rimed leaves. Untouched, as if kept behind glass.

Marta steps out of the shower, glancing at her changing form in the steam-clouded mirror; the stretch marks are vivid in the light, blue lines like veins, marking her sudden growth. She swears she's grown bigger since last night.

She places her palm, gentle, just above the concavity of her navel, tapping her index finger twice against the drum-tight skin.

For a long moment, nothing happens, and she feels stupid then; was she truly expecting her child – poor deformed thing, hanging on in spite of the doctor's intervention – to tap back? To understand her intentions, her maternal Morse-code: *tap twice if you're still alive.*

And then there's a ripple of motion inside her, like the stirring of damp, newborn wings, and she smiles, amazed at his persistence, at his struggle to stay alive. She whispers promises in the language of her mother: *Keep fighting. I will keep you safe.*

Over two months her belly grows, far quicker than it should; she lies when people ask her how far along she is.

She is twenty-two weeks pregnant, but looks almost ready to burst, abdomen ripe and round with fluid. Marta continues to go to work, because she can't afford not to, and maternity leave is a luxury she won't be afforded. She wears her old uniform until the buttons gape wide, and her boss grudgingly gives her a new one on the promise that she'll pay for it later.

Nobody asks where the father is.

Every day, Marta performs the same ritual: two taps above her navel, protruding now like a tiny thumb. And every day he answers, growing ever stronger; she feels him high in her gut, tight and coiled, shifting occasionally when his position no longer suits him. Some nights she lies in her bed, distended belly gently pulsing, and wonders if the doctor got it wrong.

Marta goes into labour on a Sunday afternoon. She's standing in the canned goods aisle in Morrison when the first contractions come; a raw, tearing sensation, like something is newly awoken inside of her, and is trying, with tooth and claw, to force its way out.

She has nothing meaningful to compare the pain to; she's never given birth, never so much as broken a bone, but she knows, as she doubles over, that this is not normal. The woman beside her pauses to stare, briefly, before returning to the infinitely more important business of comparing the calorie content of the tinned beans. Marta bites back a gasp. She drops her basket and stumbles down the aisle, wiping her streaming eyes with the back of her hand.

A warm wetness runs down the inside of her thighs. She knows it's blood. She can smell the sour tang of it, coppery and obscene. And everyone is staring at her now, watching the madwoman stagger past the checkouts, out into the cold street. Somehow, she finds her way home; by the time she gets there her vision is swimming at the edges, hands trembling as she tries to slot the key into the lock. After a few attempts Ayesha comes to the door. Marta can barely make sense of the other woman's facial features but she thinks Ayesha looks mildly irritated.

"The baby," Marta says, indicating the bulge of her belly, and the dark, reddish stain on her jeans. "It's too early."

"Go to the hospital, then," Ayesha says. Pain splits Marta through her middle; she grabs Ayesha's wrist, fingers tight. Ayesha's skin is cold and dry, rough like tree bark.

"I haven't got enough money," Marta says, through gritted teeth.

And Ayesha nods. She understands. Marta has spent long nights kept awake by the rasping, wheezing coughs of Ayesha's child in the grip of bronchitis, and Ayesha's feet thumping against the floorboards, pacing endlessly up and down.

Ayesha guides her inside, where it's only marginally warmer. The communal hallway smells of dust and old, damp carpet. She all but drags Marta up the stairs, fumbles in Marta's pocket for the front-door key. "Avanthi's asleep," she says, when Marta glances questioningly at Ayesha's door. "She'll be okay for a while."

They stumble into the bedsit, the pair of them, like drunks after a long night out.

"Where's the other one?" Ayesha asks, looking around. "The Colombian girl?"

"Deported," Marta answers. She crawls onto the bed and curls up tight. "In November. Only me now."

Ayesha leaves Marta writhing on the bed while she hunts through the cupboards, the bathroom, picking through Marta's meagre supplies for anything useful. When she returns, she's got an armful of old towels, a full kettle and a plastic washing-up bowl.

"I've done this before," Ayesha tells her, laying the towels beneath Marta. She's no less terse, but she is the only familiar face Marta knows. Though as she bleeds steadily, breathes hard, Ayesha's face seems to smear at the edges like a child's watercolour, the puffy margins of her cheeks indistinct in the bright afternoon light.

Marta doesn't feel Ayesha pull her jeans off (though she does hear the sharp intake of breath, and sees the bright gleam of panic in Ayesha's eyes, and she wonders just how much blood there is now; her little bedroom smells like a slaughterhouse). Her belly seems to pulse visibly as if it's a living thing, pale and ugly. Hot pain tears through her. She's being sliced open, torn apart. In her delirium, she imagines her belly is splitting in the middle, white skin peeling back; a bloody flower, her baby pink and pristine at the centre. She's silent throughout, soaked through with sweat but colder than she's ever been in her life. Her teeth chatter loosely in her skull, a strange percussion.

Marta hears herself moaning. She sounds very far away.

Ayesha places a fat little hand on Marta's forehead. "You have a bad fever," she says, shaking her head, dark fingers smeared with bright blood. "You need the hospital."

"I can't pay," Marta says. Her head lolls to the side. She can't lift it. Her muscles are useless, paralysed by the pain. Everything seems a too bright, a little too liquid. She peers up at the window, at the pale bird-ghost imprinted on the outside, a stark, burning white against the blue sky.

It's still there when she squeezes her eyes shut, opens her mouth wide and screams, tasting the salt of her sweat as it runs down her face. Something wrenches deep inside her; she can hear Ayesha telling her to push and she's bursting, coming apart at the seams, raw and burning and dizzy.

And just like that, it's over.

The room is silent save for her own ragged breathing. The baby should be crying. They always cry in films.

"Let me see him," she says, breathless.

Ayesha's staring down at the bloody towel bundled in her arms. "His head…" she mumbles, appalled.

"My *son*," Marta insists. Her lips feel numb and awkward; the worlds are lumpen in her mouth. "Give him to me."

108

Ayesha places the bundle in Marta's outstretched arms. He's so light, but she can barely hold him; her arms feel insubstantial as she lifts him up, seeking the face beneath the red-stained folds. He's perfect, her son; his black feathers are slick with fluids, eyes hard and unblinking. Beautiful *ptichka*, small enough to fit in the concavity of her cupped palms.

She smiles up at Ayesha, lips pulled tight over her teeth, and says, distantly: "He has his father's eyes."

The other woman's eyes are wide with horror, and bright with tears. "It's dead," she says, quiet. "Can't you see?"

Marta shifts her son to the crook of her elbow, places two fingers on the bony arch of his chest and taps, gently, hollow bird-bones reverberating. And there's his pulse, slow beneath her fingers like the ripple of tiny wings.

"No," Marta whispers. "He's still alive. I can feel his heart beating."

109

The Devil's Only Friend
By Stephen Bacon

The walk from the train station was exhausting. By the time Nolan had reached the B&B his lips were chapped, his face stung by the wind. He paid by cash and was directed to a room on the third floor: a sparse hovel, barely larger than the box he'd occupied for the past six years. At least the threadbare carpet was marginally more comfortable than those cold tiles.

He sat on the sagging bed and stared through the net curtains. The building opposite lurked sullenly, a hulking silhouette that blocked the glare of the town's neon. At some point, part of its roof had collapsed, though Nolan could see shadows flitting through the broken windows, movement beneath the exposed eaves. Probably just roosting gulls. Scaffolding and polythene sheets did their best to conceal the building's ruined state. A wooden fence surrounded the perimeter of the grounds, plastered with warning signs prohibiting entry.

It was getting late. The window was draughty, and Nolan could hear the pulse of techno music from the bar, two streets away. He felt his heart race instinctively. He was out of practice but he knew he couldn't resist the lure.

Six years was six years.

Afterwards they lay in silence on the bed, allowing the mood to slip away. Nolan's arm was under the boy's side and he tried not to imagine he was trapped. It had been so long since he'd done this he wasn't quite sure of the correct etiquette. But the boy twisted his spray-tanned torso and turned to Nolan. "This a smoking room?"

Nolan knew it wasn't but he was afraid of losing the boy so he said, "You'll be all right." He fought the urge to glance at the ceiling's smoke detector.

The boy – *Brett, wasn't it?* – leaned out of bed and fished around in the pocket of his jeans. He lit a cigarette and lay back against the pillow, exhaling a slender coil of smoke.

Nolan watched the process with his stomach in knots. Every time the boy sucked on the cigarette the tip glowed, burning with an intensity that matched his own accelerated heartbeat. He tried to remember the relaxation techniques he'd been taught in his therapy sessions but they seemed so distant it almost felt like they'd happened to someone else. Although didn't everything? They'd told him this was all part of the coping mechanism.

The boy finished his cigarette and climbed out of bed. He was skinny and hairless, well-defined arms and stomach. A nice tattoo extended from his left shoulder to the tops of his buttocks. He opened the window and tossed the cigarette-butt out. For a few seconds he remained staring through the net curtains. "'Bout time they knocked that place down." He turned and looked at Nolan, smiling provocatively.

Nolan returned his gaze through the smoky veil. He could feel the tension in his chest. The smell of smoke and his memory of the cigarette stirred excitement. Vibrant. Untethered.

The boy misinterpreted Nolan's pause. "That place over the road, I mean."

"Yeah," said Nolan expressionlessly.

But the boy continued. "Fucking place burned down years ago. Arson - so they said. Rumoured it's gonna be an Aldi, once they sort out the insurance."

Nolan shrugged. Aldi left him feeling detached, just like Ikea and all those trendy coffee-shops. In the week since his release he'd noticed them littering the high street; replacements for the shops that had closed during the period

111

of his detainment – Woolworths, Comet, Clinton Cards, Jessops – names that now sounded like relics of his old life, back when his desire felt more like compulsion than just a yearning.

His thoughts were interrupted by the boy. "So you used to live round here then?"

"Years ago." Nolan nodded. "Came here after I dropped out of Uni."

The boy walked back and threw himself on to the bed. "Too bad you weren't here in the summer. We'd've had some fun."

Nolan smiled absently and leaned forward.

The park was almost empty. Nolan had been there for almost an hour. Now the kids had gone back to school it was populated by dog-walkers and red-faced joggers, pensioners wearing thick anoraks who used the park as a short-cut to the community centre. He could hear the caw of gulls from up on the shopping arcade's roof, its glass cracked and speckled with dirt. Traffic sounds did their best to mask the distant susurration of the sea. It was as if the seaside part of the town was slowly been overtaken by shops and car-parks.

The wrought-iron bench was rusting and uncomfortable, its wooden seat warped by the elements. Nolan nursed a plastic carrier-bag, watching the house for any sign of life. Earlier he'd spotted the outline of a figure through the frosted glass of the front door, thirty seconds after the postman had departed. It was a vague watercolour-hazed blur of browns and greys. Nolan had been staring at the house for so long it felt like he was looking at a photograph. He was just about to give up and return to the B&B when he saw a man come out of the front door and shuffle along the garden path, looking directly at him from across the road. He was dressed in a beige anorak and a pair of dark trousers.

Nolan shifted in his seat and waited while the man trudged slowly across the zebra-crossing. As he drew close, Nolan could see Mark's strong resemblance in the old man's tired face. This caused a spike of regret to lance through him. He swallowed and tried to prevent his hands from shaking.

The man sat down wearily next to him. He must have only been in his mid-fifties, yet he appeared much older. He smelt vaguely of stale, enclosed rooms, like the interior of caravans or a musty attic; nothing too unpleasant, but somehow infinitely sad. His breathing was ragged. When the man finally spoke he sounded frail: "You win. Thought I'd better come out – seeing as you don't look like you're about to give up anytime soon."

Nolan cleared his throat. "Thanks for coming, Mr Wheeler." He watched a woman and a toddler feeding some ducks on the edge of the pond. "Sorry to keep ringing you like that, only – "

"Mabel thinks I've popped out to buy some milk, so I can only spare a few minutes." The man half-turned so that he was looking at Nolan. "If you've come to say you're sorry, you can save your breath. There's nothing you can say that'll make it right."

Nolan patted the bag on his lap. "I've just come to return some of Mark's things, that's all."

"When d'you get out?"

"Friday."

The man whistled between his teeth. "Wasted no time in coming back then."

Nolan ignored this, and handed the bag over. "Just some of Mark's CDs, a couple of photos, stuff like that."

For a few moments neither of them spoke. The old man took a linen handkerchief from his pocket and wiped his nose. "Mabel thinks it was just an accident. A house fire. I managed to shield her. She's never been the same since, but if she'd known the truth it would've killed her."

"Mr Wheeler - for what it's worth – I'm very sorry."

The man laughed hollowly. "Well - it's worth nothing, lad. Nothing at all."

The woman and the toddler had exited the park through the gates. There was a flurry of activity from the pond, flapping wings and squawks of protest. A typhoon of feathers.

Nolan sensed the man was about to stand up, but instead he said, "So you've learned your lesson? You're reformed?"

"I had therapy sessions in prison, Mr Wheeler. Three times a week. Mark's death was a horrible accident. But... I've been addicted to starting fires since I was eight. It's just what I did. I never meant to hurt anyone."

"Aye - they said that at the trial. But locking you up as a young 'un still hadn't cured you, had it?"

"No. Juvenile detention... just *toughened* me more."

"The judge said you were selfish and weak. In denial."

"I know. But the doctors managed to help me – showed me how to control it."

"So why'd you do it? That's something that no one was able to answer."

Nolan shook his head once. "Apparently it stems from when I was a kid. My up-bringing. No friends. A lack of control." He shrugged.

The old man pursed his lips. "I didn't even know Mark was... *that way*. He'd had girlfriends when he was a teenager."

"Me and Mark got on well. We had a lot in common."

"You're nothing like him," said the old man vehemently. He was grimacing. Nolan could feel the contempt in his voice.

"What I mean is, we enjoyed the same things – music, films, books, bands."

Neither spoke for a long time. Overhead the gulls wheeled, a car horn blasted from the promenade. Nolan could hear random electronic melodies from an amusement arcade.

"So what now - you move on, whilst we have to live with what you did?" There was a tremor in the man's voice that wasn't there before.

Nolan shrugged. "Too much has changed. There's a war being fought on these streets. I'm just another casualty of it."

"Poor you."

"Not just me. I know Mark felt disconnected from society as well. I saw men in prison who don't know anything except what it's like to commit crime. Career criminals, they call 'em. I saw a man who lost an eye in Helmand reduced to dealing drugs on the streets. There was one bloke in therapy who'd lain on the railway tracks 'cause he was being forced to work or they'd stop his benefits. He thought losing the other leg might make his disability more real, might prevent him going through the assessment."

"None of this has anything to do with Mark. He was happy at home. We had a lovely family."

"Yes." Nolan ran a hand across his stubbled chin. "So happy he was scared to tell you what he really was."

As soon as the words were out he regretted it. He was here to make his peace, not antagonise anyone. God knew he'd caused enough suffering already.

"You young people think the world owes you everything, don't you? Won't get out of bed unless you're getting forty grand a year. You want to be famous but you can't be arsed to learn a craft. Well it's not just you that's fighting this war – I was made redundant a few years back. Can't get another job. No one wants to employ a 57 year-old. Now we've got to pay more rent 'cause we've got an unused bedroom. The council don't care. So we either move to a one-bedroom place miles away from here, or rent out the room to a lodger. Can you imagine how hard it is to tell your wife she'll have to pack away all your dead son's stuff and let a stranger move into his old room? So spare me the victim card, because I'm all out of sympathy." He blew his nose with the handkerchief. He seemed to have been

115

invigorated by Nolan's presence. "And all the while the bloody energy companies are making more money than ever. The gulf's widening. The bankers are sitting on million-pound pensions and the government's moving the goalposts for me to draw my state pension. I always imagined pushing the grand-kids on them swings once I'd finished work, but now that's never gonna happen.

"Sometimes I wish it'd been me in that bloody hotel, not Mark."

A brittle silence descended on them. For ages they sat without moving. The man wiped his eyes again. "I can't bear to walk down that road where it happened. They keep talking about turning it into a supermarket. I wish they bloody well would. Once it's gone I might be able to move on."

"Look – I just came to bring you his things and tell you I'm sorry. I never meant to hurt anyone. I was messing about – just like I always did. The fire got out of hand. I managed to get out, Mark wasn't so lucky. There isn't a day that goes by that I don't regret what happened. I think about it all the time..."

The man laughed. It sounded ugly. "You'll get a job and in a few years this'll all be behind you. Well, it's not right. It's not right, I tell you. I hope this bloody well haunts you till the day you die."

Nolan stood and zipped up his coat. "It will, Mr Wheeler. It definitely will."

In the afternoon he walked along the seafront, staring at the grey churning tide. It felt like he was teetering on the brink of another world. The briney air whipped his face. Overhead, gulls soared like untethered kites. Two dogs raced across the wet sand as the wind did its best to snatch away their barks. There was a wooden hut on the promenade, from which he bought an ice-cream. Faded postcards rattled in the metal rack next to the window, threatening to leap to freedom on the breeze. He sat on a bench facing the sea, licking his ice-cream. About twenty feet away, three teenagers huddled together, isolated from one another by the attention their mobile phones demanded. Nolan watched them swiping photos across their screens, playing games, listening to music. One of them laughed at something on a pop video.

Nolan finished his cornet and took out his battered Nokia. He scrolled through the contacts list and deleted Mark's number from its memory. Instinctively he held up the phone and sniffed it. The antiseptic stench of prison still clung to its plastic case. Another relic from his old life. He stood and threw the phone as far as he could onto the beach. It landed on a stretch of pebbles and smashed, bouncing into several parts. The teenagers eyed him warily.

The six years separating the old him and the here and now felt like a chasm too wide to span. Everything had altered. Society had changed. Its features were still recognisable but there was a minute difference, an imperceptible shift that was so subtle it was hard to pinpoint. Like a waxwork dummy that so closely resembled a human it was uncanny.

In prison he'd been shielded from the full effects of the change. Of course he'd had access to television and newspapers, but this week had shown him that the old enemies had just taken on a different appearance. Bankers and multi-national companies had rushed to fill the void that politicians and footballers had once occupied. Family-friendly faces from his past seemed to be arrested on an almost daily basis; further evidence that the foundations of his childhood were collapsing. His memories felt like they were fabricated. Synthetic.

He stood quickly, anxious that his manner might betray the emotion that threatened to consume him. He turned and hurried along the promenade towards his B&B, the teenagers' mocking laughter ringing in his ears.

Nolan woke during the night. The digital clock told him it was 3:22. He turned over and faced the wall, trying to allow sleep to reclaim him. Almost at once he became aware of the smell of smoke. He sat upright and blinked his eyes in the dim light. He reached over and switched on the lamp. The room was clear, there was nothing visible in the air. The smoke detector on the ceiling continued its silent red blink every thirty seconds. He inhaled deeply, wondering if the smell was just a fragment of a swiftly-forgotten dream. He closed his eyes. The acrid stench of ash and charred wood was distinct – he had smelled it enough times for it to be unmistakable.

He stood and padded to the window. The building opposite loitered in the darkness, its scaffolding masking the desolate ruination. But he couldn't be fooled. The product of his disorder was still recognisable.

He wondered if unseen eyes watched him from the shadows. He thought about what he'd endured for the past six years. How could all those court appearances, therapy sessions, countless days spent locked in his room – how could all those endless nights have passed while the destroyed building remained in its state of suspended animation? It felt as if the hotel had been awaiting his return.

He stepped away from the window, but just as he did so he noticed movement in the street below. From this angle he was afforded a view inside the wooden perimeter that cordoned the site off to the public. Things squirmed in the shadows, reaching up with indistinct limbs. As if in supplication. Nolan could hear a dull roaring in his ears, like static or the endless churn of the tide. Darkness rippled beyond the fence. Yet the streetlights bathed the road beyond the fence in an orange glow, creating fine detail and sharp definition to everything. Once again it occurred to him that the contrast between the two impressions was acute, that he was viewing both worlds from the threshold of a doorway. *The gulf is widening.*

Nolan closed his eyes against the writhing darkness. He stumbled to the bed and climbed beneath the covers. He clicked off the lamp and lay for ages until the odour of ash returned. He knew this was just his guilt manifesting itself into something physical so he turned over. In the wake of the light's absence, the darkness in the room was claustrophobic. He opened his eyes. Someone was standing against the far wall. He could make out its shape as his eyes grew accustomed to the dark.

"Mark?"

There was no reply. Nolan held his breath. The hairs on the back of his neck bristled. He recognised the hunched slope of the figure's shoulders. The smell of burning was stronger. Nolan's eyes were adjusting to the gloom. The figure slowly lowered until it was lying on the floor. It curled into a foetal position, arms enclosed over its head. It looked helpless. Frightened. Nolan sat up and clicked on the lamp but there was nobody there.

Sunlight had bleached colour from the cheaply framed print that hung on the wall opposite the window. It looked like it been there for decades. Nolan glanced at the clock, stretching until his joints popped. It was 7:47 AM.

The room was bright. The air was clear. No smoke, no ash. No signs to indicate last night's smell of burning had been anything physical. He rolled out of bed and walked to the window. There was a weird atmosphere, difficult to pinpoint. He exhaled, enjoying the hiss of release. After a few seconds he realised what it was: there was no noise from the street.

He peered through the window. It was a bright morning. Sunlight glinted off cars parked along the road. A languid cat prowled between two wheely-bins positioned near the kerb. But there was no sound of traffic from the main road. Nolan angled his head and peered up the road to the seafront. There was nobody about. Stranger still, it was silent. The only thing he could hear was the occasional cawing of a gull from somewhere nearby. It was a plaintive, desolate cry.

Nolan dressed absently, listening for sounds of life. He let himself out of the room and descended the stairs. The reception was deserted. Sunlight poured through the window, dazzling him momentarily as he paused at the desk.

"Hello?" His voice sounded alien in the muscular silence.

Nothing.

He crossed the reception and shouldered open the door. The first thing he spotted was a hanging basket suspended from a basket. Its flowers were scorched, the petals withered and charred. The sight was disturbing.

Nolan staggered to the edge of the pavement, squinting against the sun, peering in both directions in an effort to spot someone. Anyone. He felt a surge of giddiness. Silence and the apparent lack of people created a sense of dislocation in him. Random thoughts and memories flooded his mind. He recalled an old episode of *The Twilight Zone*, the one where everyone had vanished, but this made him wonder if he was still asleep. *Surely if he could reason such things he couldn't be dreaming?*

He loped up the deserted road. Newspapers and discarded burger cartons huddled against the kerb. He paused outside a squat building, staring in puzzlement at its frontage. It was an old-fashioned tea-room boasting a sign written in a fancy Edwardian font, and a 'specials' chalkboard attached to the wall. Nolan shook his head slowly, frowning. He'd passed this very same building on his way to the B&B yesterday and had noticed the hastily-constructed vinyl cover declaring that it was the area's *Food Bank*. A local charity's name and web address had been plastered all over the sign, and covering every inch of its windows. But that was gone.

Quite suddenly he became aware of a figure standing at the top of the road, on the corner of the promenade. From this angle it looked like the figure was watching him. He squinted but the image broke up, and when he blinked there was no one there. He began to jog towards the end of the road.

By the time he reached the seafront he was sweating. The silence was eerie. Oppressive. He glanced up and down the promenade but there was no one to be seen. He was struck by an abrupt feeling of confusion. At first he couldn't put his finger on it. His eyes searched for detail in the scene, noticing the odd bird in the sky, registering that the breeze that had been present earlier had now dropped. Then he realised what it was: the sea had vanished.

He stared out across the expanse of pebbles and sand, expecting to see the ceaselessly churning tide but instead it looked like his view had been replaced with a desert scene. Brown. Brittle. Parched. A tableau of orange. Endless sand extended for several miles, running at a gentle decline before becoming more disjointed as the terrain plunged lower. There were black gaps between angled tors of similar height, gaping chasms between the plateaus. He suddenly felt like he was about to overbalance, and he readjusted his feet to counter it.

The expanse of sand quivered and broke up in the distance. Nolan understood he was seeing a heat haze. Warm air ruffled his hair, bringing with it a stench of fire and ash. It promised salvation. It beckoned him home.

He blinked at the tiny figure, stark against the lighter background beyond. *Mark.* A long way away. He was waiting. Nolan began to head towards the figure.

He hurried across the road onto the promenade. His footsteps were deafening. He was glad when he reached the beach, and the sand smothered the sound. He could see the shimmering figure, distant. The pull was immense. He began to hasten, tripping over his feet as he hurried to reach his destination. Sand stretched on forever. He remained focused on the figure ahead as he jogged, his breath the only sound in his ears. Soon he was lost to the rhythm of his movement; urgent, determined, relentless, a blur of indistinct brown swallowing him.

He thought about those nights in prison, seeing his cellmate's contemptuous face in the aftermath of suddenly waking, the threads of a nightmare still clinging to him. How sometimes he heard Mark's voice in his head, or turned over in the night to see a figure standing in the corner of the room. Nolan realised that Mark was the one thing that had accompanied him on his journey from *then* to *now*. He was the doorway.

The prison therapist had preached to him that his obsession for setting fires stemmed from childhood boredom. *The Devil finds work for idle hands.* Nolan had never understood that dogma. He remembered his stepfather's behaviour in the aftermath of Nolan's mother's death; it had left him no time for boredom. He'd yearned for someone with whom he could share the suffering, but his lack of friends had left him confined. Isolated.

The gulf is widening.

His thoughts were interrupted. The light felt wrong. Nolan stopped and turned. The distant strip of hotels, amusement arcades, food outlets, looked thin and fragile and insignificant. Diminished. Nothing moved. He felt like an actor on stage.

His eyes couldn't make out any detail but somehow he knew that the town was the version from six years ago – the one with fewer boarded-up shops, the one whose streets were patrolled by a higher number of police officers, whose hospitals were staffed by nurses who felt less disillusioned by government cuts and enforced changes to their jobs. From a time when the idea of a food bank would have been archaic and absurd. Nolan guessed that *this* town's library wouldn't yet be closed, that the community centres and NHS walk-in clinics would still exist. The town he was seeing was as distant to him now as the sun.

He was reminded of heat and flame and ash, and he glanced upward. A strange hue had flooded the sky.

Ominous and crepuscular. He blinked at the unnatural light, frowning as a series of ragged shadows patterned the floor. He turned again, to glance at the distant shoreline but it was gone. There was just a rocky slope leading away, tongues of black seaweed carpeting the ground.

And in that instant he understood that he'd crossed the threshold and the door had closed.

Silence was silence, but it had taken on a transformed quality. Like after it had snowed. Muffled. Enclosed. He glanced down at his feet. Eely fronds of weed clutched at his boots. He had the sudden feeling that he was being watched, and he turned and took a step back. His breath caught in his throat.

A sheer wall of water towered above him, so high it was impossible to see the peak. It held firm, but was liquid enough to ripple and undulate like it was a living organism.

As a child he'd owned an encyclopaedia, and had spent hours poring over its contents. There'd been one picture that had remained unforgettable: a dramatic illustration of Moses parting the Red Sea. The insignificance of those humans cowering in the vast trench had left Nolan breathless.

Now he stared up at the mountainous wall of water with a similar expression of awe and fear as those fleeing Israelites. He watched absently, fascinated at the way the sides of the water trembled. It was as if there was an invisible membrane of glass holding back the tide, hundreds of feet high. He blinked his eyes, hearing a crackling and popping in his head. It sounded like burning.

The top gave way first, appearing to teeter for a second before starting its fall. It seemed to happen in slow motion, and he turned and began to stagger. There was a futile roaring in his ears which he registered was his own voice.

The water pushed him into the ground mercilessly, forcing the oxygen from his lungs. His broken limbs became numb. He was dragged this way and that. The cold harsh weight of the sea held him in its grip. Grey darkness enveloped him, confusing him with bubbles and murk, freezing his chest. He fought to remain upright in the water. Pain tore through his nostrils and throat. In the confusion of light and sound he spotted faces in the water, too brief and infrequent to identify. The faces were formed by smoke, their features malevolent. Nolan was in so much agony he could barely register the pain. Fear clouded his mind as the smoke figures circled him in the water. It was so dark he couldn't see the surface of the sea. The cold was immeasurable. But then his desperate fingers reached the comfort they sought as a hand, welcoming and warm, found his own flailing hand and led him away.

The Procedure
By David Williamson

I t's a *very* simple procedure, Mr McNab. It should take under an hour to complete. You are a fit, healthy young man and there is nothing at all for you to worry about. I promise you, you won't know anything about it until you come round. You'll be fine, trust me."

Shaun McNab looked at the consultant's confident, smiling face and could only feel a cold dread in the pit of stomach. He idly touched at the small, round lump to the lower right of his navel, a hernia according to the diagnosis, and deeply rued the day that he had offered to help his friend move that pile of old steel girders several months earlier.

"It's…Well, it's just that I have this terrible phobia of hospitals," he replied quietly.

The consultant surgeon laughed softly and nodded his head. With his mane of dark, slightly grey-tinged hair and his finely chiseled features, he looked as though he had every confidence in his own abilities with a scalpel. Shaun realised that he was actually extremely lucky to have Mr King carry out this relatively minor procedure, and especially so in these austere times. The era of cut-backs. Shaun knew also that, had he not taken the bull by the proverbial horns and decided to 'go private', he would have had a very long and painful wait ahead of him. He just hoped that his credit card could take the strain.

He understood that Mr King was the best in his field, and was almost pathetically grateful to the great surgeon. However, that in no way reduced the absolute terror he was experiencing at that moment.

"Mr McNab, *everybody* has a fear of hospitals, including, I might add, many of us working in the medical profession! It's completely normal, I assure you. After all, nobody in their right mind wants to be cut open and messed about with about, but it's the only way for you to get well again, I'm afraid."

Shaun visibly paled at the phrase 'cut open and messed about with', but he understood that the surgeon was right of course. And he *had* been suffering with the constant, nagging pain for months now.

"Please don't worry, Mr McNab. Trust me, I'm a doctor!" smiled the medical man.

He felt as though he was swimming. Swimming slowly upwards, up towards the light. His head felt as though it had been crammed full of cotton wool as he experienced the sensation of being lifted sideways onto a steel trolley, before he was wheeled out of the brightly lit operating theatre and into the recovery room.

"There Mr McNab, how are you feeling now? ... Are you back with us?" asked a kindly faced Asian nurse as she checked his pulse, before shining a small torch into his eyes, checking the reaction of his pupils.

Shaun was still feeling very groggy as he struggled to form words with which to reply. His throat felt really sore and his mouth was as dry as the Sahara, prompting the nurse to give him a sip of water via a straw from a plastic beaker.

The water helped to ease his burning throat a little and he tried to speak once more.

"Fuzzy... I feel fuzzy... Here," he managed to say, pointing at his own head before indicating that he wanted some more water.

"Of course you feel fuzzy, Mr McNab. I would feel fuzzy too if I'd been pumped full of anaesthetic for over four hours!"

Shaun's dulled brain try to make sense of the words. "Four hours?" What had happened to the 'simple procedure' that was supposed to take no more than an hour?

"Whaaa... I...?" he tried to speak but the cotton wool pressing inside his brain blocked out all his efforts at thinking and he quickly lapsed back into a deep sleep.

The next morning, his head felt much clearer.

"Nurse... How did it go yesterday? Was everything okay?" he asked. The same Asian nurse studied his medical chart and smiled thinly.

"Mr King will be here to see you shortly. Until then Mr McNab, please, just try and relax."

The nurse fussed about beside his bed, then handed something to her patient. Shaun looked blankly at the device he had been presented with and it took him quite some time to register that it was a chip and pin card reader.

The nurse smiled tightly, a slightly embarrassed expression on her face.

"I'm terribly sorry to ask you at a time like this, but as your stay will be slightly longer than we allowed for, we need to take a further payment from you..."

The nurse raised a querying eyebrow as she helped her bemused patient insert his credit card into the reader, before turning her head away while he entered his PIN. She then handed him his receipt, picked up the card reader and bustled out of the room before he could ask her any further questions.

He lay there confused and more than a little scared and noticed for the first time, that he appeared to be the sole occupant of the ward. There were five other beds, three opposite and one either side of him, but none of them were even so much as made up, let alone occupied by other patients. Odd, he thought, to have five empty beds at a time of record hospital waiting lists? Staff cut-backs again, maybe... But in the *private* sector?

Almost an hour later, Mr King and a staff nurse, together with a couple of junior doctors came in to see him.

"Ah, Mr McNab, and how are you feeling this fine morning?" asked the surgeon jovially, as he idly flipped through his patient's chart, before handing it over to his juniors for them to study.

"Yes, I'm not too bad, thank you. But tell me, how did the operation go? Was everything okay?"

The surgeon's smile disappeared as he looked from the sister to his junior doctors and, retrieving the chart from one of them, briefly glanced through it once more before placing it back where he'd found it.

"Ah…well…" he began, and Shaun's heart began to sink rapidly towards his stomach.

"When we opened you up yesterday, I'm afraid we discovered that things were much worse than they had appeared to be on the scan we did of your injury."

Shaun looked horrified. His mouth felt dry and his head was suddenly spinning.

"*How* much worse?" he managed to ask, his face now ashen and shocked looking.

"I won't beat about the bush, Mr McNab: I'm afraid that we found it necessary to remove one of your kidneys, the right one to be more accurate, which unfortunately we discovered was quite badly diseased. I'm very sorry to have to break it to you like this…"

If Shaun had been pale before, he was now whiter than the hospital linen and he found himself trembling badly after the sudden traumatic news.

"A diseased *kidney*… But… But...?" he petered out, no longer able to think straight.

"I appreciate that this is a terrible shock for you, Mr McNab, but on the bright side, the other kidney was in perfect health, and as I am sure you are aware, it's completely possible to live a full and healthy life with just the one. Many people across the world do, you know?"

Shaun was now in a cold sweat and he was shaking worse than ever.

"I… I…" he spluttered, but could manage to say no more.

"Sister," said the surgeon pointedly, "I think Mr. Mc Nab could do with a little something to help settle him down, perhaps?"

And before Shaun could utter another word, he felt the sharp prick of a hypodermic needle entering his arm and the world started to swim before his eyes. Down, down, down... Nothing.

The next thing he knew, he was swimming back up towards the light once more, followed by the now almost familiar sensation of being lifted sideways onto a trolley, before he passed out again.

"Hello, Mr McNab... Mr McNab...?"

It was the kindly Asian nurse yet again, and Shaun began to wonder whether this was just a really bad dream or some kind of hideous *déjà vu* experience, as he struggled hard to croak some kind of a response.

"Just lie still, please, and I'll give you some water," offered the nurse, before holding a plastic straw to his mouth.

"Whaaat's happenin... Where am I...?" he managed to mumble between small sips of water.

The nurse smiled. "You're all right... You are just in the recovery room at the moment. You'll soon be right as rain, Mr McNab."

Shaun had no idea how long he had been unconscious for, but when he awoke back in the ward some time later, he looked around at the five other empty beds, and wondered again whether he was dreaming it all. He had heard how anaesthetics can sometimes lead to all manner of problems with certain people, and he guessed, or rather *hoped*, that was what was causing his confused state of mind.

Then, slowly, his befuddled brain realised that he was now hooked up to a ventilation machine. He also had a couple of intravenous drips plugged into his right arm, and his chest was now covered with monitoring devices.

He groped around for the call button above his head and pressed it weakly. Moments later, the Asian nurse (Was she the only nurse in the entire hospital? he wondered) appeared at his bed side, and he pointed to all the medical contraptions attached to him, unable to speak due to the oxygen mask which covered his mouth.

The nurse consulted his charts before speaking.

"Mr King will be along shortly to see you, Mr McNab. You've had a very lucky escape, it would seem," she said, before leaving him lying there with a thousand unanswered questions spinning around in his dazed head.

"Mr McNab, can you hear me alright? Mr McNab....?"

It was the surgeon with his usual small entourage by his side.

Shaun nodded weakly and tried to sit up.

"Mr McNab, lie still please. You've had a serious operation, and you'll have to take things extremely easy for a while."

His patient tried to pull the face mask off and speak, but he was far too weak. His arm flopped back uselessly by his side, twitching on the bed like a freshly landed fish.

"I realise that you must have a hundred questions, but please, try to remain calm while I explain what has happened," said the surgeon.

"When we sent the kidney we removed off for further analysis, the results which came back were not at all promising. They gave us every indication that the disease may well have spread further than we had at first anticipated, and we were forced to investigate the situation."

Shaun could only stare dumbly at the surgeon, tears forming in his rheumy eyes as he listened.

"What we discovered was not good, I'm afraid, Mr McNab. Your right lung had become seriously infected, and we had to remove it to stop the infection spreading further throughout your body. I'm terribly sorry."

Shaun was now shaking his head from side to side. All this because of a hernia? Surely, this had to be some kind of a nightmare... It *had* to be.

"Sister, Mr McNab is becoming distressed."

He once again felt the sharp prick of the hypodermic needle in his arm and the world rapidly started to go black. Just before he went completely under, he could have sworn that he heard music playing somewhere, way off in the distance. He recognised the tune as an old song from the 1970s, but didn't have the time to recall which one.

The next time Shaun woke up, he discovered through a mist of pain that he could now only see through one of his eyes. He was still connected to the ventilator, yet there seemed to be even more lines in his arm and a whole maze of wiring now led from his chest area to a series of monitoring devices which stood beside his bed.

Groggily, he tried to reach out for the call button, but as he groped about the headboard of his bed, he thought he heard a voice, a voice which seemed to be coming from a million miles away.

"He's coming round."

Shaun tried to focus on any one of the three faces wavering above him, without success.

"Mr McNab? Mr McNab...?"

The patient groaned slightly by way of a reply.

"Ah, Mr McNab, you've come back to us." The voice sounded vaguely familiar to Shaun, though for the life of him, he couldn't recall who the speaker was.

"I'm sorry to tell you that you've been in the wars again, I'm afraid, Mr McNab. More bad news for you alas," said the distant voice. Shaun was still trying unsuccessfully to fix his eyes on the ethereal face speaking to him, and groaned again in his frustration.

"The infection has spread, I have to inform you. We've had to remove half of your liver as well as your right eye in an attempt to stop the disease encroaching further..."

131

Shaun could only slowly shake his head in terror. He tried to speak, and struggled to sit up and focus on the surgeon, but he was too ill and too heavily drugged to move. He felt completely numb with the horror of his situation. Through his one remaining eye, he could just make out the white swathe of bandages covering his torso from the top of his chest downwards towards his waist. An anguished sob escaped from his throat, muffled by the ventilator mask fastened across his mouth.

The surgeon, who had been carefully studying his patient's notes, handed the clipboard back to the nurse.

"We'll speak again later, Mr McNab. When you're feeling up to it. I know that all this is very hard for you to take in, but we really are doing our very best for you, you know. "

And with that, he and the other medical staff left the room.

Shaun tried desperately to think. He tried to summon up enough drug-free brain cells to focus his attention on his predicament, he tried to work out what had...what *was* happening to him, but it was a losing fight. He was too doped up to string even the simplest of thoughts into any kind of logical reasoning.

He lapsed once more into a deep, dreamless sleep.

When he awoke what felt like several hours later, he was able to focus a little more clearly and, although still heavily sedated, he managed to glance slowly and painfully around the room. The still *empty* room, apart from himself and the five vacant beds.

That half remembered tune was playing softly once more, somewhere outside in the corridor, and he struggled in vain to recall the song's name. As he glanced towards the brightly lit reception area beyond his room, he noticed for the first time, a sign attached to the half- open ward door.

With the last of his strength, he managed to concentrate on the sign and read what it said.

The red, block capital letters swam before his one remaining eye, and then slowly came into sharp focus. It read:

DONOR HARVESTING INC.
STAFF ONLY.
KEEP OUT!

At that moment, the smiling Asian nurse quietly came into the room carrying a small stainless steel tray with a large hypodermic placed upon it.

Shaun's horrified brain suddenly remembered the name of the song, and one verse in particular.

He struggled to rise up from the bed, to get out of there before it was too late, but the needle slid sharply into his arm, the hypodermic's contents flowing slowly into his vein, and almost immediately he was slipping once more into unconsciousness.

"I'm so sorry, Mr McNab," said the nurse, softly. "The problem is, your credit card seems to have reached its limit and we operate, if you'll excuse the pun, for profit here. Fortunately, we have wealthy clients who really need your remaining cornea, kidney and…"

The nurse was still talking as he began to slip under completely, and that elusive tune still taunted his semi-conscious brain.

The singer sang about a hotel, and the verse told him he could check out anytime he wanted to, but he would never be able to leave.

Pieces of Ourselves
By Rosanne Rabinowitz

School-kids run through the crowded street, disappearing around corners and reappearing. They are laughing, boisterous, defiant. Surely Richard doesn't remember having such a good time when he was that age.

Richard's contingent of library workers are more sedate, but still make a lot of noise. George, his assistant on the local history archive, bellows into a megaphone. A new librarian called Sally keeps blowing a horn.

The day is cold, but bright. The bare branches of trees etch patterns of dark lace against an acid-blue sky. He's never realised before that branches could look like lace.

A group of art students march forward as they hoist narrow, towering black banners. Linked together, swaying... the banners bear splashes and bands of lavender, green and blue, a hint of grey. No slogans, only colours. How can a banner have no words? But those colours speak to him without the words, tugging at his mind. He stares as they twist and bend in the wind.

Up on construction scaffolding, young guys cheer as they drop another banner: *"We are not your slaves... Austerity, up yours!"* Richard cheers along with them. That's right: up yours!

Richard usually doesn't go to demonstrations. In his student years they were usually grim affairs, populated by dour donkey-jacketed party paper sellers. He'd much rather read a book or potter about in his archive.

But this lifts him out of weeks of stress. He keeps bumping into mates he hasn't seen in years... people from his library course, a guy from his old hill-walking group.

They are reaching the end of the march, much too soon.

134

On the other hand, he'll get to chat in the pub with Sally. Tall and olive-skinned with green eyes, Sally said she wanted to hear more about his oral history programme.

Richard's phone chimes with a new text message. He fumbles in his pocket for it. Ginny. *Couldn't find you. I'm with the nurses from Brighton, near the book bloc.*

The book bloc? Richard texts back.

You should know, you're a librarian.

Should he? He looks over the heads of the people around him, searching for this elusive bloc and for Ginny. He's been hoping to catch up with her. They have a lot to talk about. Richard faces the loss of his job. Ginny could lose *most* of hers if it's farmed out to a private firm. Once again, they confront similar problems. They should be here together.

He scans the crowd again. A scrawl on a home-made placard catches his eye: *"Work longer, Pay more, Get less... No thanks!"* Is that Ginny holding the placard?

A shove from behind cuts his search short.

One minute he's laughing, enjoying his day out. The sun still shines but everything else shifts. A roar from the crowd vies with the samba drumming and horns. Screams and shouts: "Scum, scum!"

George grabs his arm. "C'mon Richard!"

Everyone is running now. People press against him, pushing him forward. He has to run, too. But what is he running from? Where will he go? Placards and plastic crunch underfoot. Sally's horn?

Then he looks over his shoulder. A horse rearing, the bobbing helmets of mounted police. He swallows, tasting acid from his jumping stomach. He keeps running.

Up ahead, more lines of cops at the end of the road.

Demonstrators wielding improvised shields rush past him. *Our Word is Our Weapon* is the red title painted on one. A masked woman brandishes another shield in the orange, black and white of the old Penguin classics: Orwell's *Down and Out in Paris and London*.

Is this the 'book bloc'? "George, look…" Richard starts to say.

People are retreating, others surge forward. *Towards* the cops, to push them back? Purple smoke jets up from the ground, people dismantle the police barriers that run down the middle of the road.

Where is everyone?

"George…" Richard calls again. "Sally!"

But they aren't with him. None of his friends are. And in front of him…rows of cops.

"Fuck! We've been kettled," says someone behind Richard.

Kettled in a police cordon? Richard never thought that could happen to him.

"S'cuse me," Richard says to the closest cop. "I just need to catch up with my friends…" He takes a step forward, but they push him back.

"Can't go there. Exit's that way." The cop points down the road.

He stops, not sure which way to go. Other people are still trying to push against the police line. They're shoved back. Is that Ginny? He has the back view of a bobble-hat that looks like Ginny's, short black hair showing beneath it.

Two cops smack the woman-who-might-be-Ginny with their shields.

"Hey…" Richard tries to reach her.

"Get back, I told you!" A good push and smack for him; Richard falls and lands on his arse. The impact sends a crunch through his spine.

People help him to his feet. A piece of concrete rolls away from his foot and a gloved hand snatches that up. *"Under the pavement, the beach,"* someone says with a laugh. A familiar sentence. Is it from an advert?

Yes, he used to spend a lot of time on beaches… almost twenty years ago.

He repeats the phrase to himself as he rubs his back, straightening slowly. Nothing broken but damn, something hurts. He can still move enough to get up on a low wall so he can see better and search for Ginny. The crowd just below him surges and pushes, others collect in groups. Stones arc towards the police line.

"Under the pavement, the beach."

That's it. A slogan from the revolt in France, 1968. He studied European history, should've known straight away.

But those stone throwers won't get anywhere near a beach. They won't even get to the end of the street, with those mounted police behind the riot cops on foot. An empty area of road, then more lines of cops. Shit. He has to get out. And if he can't get out straight away, he has to find Ginny if she's trapped in here too.

Richard jumps down from his wall, wincing as he lands, and walks towards the alleged exit. He tries to phone Ginny again, but now her phone is off. When he gets there, other cops shouts: *"No, exit's over there!"*

Richard walks away again with dragging feet. The cold starts to bite now that the sun is setting. He hunches further into his jacket, pulling his scarf higher. People are making fires from placards and huddling about them. He can join a huddle too, breathe in the chemical scent of burning paint and let the heat beat in his face.

Richard scratches his head under his woolly hat. Through his glove he feels an odd raised area, like a bump but not quite. When he takes his hand away a pale flake spots the leather of his glove, then it's off with the wind. Perhaps it's ash from the nearest fire.

Music comes from the same direction. A hundred people are dancing around a sound system pulled by a bicycle, picking up more people as they move through the crowd.

Richard falls in step. He used to love dancing. So did Ginny. When they first met they shared regrets about their left-behind lovers; eventually they moved on to cruise bars, gigs and festivals together looking for new love. And then they found each other for a while.

Of course, he went dancing with Blanca all the time. It

137

was different music then, trancey stuff that evoked sunlight and warmth and the pursuit of pleasure. When they became submerged into the sound and movement, time stopped; or perhaps it expanded because he was so sure they could live forever in those moments. Sound and sensation, the touch of his lover amplified by a crowd of lovers around them.

It all seems so far from now, so far from where he stands surrounded by cops on a freezing afternoon just starting to darken. Figures dancing around the sound system loom in the dwindling light, jerking about to music he doesn't know. He begins to panic again. Stuck in this kettle, away from his friends.

But soon the hoods come down, coats loosen, breath puffs in vital clouds around the dancers. Faces revealed by the streetlights show joy despite the ring of steel tightening around them. The music has changed, and he doesn't know the name of it. Dubstep or grime? Slow, yet powerful.

He launches himself among the revellers. He lifts his feet, stepping with strength and purpose. No, this is nothing like that happy-clappy stuff he raved to back in Spain. Darkness pulses at the heart of this beat. It's the sound of hard times. Faster now, faster, a beat like a barrage of rocks against riot shields. It is new music to him, yet its power moves him closer to his past.

He dances on the pavement that covers the beach, and now he dances on the beach. Back to the 90s, or dancing towards a terrifying future?

Those students he saw earlier arrive with their tall banners, black splashed with colours of the sea, shades of fields and sun-baked hillsides. Richard stops in mid-step. Time contracts, expands. Twenty years of moments collide and merge.

There's Blanca, wearing shorts and a loose stripey t-shirt. She looks just as she did in 1990-something, in the summer.

He reaches back into the past... ready to touch its hand.

Blanca smiles and slaps his palm.

138

No, Blanca was never one for high-fives and palm-slapping.

He doesn't know the woman in front of him at all, though she wears a stripy top like Blanca's. She even wears shorts, along with thick woolly tights and great big boots. *Alright?* Richard nods yes to the stranger, he's alright, he *hopes*.

Does Blanca still go out dancing? What *is* she doing, where the hell is she?

They lost touch, as people did before email and Facebook. Blanca was the one who stopped writing.

She'd been talking about becoming an art teacher before he left... and teachers in Spain must be facing cuts now. Art teachers are doubly expendable. People are occupying city squares in Spain, taking over buildings.

Is Blanca among them?

Maybe they could be friends now. He knows that he hurt Blanca by leaving. But maybe they would've hurt or disappointed each other if he stayed. He keeps wondering about that now that the life he left her for feels so shaky.

These young people are dancing on even shakier ground. They have less to lose, though. Maybe that's why they seem so happy. He should learn from them, join the fun. So he throws himself into more dancing, less worrying.

He doesn't notice just when the crowd around the sound system becomes denser and much less blissful. He can't move with his earlier abandon. Sometimes, he can barely move at all. Though he is rediscovering his enjoyment of dancing, he has no desire to revisit his moshing days.

But moshed he is getting. And aren't the police line very close? When did that happen? So many cops. Surely they must have multiplied while he danced.

The police advance, flailing and jabbing with their truncheons. He wants to shout, but suddenly he has no voice. He wants to hit back. But he can't move. He is caught in a childhood nightmare, motionless before a monster.

A wedge of horses gallops into the crowd, their hooves hitting the pavement with sparks. A mounted cop lifts his club at a boy who holds his hands in front of his face, blood showing between his fingers. Richard finally steps forward as fear blazes into anger. He stumbles on the debris left on the ground... rocks, heavy metal police barriers, railings. Then he tries to pick a barrier up. The cumbersome thing becomes light as someone takes the other end. *Shove it at them!*

Dodgy back be damned, he pushes it straight into the police line.

A firework falls sizzling on the ground, short of its target. He picks it up and throws it towards the cops, only hoping to get the firework out of their crowd. But a horse rears and bolts as the thing smokes and crackles, the cop barely clinging to his steed.

Richard's heart bolts too, this time with a stab of happiness. He's not sure if he's the one who frightened that horse, but even a temporary retreat thrills him.

A boy who can't be over fourteen tugs at Richard's arm. "You shouldn't throw shit at the horses. It's not the horse's fault!"

Before he can reply, he's off his feet, several cops twisting his arm behind his back.

He's been arrested only once before when he was a student, for drunk and disorderly. But then he had a toilet in his cell and even a cup of tea later.

This is it, he thinks. He's nicked. It won't be so civilised now. Will they beat the shit out of him? Will he lose his job? But that's likely to go anyway.

"Stop the snatch squad!"

Other demonstrators move around them. One grabs his legs, others struggle with the cops. He's a wishbone tugged between the two sides. Will he break in pieces like one too, and left to litter the ground? He squirms and flails.

A woman in an orange 'legal observer' bib takes notes. *"What's your name?"*

140

Suddenly he's pulled away from the cops and sent back into the crowd. Space opens up there, as if the police line has been pushed back.

Richard tries to catch his breath, then turns around to thank one his rescuers, a bloke in a hoodie. The young man lowers the scarf covering his face.

"Hey, it's the Library Guy! You alright?"

"I'm fine, Michael," says Richard, recognising the boy. He came to a couple of oral history sessions and talked a lot about music.

Richard's legs are still shaky, but relief at the sight of a familiar face whooshes through his body and steadies him.

"I didn't expect to see *you* here…" Michael says.

"Why not? Libraries are getting cut, too. In fact, I came with a lot of library guys… and girls," said Richard.

"Look," Michael's friend interrupts. "The filth are getting ready to charge again."

"Tightening the noose." Another young guy draws his finger across his throat, smirking at Richard..

"We know a way out. Used it the last time. Come with us," said Michael.

They make their way down the road, away from the first police line. The boys greet friends, and more people join them.

"This your first demo?" Michael asks Richard. "Stick with us, we'll get you out. All that *dancing* is fun, but they won't let you dance all night. They press the crowd in tight. That's why they call it a kettle. Containing the heat… Hey! Hey! They're charging now!"

People run again…

"Don't panic," Michael urges. "Just go this way… they've not blocked it yet."

They nip down an alley. This broadens into a yard enclosed by a wall, much higher than the one Richard stood on earlier. People are already scrambling over it. Richard just looks at the wall. His back is hurting from his fall, and every limb aches. And he lost his hat.

141

"Go on, you go over first," Michael urges. "I'll give you a leg up."

Richard steps into the stirrup of Michael's hand and hoists himself up, teetering on top of the wall, then he plonks down on the other side.

Others drop down beside him, falling like autumn apples. Another gate divides this second courtyard from the street, but escapees yank it open, rattling chains and breaking the padlocks. They all pour through into the street on the other side.

Richard has to bend over, trying to catch his breath again. But at least he's safe.

"We're off to Trafalgar Square, see what's happening there," Michael says.

But Richard waves goodbye and hurries to the pub to find his friends. He's had more than enough excitement for the night.

On his way he finds a 'book' abandoned on the street. This shield had most of its stuffing knocked out, a mixture of styrofoam, newspaper and bubblewrap. He stamps on worm-like pieces of styrofoam scattered in the gutter as he picks it up.

The front cover is still there: *The Dispossessed* by Ursula K LeGuin. He picks up the shield, along with a few scuffed and tattered leaflets.

He'll take these home. He's an archivist after all, and collecting tat is what he does.

The warm air of the pub hits Richard in a welcome blast. His friends cheer and George claps him on the back.

"Did you fight your way out the kettle with *that*? Looks like it's seen some action." Sally points to his shield.

"No... I just found it on the street. And I really *climbed* my way out of the kettle. Now, I need a drink... Anyone else?"

He deposits his shield in their pile of scarves, coats and rucksacks in the corner. Then he peels off his layers and heads for the bar. Out of the kettle, into the pub. It feels so good, even with all his aches and pains making themselves known. But what about Ginny? He tries to ring her while he waits at the bar, but he only hears her voicemail again.

He returns to their table with the drinks.

"Richard, what's on your head?" Sally smiles. "Ha! Did the police do that?"

"No, no, I was pushed and shoved at and I fell on my arse and almost got arrested, but I'm OK now outside of an aching tailbone." He decides to leave out the fireworks and the police horse, just in case Sally's another animal lover. "I even got some dancing in," he adds. "So what's wrong with my head?"

Sally touches his face just near his hairline. He finds the place too. Yes, it's that odd spot he touched before. With his gloves off, he definitely can feel that the skin is thicker, with more defined edges. A crispness at the surface.

"It's kind of red," Sally says. "It's got flaky stuff on it, looks painful."

"It doesn't hurt, though. It'll be OK," says Richard. Nothing to worry about now, not when he's out of the kettle and talking to Sally in the pub.

Friends venture out and return with reports. It's kicking off here, there, or somewhere. And people are still trapped in the kettle.

Why doesn't Ginny turn her phone on? Should he go look for her? But he'd be little use if anything truly 'kicked off'. And Sally seems happy to carry on talking.

"Richard, if your job goes, d'you think you'll take time out and go travelling?"

"No," he says. "I've already done that."

But what *will* he do? As he contemplates that question, his fingers go to the bumpy skin that Sally had touched. He explores… He pulls at it. That isn't enough. He gets his fingernail just under its edge.

Then *something* comes loose.

Sally's eyes follow the path of this *something* as it settles on top of his Guinness. A thick white *flake* of skin. It almost disappears on the beige head of his pint, but not quite.

Richard excuses himself, goes to the loo and looks in the mirror. Just below his hairline, he sees that his skin is peeling in pale scales. He takes off another piece and looks.

When he was a child, he and his brother Jim used to pull off patches of skin when their sunburns began to peel. The markings on that skin had fascinated Richard. They reminded him of maps that show the height of mountains, the shapes of valleys and plains.

This is a smaller, more compact piece. This pattern is like a blizzard of snowflakes, or the static on a TV screen.

Almost reluctantly, Richard flushes the piece of skin down the toilet.

When the lesion on his temple doesn't clear up, Richard goes to the doctor. She says he has a form of psoriasis, and prescribes a cream. He dabs it on.

While he is drinking his coffee and reading the paper the next morning, Richard reaches over to his temple… and tugs off another loose bit. He leaves it on the kitchen table. This piece is bigger than the one in his Guinness. It shows the tight whorls of a hill, a wider one like a valley.

When he was a kid, he stored the strips of sunburnt skin in a drawer in his bedside table. He wants to save this fragment too. It is too *interesting* to throw away. But where should he keep it? He wanders about the kitchen and living room, ending up in front of the book case. His gaze settles on a stone box on the top shelf. It's made of smooth grey stone, inlaid with patterns in turquoise, blue and pink and mother-of-pearl, representing flowers, butterflies and birds.

Blanca bought that box for him in a street market. There were many of them on the market tables, in different shapes and sizes.

He used to keep his dope and tobacco and pipes in the box, back when he indulged. It is empty now.

He's always been fond of this box and gives it pride of

place on top of that bookshelf. Now he knows what to do with it.

He places the skin inside and closes the box with a click.

Richard and his brother had fussed over similar pieces of skin. They often bragged about their burns after a visit to the seaside or a hike in the sun.

"Ouch, I can't lie down… That's nothing, I got blisters the size of eggs."

This was before people worried much about UVA and UVB, and there seemed to be many more sunny days in the year.

The real fun came when the burns began to peel. They competed to see who could take off the biggest piece. You picked at the corner of a peel, then slowly lifted the skin up, careful not to tear it. When he removed a substantial piece he'd hold it up to the light. So fine and thin, with whirls and swirls and pits where hairs had been.

"Of course we want to keep the local history archive," a councillor says in a bright and jangly voice.

While pretending to listen, Richard reaches for that spot at his temple. The prescribed cream has only allowed the excess skin layers to grow thicker and more pliable. It is well worth the wait. He takes something off, about the size of his fingertip.

"We want to turn the library over to the community. We're forward-looking," insists the councillor.

Richard lets the skin drop to the table top, then places his notebook over it. No one has noticed, he's sure. Certainly none of this crowd, people who don't know the tip of their nose from their butthole. *Forward-looking*. Ugh. Time to wade in.

"The community already has the library," Richard speaks up, giving his view as the shop steward. He only became shop steward because no one else wanted to do it. No wonder, if the post involves attending meetings like this.

"You're talking in double-speak," he adds. "Double-speak! It's bad enough you're making these cuts, but do you have to abuse the English language while you hack away?"

"Is that a policy question?" one councillor asks, while the others remain stony-faced.

"Of *course* it's a policy question. Giving the library to the 'community', are you?" His voice rises. "Admit it, you're really selling it to some scabby bunch of profiteers. And how does 'the community' use a local history archive if it's moved to another city and the staff made redundant? The 'community' comes in droves to the archive now. Sometimes you can't find a seat because it's so busy."

Richard's heart pounds as if he's been running from the police again. But he's only talking to the 'Scrutiny Committee'. They're as bad as the police. Even worse. He'd love to throw a firecracker or something more lethal among this lot. How they'd squeal!

This meeting is such a far cry from his day on the streets. If he closes his eyes, he still sees the lace of black branches against a frozen sky… bands of blue and green from the tall banners splash across the darkness of his lids. He hears the sound systems and smells the acrid scent of smoke bombs.

If he closes his eyes again, he'll be dancing again with Blanca before she turns into a friendly stranger slapping his palm.

He sits back, sweating in the overheated room, the past filling his thoughts. The demonstration has sent memories replaying in loops, a counterpoint to his beleaguered job and evenings in stuffy council chambers.

What would Ginny say about this? She'd tell him to find Blanca.

As soon as he gets home he turns on his computer.

He looks under the two surnames Blanca uses; her professional name and her family name. He scrolls down the entries on Google, through search results on Facebook. They're both very common names. But if he keeps at it, he'll find her. Yes, dammit, he'll find her.

146

With a pop, the chat messenger appears. Ginny… asking how he fared on the demo. In the days since, they've only succeeded in talking to each others' voicemail.

"I was kettled too, I tried to find you…"

"My phone ran out of power…"

"I got out of the kettle and found the rest of the library workers in the pub."

"BASTARDS. We were stuck until the bitter end, frogmarched and squished on the bridge."

Richard pauses, then types: *"So we're bastards. And the bastards in the pub raised a glass to our friends in the kettle. I'll owe you one when we meet."*

"I'll take you up on that. So when are you coming to see us in Brighton?"

Richard stops to think, twisting a lock of hair. He finds a new layer of skin to peel, then he types: *"As soon as I can!"*

Meanwhile, Richard continues to scroll down the list of people who have the same names as Blanca.

As Ginny logs off, Richard lays a piece of skin on some paper.

When he drops it into the box later, it falls with a little sound. This makes him feel more substantial. The skin is *there*, while everything else is likely to evaporate into air.

He rubs the spot. Still some loose skin left. He keeps going over the patch until it's picked clean.

Before he goes to bed he looks in the mirror. The area on his temple is red, almost bleeding.

His brother once peeled a patch from his leg before it was ready. It left a raw and red area the shape of a fist. When the sun hit the exposed skin, it erupted in new blisters. *Blisters on my blisters.* Jim was proud of this, even when the blisters began to ooze.

Blisters on my blisters. Richard looks at the damage again in the morning. He vows not to pick at the skin and give the cream more time to work.

But the longer he leaves it, the less he can resist in the

end. The thick old skin just has to come off, and something else needs to be freed and revealed.

And so he drops other pieces of skin into his beautiful box.

Richard knows that many will regard his skin-peeling as a dirty and repellent little habit, like nose-picking. But they've not seen these pieces in the box, among the inlays. These are such an essential part of the outer body. They have patterns in them. How can they be ugly?

"Hey Library Guy!"

Michael, the boy who gave Richard a leg-up out of the kettle, strolls into the reference room along with a friend.

"Hey, Kettle Kids," Richard replies. They both grimace at being addressed as 'kids', but after a long look at each other plus a mutual shrug they decide to let it go.

"Look at this..." Michael opens a tabloid newspaper. "It's off the Met website."

Rows of photos, alleged miscreants from the demonstration. Richard feels a punch of panic at the sight of one fellow pushing a barrier against the police line.

"Don't worry, *we're* not in it. I checked. But they show some fit girls getting stuck in. Fancy any of them?"

Richard tries to laugh. "Too young for me!"

Is Michael taking the piss? Better change the subject. "But you haven't come here to find a girlfriend for me, have you?"

"No, it's about something else, more oral history," says Michael. "A bunch of us were talking about the difference our educational allowance makes, and what happens if it goes. So maybe I can interview people at my college about it. If the EMA's cut, most us won't be at college in the first place. We wouldn't be able to think about university or *anything*."

Richard wants to say that university might not be all it's cracked up to be. With his job up the spout, he is just as likely to end up with some twit at the job centre telling him to work for free at Tesco's.

Then Michael leans forward and whispers in Richard's ear. "Hey, you should've come with us. It was kicking off big time."

"I would've held you back. You saw how bad I was getting over that wall."

"But you made it! It just takes practice."

Richard chuckles. "Speaking of practice, we can have a go at recording something from you two. How about next week? I'll get the diary out."

"We could have photos," Michael adds. "My sister likes to take pictures."

"Good idea." And Richard is already starting to imagine how this project might shape up.

But management would be likely to give a thumbs down on anything new.

Richard touches the patch at his temple with one hand as he leafs through diary pages with the other. They should be able to make a few recordings before the axe falls.

"What's that on your head?" Michael asks.

"Nothing," says Richard. He snatches his hand away. "It's nothing."

If people were noticing that raw patch of skin, he should be careful. Then he has another thought: would the police see it on a video and identify him with it?

Would they add him to their photo gallery?

Then he finds more peeling skin on his inner arm. The condition is spreading. What if it takes over his body? He imagines what he'll look like, covered with the stuff. It makes his stomach lurch. But when he examines this lesion, he sees its possibilities.

He can peel bigger pieces from it and no one will see it under his long sleeves.

He puts the new skin in the box. The inlay on the lid reflects light on the skin inside it, reminding him how those stone boxes stay cool to the touch even in the hot sun. He thinks about Blanca's gift to him, and the paints he bought for her just before he left.

Back then, Blanca waitressed at a seaside café. Richard taught English to young Spaniards. It was a life. Once they had enough for rent, food and Blanca's art supplies, they relaxed.

Richard spent a lot of time reading books on the beach and in cafes. He loved books so much, he thought he'd like to do work that involved them. He said this to Blanca, who agreed it was a good idea. She probably thought he wanted to be a writer, like many of the young British blokes hanging out in Spain.

Soon the English teaching began to pay less. The work was hard to find as more footloose and usually broke Brits arrived. When Richard started in the trade, he had grand ideas of teaching eager young people about English literature while he improved his Spanish. But his clients were often businessmen, and he refused to teach words like 'incentivise'.

As Blanca grew more engaged with her art, Richard wished he had a similar vocation. He watched Blanca explore new colours, while he just taught the same lessons. He wanted to do something that would enthral him, while benefiting or at least entertaining others.

He thought about what he could do with his degree in history and geography. And he imagined books, rows and rows of them. He wanted to spread their magic, and came to the conclusion he couldn't do that in Spain. It was time to go home.

When he made up his mind, Richard took Blanca out for dinner. They went for a walk on the beach afterwards and he told her about his plans.

"I have to stay here. But if you need to leave... I want you to be happy."

Happy, wonders Richard. Is this what we both had in mind?

Then he peels more skin from his temple, then from his arm.

When another patch comes up on his leg he goes to the doctor again. She speaks more about stress, and prescribes a holiday along with another cream.

Perhaps there is even more *stress* when he has to inform his assistant of his redundancy. *"George, this doesn't come from me. I've tried to stop it and I'll continue to campaign for your reinstatement..."*

"It's alright, Richard. You're only the messenger and I won't shoot you." George says, more than a few times. But is that a curl of contempt to his lip, and disgust in his eyes?

When Richard holds up a bigger piece of skin in the light, he thinks more about those criss-crossings of his surface geography, about the lines his life has taken, bringing him to this point. Perhaps the 'lifeline' runs all along a person's body, a tangle of many lines, a spaghetti junction of possibilities... and traps and errors.

Meanwhile, he checks the police website most nights to make sure his photo doesn't crop up in the rogues' gallery. He does recognise that young woman in the striped top, the one he mistook for Blanca. *Stay free*, he thinks.

And you stay free too, Blanca, wherever you are. Live well.

He imagines Blanca standing firm in a city square, holding her hand out to him all the way from Spain. And in her hand she offers him a piece of himself, the part he left behind.

Go on a holiday, the doctor suggested. So Richard decides to visit Ginny and her partner Bron at last.

As the train leaves London he begins to relax, looking forward to a long weekend with his friends. He gazes out the window, thinking fond thoughts. Then he realises that he left something behind. The box. It's still at home. Where will he put his pieces?

When he catches the bus from the train station, he is still

thinking about that box. As he walks up the hill to Ginny's house, he continues to fret.

Though his friends live a short bus ride from the centre of Brighton, their row of houses belong to the countryside. He gazes at the rolling hills, breathes in air from the sea. Maybe that sea breeze will do his skin good.

Bron opens the door. Richard blinks. Her hair is longer, and dyed bright red. But her bus-driver's jacket rings the bell of recognition.

"You're not looking good, Richard," says Bron.

This really isn't what he needs to hear, but he forgives her when she settles him in the kitchen with a mug of coffee.

Ginny comes into the kitchen and gives him a big hug. Ginny still seems the same, wiry and intense. But her black hair is now the same red as Bron's.

Bron excuses herself, saying she needs to make some phone calls. Once Bron leaves, Richard is surprised to find himself feeling shy and tongue-tied. If he's like this after a mere year, what will it be like to meet up with Blanca again after two decades?

He asks Ginny about work, just to begin with. So she frets about her health authority's plans to tender its service to a firm known for mobile phones and pop music. "Imagine the muzak we'll have to sit through when we ring up the call centre!" They both laugh, though they knew it's no joke.

But it's enough to put Richard at ease. "It's great to see you. Sorry I've been crap about keeping in touch."

"No problem, I've been crap too. It's a shame we didn't hook up at the demo."

"Yeah, we could've had a dance like old times. And all that raving made me think of Blanca. I even thought I saw her."

"Think she's in London?"

"No, I just got in a state thinking I saw her because of this woman's t-shirt. I don't know where she is. I need to

152

find her."

"Go for it. I'm glad I finally contacted my ex in the States. We talk on Skype. Maybe she'll visit, since I can't go back there."

"It's different for you. I *chose* to leave Blanca. She might not want anything to do with me. But you were *forced* to leave your girlfriend when Uncle Sam gave you the boot."

"So? I could've taken steps to make my immigration status more regular. But I kept putting it off, and then... We all make mistakes."

Ginny is frowning, her eyes focused just above Richard's. "What's that on your temple? Near the hairline?"

"Just a bit of psoriasis," Richard explains. "Stress, the doctor said."

"It looks awful. Have you been scratching it?"

"No, if you really want to know..." He pauses. "I've been peeling it. A lot."

Ginny is looking at him as if she expects him to say more.

"And I've been keeping the pieces in a box. A very nice inlay box."

Ginny shrugs. "At least you don't eat the pieces. That's very common."

"Of course I don't," Richard says. "But the question is... what do I do before it gets worse? I'm even paranoid that the police can use it to identify me. I lost my hat in the kettle..."

"Identify you? Why, what did you get up to? *Wait...* I *don't* want to know. Loose talk and all that. But good on you. As for your skin... worrying won't help."

Ginny adjusts her glasses and assumes an erect posture. She clears her throat. "Your problem is 'dermatillomania', and like all these things, there's a spectrum. On one end, you get self-harming behaviour. But on the other, many people bite their nails, pick scabs or peel their sunburns and it does no harm."

Ginny starts to sound so professional that Richard has to laugh.

"Sorry," she says. "I suppose I slipped into work mode."

"It's easy to do. When I got out of the kettle, I was collecting leaflets and tat for the archive... Well, the archive I'll keep in my basement, if nowhere else."

Is that an attempt at humour? He must look so miserable that Ginny pours him another cup of coffee and opens a packet of biscuits as well.

"Richard, your doctor's right that worry and stress over redundancy has triggered your skin problem. But at least you're not damaging yourself. If it still bothers you, see a counsellor."

She gives him a quick smile. "But maybe what you really need is to get out and meet more girls. When was the last time you went out with someone properly?" She nudges him.

Bron returns to the kitchen just in time for this comment. She laughs and slaps him on the back. "Yeah, you need to get out more."

"I've been too busy with work," he sighs. "None of my affairs have lasted. Still, I've stayed on good terms with *most* exes, especially the present company."

It's his turn to nudge Ginny. Bron watches them with a benign smile, which has always impressed Richard. He wouldn't have liked it if Blanca's old boyfriends had visited regularly.

"And it's not only work," Richard adds. "I'm always at a meeting. Union stuff, negotiations... Mind you, I've met new people while fighting cuts in the library service!"

"Oh yes, nothing like activism to spice up your love life," says Ginny. "And why not? No reason why changing the world should be all doom and gloom and self-sacrifice."

"Tell me about it!" Richard laughs. "But I think I blew my chances. After the demo, we went to the pub and I was chatting with this new librarian I fancied. She asked about my face, joked about my battle wound. And once she

154

mentioned it I kept wanting to… dunno, kind of check it out. Then the pickings fell into my Guinness."

"Oh no…"

"Oh yes. Needless to say she wasn't impressed. "

"Well, since your habit *is* cramping your style..."

"Too right it is," says Bron. "If you're putting those *bits* in a box, maybe you're putting *feelings* in a box."

Richard remembers that Bron completed a basic counselling course in her pre-bus driving days.

She continues. "When you go home you should open the box and dispose of the skin in a… excuse the expression, a ritual."

"Like, bury them and do a dance?"

"Hah! I knew you'd take the piss. Seriously though, open that box and face your fears. Then get rid of them!"

"There you go again, Bron." Ginny gets up from her chair. "I think Richard needs dinner and a few drinks more than a ritual." She opens the fridge to survey the ingredients.

Richard offers to help chop.

When Richard returns home, he's feeling better. He's even stopped missing his box, though he did drop a few flakes in the ocean when they took a walk along the beach.

But as soon as he gets in the house he has to sit down and inspect a new patch on his arm. He finds the edge, and lifts the skin up. Slow, slow, gentle.

He holds the piece up to the light and gazes at its patterns.

Cross-hatching, shadings and pits. Is there a touch of pink to its transparency as if it still lives?

He takes the box from the bookcase. The stone is usually quite cool. Now, the surface feels just a little warm in his hands. This puzzles him.

He sets the box down on the kitchen table and opens it. He glimpses *movement* within the box, along with a slick, barely audible sound. He shuts the box before he's sure of what he sees. Maybe he doesn't *want* to see it.

No, he *has* to look. Surely those aren't maggots.

He opens the box again…

The pieces of skin have grown. They move and twitch, blind yet searching. He puts his finger out and one piece curls around it. It is thick and waxy, and damp. He flings it back into the box.

The skin he has just removed, left on the table, is still delicate and paper-dry. Has it moved too? He drops it into the box. Then he slams the box shut and takes it to the basement. He places anything at hand on top of it… an oversized art book, an old computer, and finally that battered shield with *The Dispossessed* scrawled across the front.

In the following week, he considers throwing the box in the river or a rubbish bin.

But these are pieces of himself, so he can't bring himself to destroy them.

When he was a kid he read Poe's *Telltale Heart.* The murdered guy's heart kept beating and pounding, loud enough to be heard, shaking the house.

But this is only skin. Skin that belongs to him, and he's very much alive.

Those pieces do create a sound, though. They send a stirring throughout the house, a shifting in the air that spreads from the basement. Those things *sing*, with a song no mouth could make.

Fortunately, his work at the library keeps him well beyond that song's range during the day. The project with the Kettle Kids is coming along.

And Richard stays out with meetings every night. His union, the fight against redundancies. He has to concentrate on that. And stop peeling and picking.

Sometimes he touches a lesion, but only a touch. Maybe the sight of that crawling, searching skin has cured his dirty habit more than counselling ever could.

And he begins to dream about opening his box.

In the first dream, the pieces begin to stir. They've grown wings and lift out of the box like horseflies clustered in the residue of a sweet drink. They fly at him, sticky with sugar. They buzz like drills and hit him in the face.

Then a *good* dream surprises him.

The bits of skin turn to shards of glass, reminding him of the beaded curtains that tinted the light in the room he shared with Blanca. These glass pieces erupt in more hues than a Dulux paint display. He fills his hands with them and flings them upwards. They bathe him in their colours. He looks up to the cool touch of turquoise and green on his face.

After that vision of colour and light, Richard lets his guard down in his next dream.

He flings open the lid. Fleshy moths fly out of the box and fill the air. One plump insect flies straight into his face, filling his mouth and nose with dust smelling like the bottom of a birdcage.

He wakes with his heart pounding. He can't get back to sleep. He finally gets out of bed and makes himself coffee. It's already morning. He has a meeting first thing at work. He touches the back of his neck, and peels some skin.

Instead of putting it in the box, he opens the window and lets the piece fall. A breeze lifts it for a moment, then it dissolves. If it hits the ground, he certainly doesn't hear it.

But he does hear the 'singing' with no words, drifting up from the basement.

Did he imagine what he saw in that box? Does he really hear that sibilant whispering through the house, infiltrating his thoughts and dreams? Bron urged him to 'face his fears'. So maybe he should. Then he'll throw the box out.

When he brings the box up from the basement, he puts a domed cake tin next to it. If something foul comes out, he'll just clap that over. The tin was a present from Ginny. She'll be glad he's finally using it.

He puts on the TV, an everyday sound to soothe his nerves.

He just has to keep one hand on that cake tin and lift the lid off the box with the other.

It's empty.

Empty. Richard slumps, the tension leaving him.

All that fuss over an empty box, eh?

Then he sees something scrunched in the corner. A tight, contracted bundle like a ball of fine yarn. It has a clear colour, with tints of pink and purple, the delicacy of an orchid petal. Though it is quite pretty, he hesitates to touch it.

But when he does, the sensation is silken and smooth.

Feeling bolder, he lifts a strand from the ball. It comes away like a piece of string. He pulls at it more, until he holds a shining skein at arm's length. He smiles. This is not horrible at all, but strange and beautiful like the coloured glass that came out of the box in his good dream.

Curiosity blooms in his mind, spreading slow petals. He holds a mystery in his hand, and he must get to the centre of it. He pulls and pulls, letting the filaments float, swirl and settle around him. When the skein of skin touches him, it is gentle.

But the thread of matter only seeks itself, pulling together, adhering. Then it floats apart again, weaving and coalescing in a dance.

First Richard sees a hint of an arm, a leg, a torso. Then the threads swirl into formlessness again, only to define something more. A figure. A man.

This figure, this man, is naked. Yet its own skin suitably covers it. The wall shows through. The TV shines a light through its chest. A photo of Richard with his hill-walking friends flickers in the figure's eyes; its mouth contains the light switch.

Yet there's density to the space within the figure. Its eyes hold the same tint as Richard's, but semi-transparent. The figure stumbles, as if trying to get its balance. It sees Richard and recoils. And it stumbles again, as if in fright.

Richard's heart is also beating fast. He feels a cold finger down his back, the jab of the unknown. But this isn't the crawling flesh he dreaded so much. Instead, gazing on this figure is like looking into an incredibly old and warped mirror.

What is this?

Fascination fights with fear. His counterpart seems terrified too.

Terrified... of *me*?

Richard puts his hand on the box, seeking its familiar surface. The figure sees where Richard's hand rests.

"That's Blanca's box!"

Has the figure spoken? Words register in Richard's mind, carried in a voice like the creaking of a branch, the run of a river, the mellow tones of a French horn.

"Blanca?" Richard repeats the name. "You know Blanca, then?"

The figure that looks like Richard sighs. The sound is so sad, so yearning. As if...

Why can't he find Blanca on Facebook, or anywhere?

Where is she?

"Look..." Richard begins. How should he start? "Look... What do I call you?"

"I have the same name as you. You must know that."

No, I bloody don't.

Something in the tone annoys him. Smug, is it?

"But my Spanish friends call me Ricardo," the figure adds. "You can too, if you want."

"Ricardo... sure. So look, sit down, relax. Where do you come from? Do you remember how you got here?"

"Only fragments. Shimmering, like mother-of-pearl... dove grey, a rose-blush and glimmer of green. Yes, it was the box. This box. When I found it again, I was thinking of Blanca. It's been five years. When I closed that box five

159

years ago, it was in the hospital where I saw her for the last time."

The last time?

"You alright, Richard?" Ricardo extends a hand toward Richard, then puts it on the table. Almost, but not quite touching his.

Ricardo's hand shows the pits of pore, light hairs... so much like the skin Richard stashed in the box.

But other parts of Ricardo seem fainter. His face flickers, coming into the focus and then receding.

Ricardo touches the box on the table. "Blanca gave this to me. But we shared it. I kept my dope there, and she put her bits and pieces and treasures in it..." He strokes the inlay on the cover. "What did *you* put in this?"

"I also kept my dope in there, years ago," says Richard. "Much later... several weeks ago. I put pieces of skin in there. It came off this patch of psoriasis, or whatever it is." Richard rolls up his sleeve and points to the lesion on his arm.

Ricardo reaches forward to touch the spot. Richard first wants to pull away, but he makes himself stay put. *Face your fears.*

Ricardo's fingertip feels like a breeze or a faint kiss. Richard shivers, not in an entirely bad way. The sensation reminds him of... reeds, sun shining off water? Still water, not the sea. He has an urge to close his eyes, as if it will help him see what he needs to see. Then Ricardo withdraws his finger.

"Does that look strange?" Richard asks. "Did *you* have trouble with your skin?"

"Not really, but I kept my sunburn peelings when I was a kid."

"So did I. Except by my skin problem is now caused by stress, not sunshine. They've been cutting my department at work, you see... With each cut, it feels like a bit of myself is about to go missing."

Ricardo winces. "I did something like that when Blanca

was ill," said Ricardo. "I took her things out of the box so she could see them on the table near her bed. I was so worried about her, I started pulling some of my hair out... and put that in the box."

The last time. That could mean anything.

"If Blanca was ill..." said Richard. "Is she OK now?"

The last time Richard saw Blanca, she was fine. They were saying goodbye at the airport.

"OK?" Ricardo is surprised at this question. "Don't you know?"

Know what?

"Blanca died five years ago. She had cancer."

Though Richard has had a sense of something deeply wrong, hearing this still knocks the wind out of him. He can't breathe. He thinks he will die too. Then air fills his lungs again in a rush.

Blanca is dead?

Don't you know, this guy asks.

"How the hell would I know?" Richard bursts out. "You should've told me!"

"Told you? And who the fuck are *you* anyway?"

Argumentative bastard. But the same could be said about himself, Richard is thinking. That's why he became shop steward. Yet he also knows how to negotiate.

"And *you*..." Ricardo accuses. "You left Blanca, didn't you? How could you?"

"It's not that simple," explains Richard. "There wasn't enough teaching work. I had to leave, and Blanca didn't want to come with me. I needed to do something more with myself. We kept in touch for a while, but then she stopped writing."

"So you wanted to do *what* with yourself? I managed. I found other work... labouring, cleaning, whatever. Sure, things were hard... especially since Blanca was made redundant, then rehired as a casual with no sick pay... But you know, we got by."

Ricardo looks like he's about to say more. But instead

161

he just leans his head against his hands, eyes closed. Richard wonders if he's crying. He reaches over to touch Ricardo on the shoulder, then stops. "I'm so sorry," he finally mutters.

Ricardo nods. "I'm sorry too. You were close to her and you've lost her… *twice*."

"I'm… I'm stunned. But it must've been very hard for you."

"Yes, it was… I lost a part of myself, as you put it. But then, I'm still here."

Barely. Richard is seeing much more through Ricardo's body. The TV footage from the 'student riots', playing within Ricardo's outlines. There's that poor bloke with the police barrier again; a girl throws a crate at a departing limo. Richard feels that familiar leap of his heart, beating with the day's exhilaration and its fear. But Ricardo is oblivious.

So *there's* a difference between them. Richard gets up to turn off the TV.

"Blanca would've been fascinated by you," says Ricardo at last. "I'm sure she'd tell us to stop bickering, or to sit still so she could paint us. And she'd want to know what you're doing. So do I. Tell me more about your job. I mean, I've had jobs and I've lost them. And I've been skint. But you're not just worried about money, are you? It involves who you are. But why pick yourself apart over it?"

So Richard talks about his archive. "It's about much more than books and paper," he tells Ricardo. "A lot of people come to our events, people who never thought of using an archive or library before."

He describes the pleasure of nurturing a project and seeing it change peoples' lives for the better. "My friend Ginny, she's a nurse, did a study on libraries and community health. Just having a warm safe place to read or think makes a big difference to many people."

Ricardo smiles when Richard tells him how he met the Kettle Kids and the work he started with them.

162

"But now *you* have to tell me something," Richard adds. "Tell me about Blanca. How was her art going? Just before I left, she'd been talking about doing more abstract stuff."

Ricardo describes those paintings, full of greens and blues and luminous grey mists. "She laid on layers of oil paint with a palette knife, stirred and smoothed them like plaster. She was mad for green and blue, all shades of it. With touches of lavender and grey."

Richard recalls those colours, settling over him in the dream. He remembers tall banners banded and splashed with greens, blues, pearl-grey and lavender mist.

Now he knows why those banners had drawn his eye, provoked such feelings. They bore the colours Blanca splashed on canvasses he has never seen, but recognised.

"She loved her paintings," Ricardo says. "She sold a few, but in the end she hated to be parted from them. Instead of trying to live from selling her work, she trained to teach art. So I still have some paintings." Ricardo's gaze turns inward. A smile plays on his lips as memories surface.

A pang of envy and regret stabs Richard. *We would've stayed together if I hadn't left to do my course. We would've been happy after all... until Blanca died.*

But he can't be jealous of *himself.* And Ricardo is right to say that Blanca wouldn't have wanted them to quarrel.

"I wish I could've seen those paintings," says Richard. He moves the box so the inlays catch the light. "Blanca's favourite colours make me think of this box. Is there *something* about it? Or could it be the way we put pieces of ourselves into it... my skin, your hair?"

"Maybe. The box is a link, but what kind? Maybe we have other versions of ourselves hidden in our DNA... Or perhaps I *am* a ghost." Ricardo speaks slowly. "Maybe we don't have to be dead to haunt someone."

He is staring at the mirror behind the TV. "I don't see much of myself there." Ricardo looks at his hands, his arms, his legs. "And I think there's less than before."

"Maybe it's just the light," Richard suggests. But his

163

voice lacks conviction.

He doesn't want Ricardo to disappear. They still have more to talk about. He's beginning to *like* Ricardo.

"If I put more skin into that box, maybe it'll make you more solid," Richard suggests. He rolls up his sleeve, and finds the patch. Since he has resisted peeling for a while, it is good and thick. "I know this is far-fetched and desperate, but what can we do?"

Ricardo nods. *What can we do?*

Richard's fingers are trembling as he peels the skin off. Then he places it in the box and closes the lid, leaving it on the table between them.

Ricardo puts his hands on the box, and Richard does the same. This box has brought them together, so it feels like the right thing to do.

Richard clasps Ricardo's hand. It's like bathing his hand in silk instead of water. The contact flicks on images in Richard's mind. They are sharp, as if lit by strip-lighting. They have the quality of a clear winter morning, though some show summer.

Blanca in hospital. Then a scene on a beach, which Richard remembers. It's the day he told Blanca he wanted to return to England for his library course.

But in *this* scene, Ricardo's scene, he doesn't talk about courses.

Richard leans closer and put his arm across Ricardo's shoulders, resting against the chair. He sees a lake in south-eastern Europe that Ricardo and Blanca visited during a heavy damp summer. Dragonflies rise from the lake and one rests on Blanca's hand. Its translucent wings hold tints of the water and the sky. They are as fragile as that piece of skin Richard had dropped out the window, as transparent as Ricardo himself.

Will Ricardo dissolve on the wind, or drift apart in the still air of this room? Perhaps he'll go back to Spain where the rest of him lives… along with Blanca's paintings.

The paintings. "Ricardo, you said you kept *some* of

Blanca's work. Where's the rest?" Richard speaks as if the air expelled with his words could scatter his counterpart in pieces again.

"After Blanca died, I had to move to a smaller place, so I didn't have room for all the paintings. But I gave one to a museum, and others to the local library."

He gave Blanca's paintings to a library. Richard smiles at that, and can't stop.

Ricardo brightens, as if the same idea has occurred to him. "So we have something in common."

Richard nods a passionate *yes*, for their lines of departure have finally met in a circle.

But he also hears Ricardo's voice grow faint. Richard draws him closer. A vapour like breath mingles between them, or it could be part of Ricardo himself.

Again, he sees Blanca in the hospital, sees her through Ricardo's eyes as he stays with her to the end.

He has to do the same for Ricardo. Stay with him as he leaves. Richard tries to tighten his grip on Ricardo. But the substance of Ricardo only slips through his hands; a puff of air, the threads of silk unravelling.

And then Richard is alone with the box.

Finally, Richard opens it. It is empty except for a ripped dragonfly wing. Or it could be a piece of his skin, a piece of himself.

A Simple Matter of Space
By John Forth

Look, if I've gone over this once then I've gone over it a thousand times, but if I must explain again then I will. Last month one of your *housing officers* came by to inspect my home – that is to say, the home I have shared with my wife for some forty years – and according to this *housing officer* the house now has too many rooms. To him I say, 'The house has as many rooms as it used to, now it simply has less people,' but he shakes his head and says no; he says that I have too many *rooms*. I have too much *space*. Honestly, have you ever heard the like? Too much space! He says I must pay for the space. I say I do not want the space, I simply want my wife back to fill the space again. Then today I receive this in the mail." The old man brandished a neatly-folded letter, holding it by the corner as if it was infected with some filthy disease. With no little ceremony, he slammed it against the Plexiglas partition separating Cora from the waiting room. "This. You say you are charging me for space. Well, I tell you, you can have your space. I do not want it. I do not!"

Throughout Leibniz's rant, Cora had been slowly pushing herself against the back of the chair. Now she pushed hard enough to wheel herself a few inches from the desk. She needn't have worried, the shatterproof glass held, but it was difficult not to be impressed by the force of Leibniz's fury. For a moment there she'd thought the sparse hair on the side of Leibniz's otherwise bald head was about to burst into flames.

Cora glanced right and then left. Paul Keogh, in the next booth, raised his eyebrows; Karen Foyle, to Cora's left, shook her head in despair then went back to dealing with her own client. That was one thing about the Hexmouth

Housing Department; it wasn't exactly what you'd call a supportive workplace.

"Well?"

Cora swallowed, acutely aware of the crowded waiting room behind Leibniz. According to the ticket counter on the wall there were exactly fifty-seven people waiting to speak to Cora or one of her colleagues, and she was sure that every last one of them was watching to see what happened next. She would have to deal with the situation very carefully indeed. Handled badly, this was the sort of thing that made it into the newspapers, and the Grade Fives, well, they didn't much like press attention of any kind.

"Mister Leibniz," she said, quietly but firmly, "if you'd just like to take a seat..."

Leibniz's eyes flared. He crumpled the letter in one crooked hand. "Take a seat?" he said, gritting his few remaining teeth. "Take a *seat*? Oh but that is *space*. That is *space* in your precious office. Will you charge me for that too? Will you?" Now he stood upright, as if to attention. On the strip of shirt visible between the lapels of his ragged jacket, Cora saw old yellow stains and the outline of Leibniz's ribcage. "Well, I will not be charged any longer. I am tired of this and I am tired of you." He turned to face the waiting room. "All of you, with your... your *conservatories* and your *McDonalds hips* and your... your *twin-child prams*. You are the fat in the arteries of the world! You are the choking death of this planet, and I will STAND FOR YOU NO LONGER!"

With which he turned, threw the balled letter ineffectually against Cora's partition, and stalked out of the room.

"Well," Paul said after a silence in which Cora could hear only her beating heart, "that was one angry old Nazi."

"Jesus, Paul," said Karen, shaking her head.

Cora looked across the waiting heads to the windows on the far side of the room. She could see movement on the pavement outside, but of Leibniz there was no sign. Still, she asked, "Is he gone?"

"Looks like it," Paul said. "Christ, I think you win 'nutter of the day'."

"I dunno," Karen said out of the side of her mouth. "It looks like there're a few candidates out there." She fixed a grin and pressed a button to show the waiting room she was ready for the next case. "Can I help you?" Cora heard her ask.

Impatient eyes watched Cora from the other side of the glass, but she didn't feel ready to take on another case yet. "I'm going for a drink of water," she told Paul, wheeling her chair back and pushing herself unsteadily to her feet. He nodded, and turned back to his own client, a thin-faced young woman with children crawling up her like some horrible, pink ivy. The woman looked familiar, and Cora briefly wondered if she'd been to school with her. She thought on this as she walked to the break room, mainly to avoid thinking about the confrontation with Leibniz. The poor old bugger. She'd only had the briefest chance to look at his file before he lost his temper, but she could see why he was so upset. No sooner had he lost his wife than Cora's colleagues in the back office had started bombarding him with letters informing him that if he continued to live alone in a house with three bedrooms, he would be charged based on each empty room. They had offered him a maisonette, which he had refused; efforts to give him a flat on the new estate out by the all-night supermarket had been similarly rebuffed. She could hear his heavily-accented voice in her head still. *It is my home. It is my home.*

Cora sighed and turned to head back to her desk. Trevor would complain if she abandoned her post for too long. There were targets to be hit, after all. *Well, let him complain*, said a rebellious voice in her head. After all, when was the last time he'd sat with a case personally? Officious, little jobsworth pri—

"Cora, a moment?"

He stood in the hall that connected the front and back offices. Cora glared for a moment before catching herself. "Yes, Trevor?"

"I, ah, I hear there was a bit of difficulty just now with a certain Mister, ah..." He consulted the file he held in one hand, "Leibniz."

"No difficulty, Trevor," Cora said, aware of how defensive she sounded. "He was just a little angry."

"From what I heard he was more than a, ah, little angry. He was, ah, a lot angry."

"He had something of a rant, yes."

"You realise of course that you should have escalated it to me immediately."

Cora almost scoffed at that. What could Trevor have done? Tremble Leibniz into submission? The words crowded her mouth, desperate to throw themselves in Trevor's face. She choked them down. "Yes, of course, but you see there was no time. He—"

Trevor cut in, as if she hadn't even been talking. "You have to take control of these situations, that's the thing. You're a good officer, Cora, but you need to show a little more backbone. If you don't, these people will walk right over you."

"It's not a fight, Trevor," Cora said, exasperated.

"That's where you're wrong, Cora. We're the front line. We're responsible for making sure that the rules are obeyed, that people don't take advantage. Without us there'd be anarchy, Cora – anarchy!"

"If you say so."

"I do. So you fortify yourself, Cora Ellis. Fortify yourself and get back out there." His skinny, clenched fist reminded Cora of a dead spider. "Fight the fight."

With a curt nod, Trevor turned and walked away, leaving Cora both bemused and furious. The day, which had started badly, had taken a turn for the absurd, and it wasn't even lunchtime yet. She would pray for an early home time, but she knew that any prayer would be intercepted by the Grade

Fives upstairs long before it reached its intended destination. Such was the way of things around here. There was God, there was the Government, and there were the Grade Fives. There would be no early finish for Cora today.

Resigned to an afternoon of misery, Cora returned to her desk. She was preparing to call forward another case when Paul, off to her right, let out a spluttering laugh. "Brace yourself, Cora," he said, "your boyfriend's back."

She glanced towards the door. Sure enough, there was Mister Leibniz, reversing into the waiting room. Why he was coming in backwards was a mystery, one hardly solved when he turned around. For some reason he was holding his arms out in front of him, palms upturned, as if he carried some invisible load. As Cora watched, Leibniz stumbled, legs buckling beneath the weight of whatever he was pretending to carry. Recovering his balance, the old man staggered towards the centre of the room, jostling a long-faced youth perched on the end of one of the waiting room benches. The youth growled and pushed Leibniz's hip, sending the old man into the back of an elderly woman sitting on the next bench. Leibniz barely seemed to notice. His attention was focused on the partition behind which Cora sat. "You see," he called, arms still held out ahead of him. "You see, I have your precious space. I have *all* of your precious space. Take it back. I do not want it!"

He let his arms fall to his sides.

The effect was much as if someone had detonated a bomb in the middle of the room, except there was no flash, no explosion, only a sudden shockwave, emanating from Leibniz's arms. Leibniz himself was thrown back against the far wall, skull cracking against waiting room window. The elderly woman against whom he'd stumbled was blasted to one side, where she tumbled over a crowd of splayed bodies. Benches were torn from the floor and hurled in the direction of Cora's partition. The man who had been talking to Paul was thrust forward, his chest caving against the desk, a spray of blood speckling the Plexiglas. Paul

170

threw himself back, falling off his chair. "What the Christ?" he said. "What the Christ?"

The waiting room was a disaster area. Bodies lay everywhere, buckled and broken by the force of the explosion. Twisted plastic chairs lined the edge of the room. At the core was an empty crater where Leibniz had stood. Still not certain what had happened, Cora surveyed the room through her cracked partition. Leibniz lay almost directly opposite, slouched against the wall. A red veil hung across his face. At first Cora was sure he was dead, but after a moment Leibniz coughed and pushed himself unsteadily to his feet. Blood dripped from his chin. Through the red, his eyes were a blazing, sickly yellow, and focused solely on Cora. "Take it," he said, weakly, raising his arms. "Take it."

Leibniz thrust his arms forward, a conductor facing an orchestra of destruction. The windows behind him exploded inwards, filling the air with glittering shards of glass. Empty space rushed in to the room like a tidal wave, picking up the scattered chairs and bodies and throwing them towards the partition. Leibniz, too, was caught in the rush. His frail form was picked up and pushed violently towards Cora's partition. She recoiled mere moments before his face was dashed against the Plexiglas, which cracked further beneath the pressure. Through the red impact splash she could see Leibniz's skewed eyeball, still watching her. With a series of damp *smacks*, other men and women were smashed against the glass. Before long Cora was staring at a wall of crushed bodies, crushed faces. Blood seeped through the partition and pooled across her desk.

From the groans and cracks it was clear that the partition would not hold. Blinded by tears, Cora dragged herself to her feet and began to scramble towards the door. Paul was already there, shock on his slim, handsome face. Driven on by the increasing intensity of the sound, Cora reached him in moments. "Close the door," she screamed, pushing past him into the corridor. "Close the door."

"What about Karen?"

Cora glanced back. Karen had been a few steps behind her, but had fallen. She lay in the dust that had been shaken from the ceiling by the explosion, an expression of sheer bewilderment on her face. After a dazed moment, she started to get back to her feet. Paul stepped forward to help. Realising what was about to happen, Cora reached out and seized back of his suit jacket before he could step through the door. She tugged at the exact moment the partition gave way. One moment she was staring into Karen's uncomprehending eyes, and the next there was nothing save the rush of bodies and debris that had pushed through from the waiting room. She heard Karen let out a single, alarmed squawk before the door was slammed shut by the force of the wave.

Still, they were far from safe. Almost immediately, the wall began to groan at the great pressure being placed against it from the other side. Grabbing Paul's arm, Cora started along the corridor. Doors to the offices on either side were already open, concerned and confused faces staring out. Cora shouted for all of them to get out, to leave as fast as they could, but she did not stop to explain or to help them. There was no time. Cracks were already appearing on the wall. Leibniz had brought back the space they had tried to tax him for, and he had brought it with interest. Before long the great rush of emptiness he had conjured would push the housing office out of existence.

Cora had no intention of being there when that happened. The pathetic amount she was paid was barely enough to compel her to take the flak the public fired her way, let alone convince her to die in the office. Dragging Paul behind, she fled along the corridor, pushing the back office staff out of the way. The ground was trembling now, and the deep, angry roar of the collapsing building drowned out all but the shrillest of screams. Out the back door, across the parking lot, that seemed the safest way. Cora took the next turn, flinching away from the chunks of ceiling that

172

were starting to fall from above. A great chunk of masonry shattered on the linoleum ahead of her. Another just ahead of that. From behind she heard a wet thump, and Paul's arm pulled away from her. She turned, saw his gaping, bubbling mouth; saw the hunk of concrete embedded in his skull all the way to his eyes. He made a single sound, "Muh," then fell to his knees. By the time his shattered head hit the ground, Cora already had her back to him, was already another three strides closer to the back door.

The wall gave away. Cora heard it slamming into its opposite number, the sound not quite able to obscure the cracking of bones that accompanied it. Abruptly, Trevor appeared in the doorway ahead. There was dust in his sparse, dark hair and desperation in his eyes. He seemed to be considering closing the door, as if that might in some way hold back the rush of devastation. Seeing Cora he paused, long enough for her to push past him and into dust-obscured daylight. She fell through the door, skinning her palms on the rough tarmac of the car park. Rolling, she looked back at the red brick rear of the council offices. The brickwork breathed, straining to constrain the influx of extra space within. Cora scurried back, shouted for Trevor to retreat. He only stood there, staring at the building as it took a deep, final breath. Finally, when Cora was some two dozen feet away, he turned to run. The building exploded, throwing shrapnel in all directions. Trevor's body was buffeted by spinning bricks. He twisted under the onslaught, every bone in his body broken within a moment. To Cora, it looked almost as if he was melting, his skull collapsing within its skin, eyes sliding at odd angles. His arms flailed like loose rubber tubing, fingers twisted twigs. Finally his ribcage caved and his torso folded in on itself, with his legs following suit. He became a puddle of flesh and fabric, soon buried beneath what remained of his workplace.

Only when the dust settled and the rubble ceased skittering across the tarmac did Cora stand. Where the housing office had once stood was now a wall of detritus

173

and tangled corpses. Although she could not see from where she stood, Cora could imagine a great circle of empty space away from which the rubble had been pushed. She thought of Leibniz, of the rage the old man must have summoned in order to achieve such destruction. Who was he to have been capable of this? Cora supposed she would never know. On shaking legs she made her way to the exit of the car park. When she saw what remained of the street, she had to support herself against the low brick wall. The buildings opposite the housing office had been pulled forward from their usual positions, piece by piece. Overturned cars, masonry and bodies lay strewn across a road along which a long, cracked ridge had appeared. Several of the smaller buildings on either side had collapsed completely. A fine dust hung over the street.

Every road she followed had been narrowed by half. What was left had been rendered mostly impassable by the ruin of the buildings on either side. The further she walked, the clearer it was just how devastating Leibniz's transference of space had been. She passed roads bunched up like badly lain carpets; traffic lights canted at an angle that reminded her of trees she had seen on the Cornish coast, eternally shying away from the ocean wind. She saw drifts of bodies, heaped high and still squirming as the survivors tried to push themselves free. When she could take no more, she lowered her head and walked on. Eventually she arrived at the block of flats where she lived, but it too had succumbed to the emptiness that had rushed to fill the space Leibniz had taken. Exhausted, footsore, she continued on her way.

Finally, she cleared the town limits. On the motorway she crested a hill of cracked road and looked out across the lowland hills. In the distance she could see the bridge across the river, torn and twisted, pointing red fingers at the sky. Further on she passed a set of cottages that had been crushed together like the bellows of an accordion. An arm hung limply between two of the cottages, fingers trembling in the breeze. After an hour she passed a sign for the city. Only then did she veer off the road, down a gravel path leading to a farmer's gate. She kept walking until she reached the middle of the field, where she lay down with a deep, exhausted sigh. The sky turned above. She could not go on to the city, nor could she return to the town. For now she needed space. Just space. Without it, she feared she might go mad.

The Privilege Card
By David Turnbull

I had this letter," said Tom, holding out the crumpled envelope for the well-dressed woman seated on the opposite side of the desk to see. The enamel name badge pinned to the lapel of her designer jacket declared her to be *Mona McAllister – Loyalty and Reward Consultant.* She waved the letter away with long fingernails that were painted a deep shade of glossy red.

"No need to show me that," she said. "Your appointment is in the diary."

"Have I done something wrong?" asked Tom. He'd been losing sleep since the letter landed on his doormat. He'd never heard of the UK Citizens' Agency – but they sounded official and in his experience anything official usually meant some sort of trouble.

Mona McAllister smiled, lipstick as red as her nail varnish.

"Nothing to worry about," she said. "In fact I think it's entirely possible that you will leave here with a positive outcome."

Tom didn't feel reassured. He looked at the plush décor of the office, the potted bonsai plants, the expensive blinds, the artwork hanging on the walls. This wasn't the type of place a person like him was called to unless there was trouble of some sort.

"What's this about?" he asked.

"UKCA is a private concern," replied Ms McAllister. "We are a sub-contractor of Her Majesty's Revenue and Customs. What we're engaged in, and what we are inviting *you* to become engaged in, Mr Riley, is a regional trial of a scheme that it is hoped will be launched nationally before the end of the year."

Tom shifted in his seat. When they announced *trials* at work it was usually the staff that lost out. He loosened a button on his polo shirt.

"What kind of scheme?" he asked

Ms McAllister smiled again, lipstick gleaming in the glow of the concealed lighting. "I take it you're familiar with the concept of the *Privilege Card*?"

"Like the ones you get from the supermarket?" asked Tom. "With special offers and stuff?"

Ms McAllister nodded and took something from one of the drawers in her desk.

She slid it across the desktop towards Tom.

It was a little plastic card.

He picked it up and examined it.

Running along the top were the words – *UK Citizen Privilege Card*. Along the middle ran a series of letters and digits that Tom recognised as his National Insurance Number. On the bottom left was his name. On the bottom right a silver hologram of Britannia, spear in one hand, shield in the other. The backdrop was an unfurled Union Jack flag, fluttering resolutely in an imaginary wind.

"These are difficult times," said Ms McAllister "We've all had to tighten our belts."

Tell me about it, thought Tom. *I haven't had a pay rise in three years.*

"But the Government is determined to look after hard working families," she assured him. "It is minded to develop a scheme which recognises *loyalty* to this country and all that it stands for, through a system of very real and tangible rewards."

Tom turned the card over. On the back there was a little electronic strip, like that on a credit card, and a space to sign his name. "I don't understand," he said.

"It's a simple concept," said the woman. "You accumulate points on your card in the same way as you would with a retail or department store card. And then you exchange those for rewards."

"What kind of rewards?" asked Tom.

"Rewards that are of great practical value to hard working families in these austere times," replied Ms McAllister. "Tax relief for one – Council Tax rebates for another. Pension Credits and guaranteed acceptance on the Enhanced Mortgage Assistance Programme will shortly also be on offer."

She leaned across the table and the heady smell of her perfume made his nose twitch. "There are things in the pipeline," she told him. "In the autumn new regulations are coming in which will require everyone to pay a one off fee of £75 to remain on the register of their local GP. And the spring the new £25 appointment fee is going to kick in. But if you earn enough points on your Privilege Card you could use them to apply for an exemption to such fees."

Tom looked down at the card.

"So how would I earn these points?"

Ms McAllister leaned back in her chair.

"We're all in this together," she said again. "That's the fairest way to do things. If we all take a little bit of the pain we can reduce the deficit and encourage inward investment to secure the future of this great country. But you and I know, Mr Riley, that there are those who simply will not play their part – benefit cheats, petty criminals, illegal immigrants and the like."

That certainly struck a chord with Tom.

But he was still at a loss as to where this was going.

"These people are dragging the country down," she went on. "Costing the tax payer billions. And that's where good citizens like yourself can play your part. If you see someone who's fit as a fiddle and still claiming disability benefits, you tell us. If you hear about a council tenant on the estate where you live who is sub-letting their property and maybe claiming housing benefit into the bargain, you tell us. If you go into your local kebab shop and the person behind the counter looks like an illegal immigrant, you tell us."

"You want me to be an informant?"

He could hear his dead father's voice resonating from the grave.

Never be a grass, son. A grass is almost as bad as a scab.

"We want you to be a loyal citizen," said Ms McAllister. "Every time you supply information points will go on your *Privilege Card*. If that information leads to a suspension of benefit, a conviction or a deportation, even more points will go onto your card. And what do points make, Mr Riley?"

"Rewards," he replied.

"Exactly," she said and handed him a pen. "Just sign the strip on the back and I'll have your card registered on the system."

Times have changed, Dad, thought Tom, engaging, as he often did, in an internal dialogue with his departed parent. *Nowadays people have different sets of values.*

An image of his father materialised behind Ms McAllister. Whenever this happened Tom could never decide whether he was actually seeing a ghost or whether his mind was somehow generating a dreadful hallucination, hatched from the raw grief that still festered within him.

His father looked disappointed by what Tom had said. Tom blushed a little. Then it happened – the dreadful, sickening thing that always happened whenever this vision appeared before him. The cancerous tumours that had so thoroughly devoured his father's body came burrowing out of his flesh to squirm and writhe like bloated, blood soaked leeches.

Tom squeezed his eyes shut to blank out the horror of what he was seeing.

Ask her why - said his father's voice.

When Tom opened his eyes the image was gone.

He looked across at Ms McAllister.

"How did I get selected for this?"

"You may recall that a couple of months back that you took part in an opinion poll that was being conducted in your local shopping centre," she replied.

Tom nodded.

"Well, when we analysed your responses on the key indicators it was clear that you were exactly the type of person the Government wants to give encouragement to. You have a low tolerance for scroungers and cheats and a good grasp of the economic and social challenges this country needs to get to grips with."

Tom picked up the pen, but still found that he was hesitating.

"You have two daughters, don't you, Mr Riley?" she asked him.

"Fifteen and twelve," said Tom.

"Don't you aspire to something better for them? Don't you aspire to something better for the type of society they're growing up in?"

Tom nodded again.

"Then the *Privilege Card* offers you the opportunity to make those aspirations far more than just a pipedream."

Tom closed his eyes before his father had the chance to appear once more.

Tom worked as a forklift truck driver at his local DIY superstore.

He loaded and unloaded vehicles; moved stuff around in the warehouse, put stuff up on the racking, took stuff down from the racking. It wasn't the best job in the world, but it was better than sticking on price labels or working the tills. There was even a public announcement that heralded his arrival whenever he was required to transport heavy items around on the shop floor

"Our forklift truck is operating in aisles fourteen and fifteen. In the interests of health and safety customers are advised to exercise care and caution when browsing in those aisles."

It was during a tea break on one of his shifts that the opportunity to try out the *Privilege Card* first presented itself. He'd put himself down for overtime that coming

Sunday, but on checking the roster he found that his name had been scratched out and replaced by one of the Sri Lankan students the store had been employing in increasing numbers on zero hour contracts.

Tom had heard some of the other staff grumbling that overtime preference was being given to zero hour staff – because they were only paid the minimum wage and didn't have the right to premium payments. Given his particular skill base Tom had never expected that this was a problem *he'd* have to contend with.

"You can't give him my hours," he protested to the Team Leader. "He doesn't have a forklift truck license."

"He does," the Team Leader assured him. "He passed his test at head office last week."

"How many hours has he done this week?" demanded Tom.

"That's none of your business," replied the Team Leader.

"He's on a Student Visa," said Tom. "He's not allowed to work more than sixteen hours a week."

"It's none of your business," insisted the Team Leader. "Just be thankful you've got a job. There are people queuing up out there to take your place."

Returning to the canteen in a foul mood Tom took out the *UK Citizen's Privilege Card*. From the corner of his eye he became aware of the materialisation of his father in the seat next to him. *My terms and conditions of employment are being undermined,* he muttered defensively, attempting to silence the disembodied nagging before it *really* got started.

You want to join a union, said his father. *Get yourself organised. Stand up for your rights. Stop the company from exploiting poor migrant workers.*

Tom almost blurted his reply out loud.

181

What good did the unions ever do you?

A cancerous leech dropped onto the table and squirmed before him in a pool of dark blood.

When Tom logged on to the *Privilege Card* website with the password Ms McAllister had issued to him he found that five points had automatically been awarded to him when he reported the student, a further ten were due to be added when his Visa was suspended pending an investigation, and a further twenty were promised if a deportation order was successfully obtained.

Tom scrolled down, looking for what rewards he might be able to apply for with thirty-five points. There was nothing immediately within his reach. But if he could get to fifty points he could apply for an adjustment to his Tax Code. He liked the sound of that. It would substantially increase his take home pay.

I'll stop then, he assured his Dad, when the voice started niggling at him.

He didn't dare to turn around in case his father was hovering behind him, smothered in foul and ravenous tumour leeches.

All I want is a bit more cash, he insisted. *Decorate the front room. Maybe take your granddaughters on a decent holiday for once.*

It occurred to him that Mick Rogers, who worked the forklift truck on the opposite shift to him, did a lot of moonlighting in his spare time, using his staff discount to buy materials for cheap and then installing bathrooms for cash-in-hand payments that were never declared to the Inland Revenue.

He was given three points for reporting that one and a further ten when charges of tax evasions were laid against his work colleague. When Mick was dismissed for abusing his staff discount all the overtime went to Tom. A little added bonus he hadn't expected.

I'm only two points short of my target, he replied when his Dad's voice attempted to admonish him.

He easily exceeded his target after a family wedding where one of his cousins made the mistake of drunkenly boasting about how he was wangling long term sick benefits as a result of faking whiplash injuries following a minor shunt in his car.

"Haven't worked since," bragged his cousin. "And any day now a big fat compensation cheque is going to land on my doormat."

Despite the protestations of his father's spectral presence Tom reported his relative's scam. He used his accumulated points to apply for the Tax Code adjustment and was left with a balance of eighteen points on the card. It seemed such a shame not to push on for the next fifty that would also afford him a Council Tax rebate.

He scoured the estate, kept his ears open at work, listened to gossip from his wife and his mother. Anything up to five points could be accrued for simply reporting someone for suspected wrongdoing. So he reported frequently, even if there was no real evidence to support an allegation.

With his extra overtime, his lower tax band and his council tax rebate he was able to start saving for the first time in his life. He had eighty-five points on his card when he seriously started to consider applying for Enhanced Mortgage Assistance. All you needed was two hundred points for that particular reward.

Don't start, he told his Dad while logged on to the website. *It's within my grasp to be the first person in this family to own a property.*

Something flashed up on the screen as he was scrolling through it.

"Double Bonus Points for information concerning potential extremist groups!"

His eldest daughter came home from school one day, rambling on about some sixth formers who were going to organise a boycott of a Coffee Shop in the town centre that was part of global chain, suspected of not paying its taxes.

Good on them, said his father's voice. *Those are the real villains.*

Tom thought that he saw his father's ghoulish image reflecting back from the computer screen, face seething with swollen leeches, spinning spiral trails of blood on his grey flesh. He blinked and the image was gone.

Tom reported – *anti-capitalist group active in my area* – and gave the names of half a dozen teenagers he'd managed to prise out of his daughter.

Then his wife started raving about some book one of her workmates had put her on to. Apparently the work colleague had read it as part of a Muslim women's book club that met at the local community centre. The book seemed harmless – some sort of historical romance. But Tom started wondering exactly what it was that these women were *really* reading and what the book club might be a front for.

Now you're being ridiculous, rebuked his father and Tom could have sworn that his shadow fell against the wall of the room where the computer sat on the new self assembly unit he'd bought from work with his staff discount.

Tom reported – *Possible Islamic radicalisation at secret meetings.*

Soon they were packing up the removal van, ready to leave the council estate and set up in their new mid-terraced semi-detached property in a nearby residential area.

"Have I done something wrong?" asked Tom.

He had been summoned once more to an appointment at the offices of UKCA.

"Not at all," said Ms McAllister, full of red lipstick smiles. "In fact you're doing so well that we want to offer you an upgrade."

"An upgrade?"

184

You promised you'd stop once you got the mortgage, reminded his father's voice.

Just let me hear her out, replied Tom.

His father materialised behind Ms McAllister. The tumour leeches gnawed their way through his flesh to slide and glide on wet films of blood. Tom bowed his head and stared at the tabletop.

"The card we issued you with could be said to be the Bronze version," Ms McAllister explained, her thick perfume again irritating his nostrils. "We want to give you the opportunity to move up to the *Silver* version."

Tom took out his card.

"What's the difference between this and the Silver version?" he asked.

"Better rewards," she replied.

"Like what?" asked Tom.

"Rewards designed to motivate people from hard working families who truly wish to aspire to something better," she said. "Under our Silver scheme you can exchange your points for vouchers. And these vouchers can, in turn, be exchanged for privileges such as private health insurance, private education, private pensions and such."

Not for the likes of us, warned Tom's father, leaning in so that his leech infested face was level with Ms McAllister's.

Shut up, Dad, snapped Tom internally.

"So what sort of information would I need to provide you with to accrue these points?" he asked Ms McAllister.

Ms McAllister drummed her red fingernails against the desktop.

"Silver Card holders are required to be somewhat less passive and more proactive," she replied.

I knew there would be a catch, said Tom's father.

"Passing on information and leaving it to the authorities to act is tantamount to expecting something for nothing," she said. "I mean all you've been doing so far is reporting wrong doing. As a loyal citizen it might be said that you should have been doing that anyway."

"So how do I become more proactive?" he asked, ignoring his father's panic-stricken warnings.

Ms McAllister smiled and leaned across the table.

"What are your views on euthanasia?" she asked.

Tom raised an eyebrow.

His father scowled at him.

Several leeches dropped wetly from his face onto the table and seemed come squirming towards Tom. Hurriedly he dropped his hands down onto his lap.

"We have an ageing population," said Ms McAllister. "People used to die in their mid sixties. Now they live on till to be eighty and ninety, drawing on the state pension for twenty or twenty-five years longer than anyone ever expected. They get all sorts of ailments - dementia, diabetes, Parkinson's. This places great strain on social services and the NHS."

"What has this got to do with upgrading my Privilege Card?" asked Tom.

"We would like you to help relieve some of these people of the burden placed on them by their unexpected longevity," replied Ms McAllister. "And in doing so relieve the state of the burden of having to look after their welfare."

"You want me to kill old people?" asked Tom.

The voice that blurted out the words sounded exactly like that of his father.

"We would like you to assist them to pass peacefully over," said Ms McAllister. "We estimate that substantial savings can be made if a reasonable proportion of pensioners are given a little nudge on the way."

"A nudge?"

"It would require a change in career," said Ms McAllister. "But we would give you free access to training, as well as supplying the necessary equipment."

You know who used to gas people that they found inconvenient, don't you?

Tom's father had appeared in the passenger seat of the new transit van that Ms McAllister had arranged to be delivered to him once he'd received his certificates as a qualified gas engineer. From the corner of his eye Tom observed the grotesque re-appearance of the disease-addled leeches as they squeezed out of their fleshy boreholes.

Shut up, Dad – he said.

His father's face materialised in the rear view mirror and Tom realised that the apparition was now seated behind him in the back of the van.

What are you going to say when this all comes out? I was only obeying orders?

It won't come out - said Tom. Ms McAllister had assured him that the Official Secrets Act covered this part of the programme.

All I'm doing is helping some poor old dears on their way – he continued. *A few little adjustments to the valves and the ventilation outlets, that's all it takes. Carbon Monoxide poisoning kills around fifty people every year, what difference is a few more going to make?*

It's murder – said his father.

Tom thought he heard the squelch of a leech falling onto the headrest of the seat.

He tightening his grip on the steering wheel and quoted directly from the wisdom of Ms McAllister.

It's good housekeeping.

Blood coloured foam seem to bubble up on his father's dead lips.

And what if someone like you is sent to help your mother on her way?

That won't happen – replied Tom. *My Privilege Card rewards are going to buy the best private health insurance going. If her health deteriorates I'll be able to provide for her in a top of the range Care Home.*

187

Private health care – spat his father. *What's wrong with the good old NHS?*

What good did the NHS do you? – Tom spat back. *You died in a seedy ward at forty-nine and you didn't even have an insurance policy that would have allowed us to pay for a funeral that was half way decent. At least through my hard work my kids are going to have a better life than you ever provided.*

I worked hard – insisted his father. *And I didn't sell my soul in the process.*

Look where that got you – said Tom.

"How many?" asked Ms McAllister when Tom was invited back for another interview.

Tom shrugged – he'd lost count.

The arguments with the ghostly manifestation of his father seemed to bicker endlessly on inside his head. On top of that he hadn't been sleeping properly. In his dreams he was having lurid visions of leeches. These were not the fat, black leeches that burrowed out of his father's flesh. These leeches were bizarrely liveried in the patriotic red, white and blue of the *Privilege Card.* In his fevered nightmares they multiplied at an alarming rate – gnawing at his heart and colonising his soul.

He knew he had visited many seedy flats – filthy hovels that reeked of urine and excrement. Hovels occupied by pathetic trembling skeletons, too weak to raise themselves up out of armchairs whose cushions were barely dented by their frail birdlike frames. They'd watch him through rheumy eyes as he made adjustments to valves and flues on their gas fires and hot water boilers. He'd leave them with the slow gift of seeping, odourless toxins to lull them into endless sleep.

"We were hoping that you would reach twenty-five," said Ms McAllister. "But you actually exceeded that by three."

"Is that good?" asked Tom.

Well done – said his father. *You're up there with the most notorious serial killers in history. Hope you're proud of yourself.*

His form materialised behind Ms McAllister, tumour leeches and all.

"It's excellent," replied Ms McAllister, lipstick lips curving to a pronounced smiley face crescent. "And we know that you're reaping the rewards. How are your daughters settling in at their new school?"

"I think the boarding was a bit of a shock at first," replied Tom. "But they're getting used to it."

"In the long run they'll thank you," Ms McAllister assured him. "They'll have considerable privileges in later life. Speaking of which, are you ready to upgrade to a Gold Card?"

"Gold?" asked Tom.

"Why else do you think I invited you in?" she asked back.

You promised – said his father, leeches devouring what was left of his ravaged features.

"I was thinking of calling it a day," Tom said.

Ms McAllister raised a plucked eyebrow.

"After you've come so far?"

After you've sunk so low – countered his father.

"Maybe I've come as far as I want to come," said Tom.

Ms McAllister scowled at him.

"We wouldn't want to see you sinking back down," she said. "How would your wife and daughters feel if you all ended up back in a council flat, you on the dole, your daughters back at the local comp?"

"That's not likely to happen," said Tom, avoiding the glare his father was giving him.

"But it is," insisted Ms McAllister. "It's in the *Privilege Card* terms and conditions. Privileges awarded can be withdrawn at the sole discretion of the company. Penalties can be imposed. Once that happens we may not be able to guarantee your further immunity from prosecution."

189

Tom could feel a headache coming on.

His father's voice prattled on amongst his panicking thoughts.

Didn't think to read the small print, did you?

Too damned greedy, weren't you?

Hook, line and fucking sinker!

"Couldn't I just downgrade to the Bronze Card?" he asked. "Pick up where I left off? Reporting stuff and accumulating points?"

Ms McAllister sighed and shook her head in obvious disappointment.

"We've given you upward mobility, Mr Riley. Where is your drive? Where's your ambition? What happened to all your aspirations?"

Tom bowed his head.

"It's just – well – the things you've had me do – "

"Things in the long term interest of this country," she reminded him.

Tom said nothing. He could feel the cold slither of leeches squirming in the sweating running down his down his spine.

"How about if I give you an idea of the type of reward you can expect in exchange for Gold Card points?" she asked.

Tom shrugged, head still slightly bowed.

"Company shares," said Ms McAllister. "Gold Card holders get privileged access to company shares."

Tom looked up.

Behind Ms McAllister his father was furiously shaking his ghoulish head.

"Our share holders receive competitive dividends and attractive bonuses," said Ms McAllister. "We are not registered in the UK – therefore our corporate taxes are lower than average."

"But isn't that?" Tom blurted.

"Tax avoidance and tax evasion are two entirely different things," she insisted. "We are simply taking prudent steps to ensure our investors get the best return."

The ghost of Tom's father was fuming.

Where's the fucking loyalty in that?

What happened to us all being in this together?

"With the income from the shares you'd soon be able to move to a bigger house," said Ms McAllister. "Maybe buy that Ferrari you've had your eye on."

"So how would I accrue Gold Card points?" asked Tom, curious now, despite his father's rage.

"Single parents are a perennial problem," said Ms McAllister, examining her red fingernails. "Those young mothers – little more than children themselves. They have no parenting skills whatsoever. Their sons and daughters end up draining the resources of social services. They grow up to become involved in petty crime, gang culture, binge drinking, recreational drugs – placing an undue burden on crime prevention resources. Sooner or later the boys end up impregnating some girl, and the girls end up getting pregnant. And so the whole sorry circle starts all over again."

"You want me to kill teenage mothers?" asked Tom.

"Not the mothers," replied Ms McAllister.

Infanticide! – Dozens of the tumour leeches fell from Tom's father's face and arms to slither in trails of blood across the tabletop.

"Carbon Monoxide?" asked Tom.

Ms McAllister shook her head.

"Our cost analysis suggest that would prove too expensive. All it really takes to suffocate a baby is a gentle hand over the lips and a little squeeze on the nostrils with a finger and thumb."

Tom bowed his head again.

You can't – pleaded his father. *Please tell me you're not actually thinking about it.*

"How would I get to them?" asked Tom.

"There are a growing number of midwives and health visitors who have been issued Bronze Privilege Cards," replied Ms McAllister. "Hard working professionals who know first hand the extent of this particular problem. They would contact you to arrange access."

You can't – repeated his father. *Little babies - helpless babies.*

Tom looked across at Ms McAllister.

"I'm not sure about this," he said. "I mean assisting old folk on their way was one thing. But this?"

"Do you like animals, Mr Riley?" she asked him.

"Not particularly," he replied.

"Neither do I," she said and launched herself into a rant.

"These people, these welfare scroungers – they're no better than animals. You lived on a council estate. You saw with your own eyes they way they lived – the squalor and the chaos of their lives, their lack of morals, their propensity to violent, anti-social behaviour, the disrespect they show towards hard working people like yourself. Drug addicts producing another generation of drug addicts – sponging off the likes of you and me – thinking the world owes them a living. Think of the culling of seal cubs, Mr Riley. They do that for the greater good of the wider seal population. That's all that we're asking you to participate in here. A little culling of the chavs for the greater good."

Tom looked across at the image of his father, wan face alive with bloated tumour leeches. This time there was no lecture – just two simple words.

Please, son.

Tom felt an eerie twitching in his belly as the alternative nightmare version of the leeches that had metaphysically settled there came suddenly awake. They began to writhe like a seething pit of vipers, the overwhelming force of their voracious hunger decisively winning the battle for his conscience. *A bigger house*, he thought – and experimentally pinched his thumb and finger together.

The Ghost at the Feast
By Alison Littlewood

David could still remember the number of steps it took to get from his sofa to the kettle (four) and the number it took to get from there to his bed (seven). It took another step to reach his wardrobe, or two if you counted the shuffle across his double bed. From there to the toilet: four again. To the mirror to shave: zero (he just needed to turn around and look in the mirror – wrinkled forehead, sallow skin, faded eyes) and zero again to reach the shower, since the nozzle was pretty much straight overhead and he had to stand under it to shave anyway.

The flat was small. It was still too large.

Now he spread himself along his narrow bed, the slats of the bench driving notches into each rib, and he looked across the park at the acres of grass. He folded his arms around his chest. The day was warm, thank all the gods, but the cold was in deep now: it took a long time to uproot it. His chest ached. It felt like there was a physical thing nestled in there, solidified to about the size of a fist. He glanced down at his hands. They were shaking. He had sworn he wouldn't do it, wouldn't become the thing they mocked and pointed the finger at all the time he was descending that greasy pole, but Christ, he could use a drink.

Dole bludger, he thought. *Scrounger. Drunk. Waster. Parasite.* If he forgot the words, the headlines of the discarded newspapers he sometimes stuffed down his jumper for warmth would soon remind him.

The sound of children's laughter drifted across the still air; there was the flash of a frisbee and a scream of delight. He closed his eyes. *Maddie.* He'd paid every penny they'd needed, the maintenance and child support, and then he'd

193

paid them some more, for as long as he could. That was why he'd done the overtime, clawing his way up the pay grades until, when the crunch came, he was too expensive to keep. John and Ted had stayed, the plodding lazy bastards, while he'd got his marching orders. *Can't carry the dead wood* was the message they gave, and he grimaced, shaking the thought away. That had been another life, another person. It wasn't who he was now.

Parasite. Waster. Dole bludger.

Except there was no dole: there was no dole because there was no address, and there was no address because he'd lost the house and the flat he'd downsized to was just too – fucking – big. *Three steps*, he thought. *Three steps from his sofa – where he was supposed to have been playing X-box all day on the state, if you listened to them – three steps to the front door when the eviction order came.* And it was still too many, at least after the Square Footage Tax, the SFT, or the Stand Fucking Tall and Don't Move Tax because that was what they wanted, wasn't it? Everyone to fit into their allotted cupboard and stay there, not taking up any room, not even breathing, taking air from the rest of them, the ones who deserved it.

They'd charged extra for the space taken up by the double bed, since he was on his own and didn't actually need one. He couldn't afford a smaller bed. He couldn't afford to move, but he'd tried to get a smaller place; there were no smaller places.

Except this one. He shuffled on the bench, trying to get comfortable. He closed his eyes, feeling the sun break through for a moment, warm on his eyelids, like comfort. Then it was cut off and he heard the grit of shoes against earth. He opened his eyes to see a man and a woman looking down at him, wearing business suits and matching expressions of disgust. He swung his feet off the bench and sat. They didn't move. The woman was looking at the man. "I thought they weren't allowed," she said. "They're not allowed, are they?"

David sighed and pushed himself to his feet. His knees and hips had seized and it took him a while to shuffle away. *Thirty steps*, he thought, *to the exit.* He lost count after about seven; he was half listening to the couple's argument about whether the bench was clean enough to sit on. He waved a hand over his shoulder, not bothering to turn and see if there was a response.

The faces around David seemed to be lit in the lurid light of hell. His own back was cold but his cheeks and nose were flaming. Someone threw a handful of garbage onto the brazier and it flared higher, but David didn't flinch. None of them did. The man standing next to him – he didn't know his name, though he could smell him, his armpits, his unwashed crotch – wriggled his elbow and David shuffled aside. If he took more of the heat, he'd only be stealing it from somebody else. They had to keep the circle, letting the fire build inside it.

Another cough rooted itself inside his chest. He knew there would be blood in it. He wanted to sit down, but if he did, he'd be out in the cold: someone else would take his place. He might not get back into the circle. He was dying in the stinking back streets of the town where he'd once lived, and there was nothing else to do but to stand a little closer to the fire.

When David woke he wasn't cold any longer and he wasn't hot. He opened his eyes. Everything seemed grey, as if the colour had been leeched from the world. He was in the same alley as before, lying by the wall. The brazier was still there but the fire had gone out and the others had gone. He looked up and the sun glared into his eyes, but there wasn't any pain. When he banged a fist against his chest, he felt nothing.

"Tha'll not feel owt," a voice said.

He looked around and met the eyes of Eddie Jowitt. He blinked. He couldn't be seeing Eddie, not really, because he

195

knew that Eddie Jowitt was dead. He rubbed his eyes. He put his hand to his chest again, wondering vaguely if he was suffering a heart attack. He wondered this with curiosity but without fear.

Eddie chuckled in just the same way he used to when someone took a half bottle of Jack from their coat. For a second David remembered the harsh burn of alcohol. He was suddenly thirsty, in an odd sort of way. He didn't actually feel the need for a drink, but that didn't stop him from wanting it.

He looked at Eddie again, really *seeing* him this time, and he started. Eddie slapped his thigh and laughed. "Your face," he said. "Still, I reckon mine'd a been t' same. Priceless."

Half of Eddie's cheek was missing. Shreds of skin hung from it. It looked as if it had been nibbled at by rats.

Oh crap, David thought.

"Aye, this *is* all there is. Tha's what you're thinkin', in't it? Short-changed again." Eddie let out another of those sputtering laughs.

David closed his eyes. Eddie Jowitt was still there, behind them. Then he heard: "Dun't 'ave ter stand fer it, though." He opened his eyes. Eddie seemed to be waiting for an answer. He wasn't sure what the question had been. *Story of my life*, he thought, and grimaced.

"Bunch of us off ter Coleman's gaff," he said. "Seein' as it were 'im put most of us on t' streets in t' fust place."

Coleman's real name wasn't Coleman. It seemed to be the fashion these days for MPs to adopt a name to match their principles, or to mask them, David wasn't sure. Coleman – *Coalman*, is what he wanted folk to think – billed himself as a 'man of the people.' He even had friends who were common: he made a point of saying so. He numbered some ex-miners among them. David could remember his last speech: *There's no better company than the working man's,* and he remembered the way he'd rubbed his hands together as he spoke, as if he were rubbing them clean.

It was Coleman who'd brought in the SFT.

David let that thought burn within him as he walked. The anger was comfortable, something he understood. It pushed the rest of it – his death, what he was doing, what he was doing *here* – to the back of his mind, and that was fine with him. Each step he took put another brick in the wall in front of it.

Eddie shambled along in front of him. He looked a mess, his clothes ragged, though David supposed he didn't look any better. At least – small mercies – he couldn't smell him. He couldn't smell the hedgerows they were walking past either, though he could see the dog-roses blooming and hear the bees buzzing in and out. The colours hadn't come back, not fully.

Then Eddie stopped. "There 'tis," he said.

David looked across the hedge. There was an expanse of green, only that, and then he saw what Eddie meant; there was a house – no, a mansion – set into the hillside opposite. It was the only building in sight. Despite the haze across his eyes he could see that the stone was mellow and beautiful in the afternoon sun, and the pillars were grand, and the windows were gleaming. He swallowed something that tasted a little like bile, but not quite. Like colours, taste had faded.

"Bastid." Eddie spat, a fat gobbet that flew from his mouth but didn't land; it disappeared before it could reach the leafy hedge.

David didn't know how many steps it was from the grand doorway through the hall and up the stairs to the bedrooms. There were too many stairs to choose from, for one thing, and too many bedrooms, and anyway, there wasn't any point in counting. He couldn't feel the marble beneath his feet or see the colours or taste the food. He couldn't sleep on the soft beds; he didn't seem to need to. He lay awake

197

through the dark hours, wondering why he hadn't simply moved on somewhere else. He couldn't enjoy the space around him. All he could feel was a kind of hollowness, as if all that empty space were slowly creeping inside him, filling him up with nothing.

Eddie had taken to sitting slumped in the hall, barely raising his head when the maids walked through him. When they did they would pause, as if they'd just remembered something important, and then they'd shake their heads and walk away. Sometimes Eddie would concentrate really hard and will himself to glow a little brighter, and then a maid would see him, really *see* him, and would run. At first that had made Eddie laugh. Now he didn't laugh. He sat.

The other ghosts milled around, walking the corridors, standing in corners as if waiting for something. They didn't talk much, didn't seem to have anything to say.

David had only seen Coleman once. This was the MP's second home, after all. He knew when he was coming, though, from the shudder that ran through the place. The ghosts stirred. He could feel their hunger, something that had awakened as the thing that could slake it drew closer. He heard the crunch of tyres on raked gravel and he edged towards the door. He had to stand tall to do it; there were a lot of ghosts now, mostly people like him with untidy clothes and blank expressions. Now there was something else in their eyes: something akin to hope.

The doors swung wide and Coleman stood there, the sun behind him, his waistcoat stretched across his belly. His suit was pinstriped, his tie neatly tied, his dark hair – dyed, probably – shining with oil. There was a smile on his face. It did not fade at the sight of the ghosts ranked before him.

David felt the concentration as the assembled throng willed themselves to shine more brightly; to be seen. He looked around and found himself brushing into – no, *through* – the ghost standing next to him. The tall, thin man flashed his anger before turning once again to Coleman, and David shuddered. It wasn't impossible to touch another ghost, or even, he supposed, to occupy the same space, but it wasn't pleasant. It wasn't *right*.

He stood shoulder to shoulder with his fellows, willing himself visible, and he waited.

Coleman blinked. There was no fear in his eyes. He turned towards David for a moment and his smile drew a little broader, and then he stepped forward, into him, *through* him. David whirled around and watched as he headed for the stairs. There were other ghosts, gaunt and softly glowing and *there*, and Coleman didn't see a single one of them. He didn't even pause, didn't seem to feel the cold rising from them. He turned and looked out across the hallway as he left; he looked genial, comfortable; happy to be home.

"It didn't mean anything," David said. "None of it. Nothing at all."

Eddie grunted.

"I just wanted him to know what he'd done. And he didn't even know we were there." He stared down at his hands. They had faded to the faintest of greys.

He could hear the cooks clattering pots in the kitchen. They seemed to be preparing something special; occasionally he caught the waft of the scent of baking, so faint it seemed to be coming from a long way away – almost from a memory, something from the past. It made his mouth water anyway. He could remember the flavour of the things he smelled – his mother's scones, her apple crumble – but he knew he would never taste them again.

Soon there were other smells, roasting game and fowl, boiling ham, and there were sounds: the spit of bursting skin, the hiss of something searing, the bubbling of water. It seemed that Coleman was having a feast. David gave a slow smile. *And we're all invited*, he thought.

They would freeze Coleman's heart. They would glow so brightly he couldn't help but see them; he would quake with fear. They would show him the work of his hands, the things he had wrought. They would squeeze the vitality from him, sap the joy from his flesh and the life from his bones. They would give him their hate and make him eat it, piece by piece, until he was so full with it that nothing else remained.

David practically drooled.

The feast was being brought to the table. Coleman had one of those long banqueting tables, all polished wood and candelabra, and it was groaning with roast pheasant, boiled ham, tender cuts of beef, rack of lamb, slices and skewers and joints. There were glazed carrots, confit potatoes and dauphinoise, plum sauce, pepper sauce, sauce in which shreds of flesh floated. As the waiters brought dish after dish, David's anger began to be replaced by something else: longing. *One more taste*, he thought. *Just one.* Or even just to be able to smell it properly, not this hollow echo of what had been. He looked around and knew that the others were thinking it too. Eddie's lower lip was gripped between his teeth; soon saliva would drip from his chin. He glanced at David and looked away.

David was so spellbound by the feast that it took him a while to realise something odd: although the table was full, there was only one place set.

The food sweated and cooled and bled. There were no more waiters, no one there except the ghosts. There were more of them now. They pressed in close, drawing themselves inward to make room for the others. All that space in the house, but for them it was the same old, same old.

When Coleman came in his smile was, if anything, a little more smug and greasy than David had yet seen. He looked across the room and David had a tremor when he thought, just for a moment, that it had worked; that he had seen them, these hungry ghosts he had created – and then the man smiled a little wider and settled into his seat, adjusting the lay of his silver knife and fork, and he placed a napkin carefully upon his lap.

At first it was ordinary, all cutting and slicing and moderate mouthfuls, but gradually it changed. Coleman began to tear at the flesh with his fingers, cramming it between his red lips, pushing it into his face as fast as he could. His cheeks bulged. His face shone with smears of fat; runnels of grease ran down his chin and darkened his shirt. He smiled and a bright, crazed light shone in his eyes.

Eventually – it seemed a long time to David – he stopped. He leaned back in his chair, placed both hands on his bulging stomach, and he belched. Then he lowered his gaze and glanced about the room. A slow smile crept across his face.

"Friends," he said, "Romans, countrymen." And he laughed, his eyes focused on nothing.

There was a long pause. David glanced around, but no one looked at him; they were all watching Coleman. No: they were transfixed.

Coleman slowly stood. He could barely lift himself from his seat. "Thank you," he said. And he made as if to leave the room.

There was a murmur from the gathering. David frowned. The chefs, the waiting staff, the maids were all absent. Who was it that Coleman had thanked? And then he realised, and his stomach roiled, hollow and empty.

As if in confirmation, the MP turned. His cheeks still shone from his gluttony, and that light remained in his eyes. This time, when he looked around the room, he took his time. He focused on every face ranked before him, one after the next. He smiled, revealing slick white teeth.

"Meat is all the sweeter," he said, "when it is seasoned by other people's want."

The room was silent.

"Thank you for sharing it with me." His smile broadened. "I was always so fond of *the people*." He waved a hand around the room, taking them all in; the contempt in his voice was plain.

He can see us, thought David. *He always could.*

"I do so enjoy the company of those so stupid they have to work with their hands. It – amuses me."

He spoke as if he was making a speech. The tones, the cadences were just the same.

"I have so much," he said. He was starting to laugh, barely able to hold the humour inside now that he was crammed full. "And you have so little. *So little* . . ." The laughter swelled, spreading across the room along with the prickles of anger and hatred and fear.

Coleman straightened. "You feed me," he said. "You *feed* me." And he started to walk, not towards the door at the back but down to where they stood, not stepping around them but walking in a straight line, *through* them, going wherever he wanted to go, and he did not pause and he did not shiver. He had all the space he could desire. He could take all the steps he wanted, because he just – didn't – care. David closed his eyes. The thought of the man touching him made him feel sick, properly *sick*, the clearest sensation he had experienced since he died.

He opened his eyes in time to see Coleman's smiling face, up close, just before he stepped into him. The MP didn't flinch, didn't seem to feel the cold. On the contrary: he looked as if he were feeding on it. *Our souls,* he thought, *He's feeding on our souls, because he's empty inside; because he has none of his own.* Then the man was walking away, having taken what he needed, leaving nothing of himself behind.

David stood there, his eyes closed, while everything and everyone dispersed around him.

The doorway was open, light slanting in. It wasn't summer light but something paler, almost silver; like moonlight but much, much brighter. David didn't know what it was. He had never seen light look that way before.

He looked across the marble hall. Ghosts stood in corners or lounged on the stairs or simply sat, staring at nothing. More of them arrived every day, but there was no point in trying to tell them how things were. They would have to discover it for themselves.

Now there was this: something new, something different outside the door.

He swallowed. Like colour and taste and the world, the whole *world*, his emotions seemed to have faded. There was nothing left to cling to but his hate. Now he could step outside. He could leave, and discover what might come to replace it. Maybe that thing would be nothing. Maybe it would be everything. One day, perhaps he could find a place where Maddie was waiting for him, a smile on her face, her hand stretched out towards him. Maybe she was there already. He had no idea how much time had passed since he came here, but he thought it might have been a lot.

He looked back at the door, at that weird light, and he shivered. *Just one step*, he thought. *One fucking step*: but somehow he couldn't seem to bring himself to take it.

The Opaque District
By Andrew Hook

J ay knew it was getting bad when he saw there were queues to join the queues.

He hadn't watched television for some time. The news held so many cuts it seemed like the government was falling through brambles, although Jay held a suspicion that the government's stance was akin to Brer Rabbit pleading not to be thrown into the briar patch. The government could handle the cuts, alright. Its job was to pass them onto everyone else.

Pale sunshine had filtered through his thin torn curtains that morning. The paucity of the light seemed reflected by the economy, as if everything, the entire reality of the world, had been stripped back to basics.

He had heated some water in a saucepan on a hob that had seen better days, then felt around in the glow of the flame for yesterday's tea bag. He remembered the luxury of steeping a bag for a full two minutes, before adding a healthy drop of milk and three unhealthy heaped spoons of sugar. Now he had got used to the tea from a bag he barely allowed to get wet, and milk and sugar were sweet reminders of times past.

It had happened quickly. The world banks had called in their debts. Then everything had folded like a birdcage in a magician's trick. Provisions were rationed then fought over. Jay could remember seeing his first ever street fight. It couldn't have been more than two months ago, although it now seemed folklore. The man had been outnumbered. His grocery bag had split, and the newspaper he had stuffed around the edges to conceal the contents flew out at the sides like Marilyn Monroe's skirt. Five tins – corned beef, peas, carrots, a Fray Bentos pie, and something Jay couldn't quite determine – hit the ground and rolled, their bent sides describing a disjointed arc. They were pounced on by three men, and when the owner had raised the quietest of objections he found himself with a broken nose lying on the ground scrabbling in the recent blood for his missing teeth. Jay could only speculate on what he intended to do with them.

Scuffles had broken into looting, looting into shooting. That two month burst of panic had spread like shotgun pellets until the only things which were left were those at the ends of the queues. That was when it quietened down, when the shuffling started, when the reason for being was reduced like the sauce in an old cooking pan to the barest extract of what it had previously been. That was when Jay had realised there were queues to join the queues.

The thin tea – no more than hot water with colour – gnawed at the inside of his stomach. He held back from vomiting. He couldn't dispel the recent memory of seeing a woman sick up in the street, and then watching her find two pieces of cardboard to scrape it off the dirty pavement and into a carrier bag. Nothing was left to chance anymore, nothing was wasted. He had known she would fry it for her tea.

He locked the door to his apartment and headed towards the High Street. Even before the austerity measures had hit, the High Street had begun to crumble. The major supermarkets had their suburban outlets and customers fled the traditional shops to bask in what seemed like a utopia of convenience. Places – and names – that Jay had considered staples of life had been boarded up, then replaced by temporary shops with rudimentary signs and badly-spelled window displays. In retrospect they should all have seen it coming. When power is in the hands of the few then there's not much left for the many. And if that power is held high enough, no matter how hard you jump you won't be able to reach it. Jay had held sway in the pubs with these conversations, yet had been shouted down by fools who knew he was right but who didn't care about it. He saw one of those fools recently, Gavin his name was, sleeping in a shop doorway, his red hands clinging to a yellow blanket to stave off the cold. In the old days Jay would have lobbed a coin to someone in that state, but now he had to keep his coins to himself. Coins were all that they had.

Where the butcher's used to be, the window was smashed and the replacement 99p store had been looted. It was there that the queue began.

Jay dug his hands in his pockets and joined it.

The queue didn't normally start this far up, but it was a little later in the day and he wondered if he was usually further along the line. Yet when he stuck his head out and followed the queue into the distance he realised that by Scallion Square it split in two. In one direction lay the soup kitchen that he had been heading for, in the other direction was the government shop. The queues usually weren't joined.

A woman in front of him had a blanket over her shoulders and a threadbare 'bag for life' over one arm. Jay considered speaking to her, but no one really did that anymore. People were guarded. Their heads down, their feet shuffled. The camaraderie from moaning about the bad times, or reminiscing about the good old days, had quickly been ground down. It was almost as though you couldn't admit to *be*. And to acknowledge anyone else acknowledged competition for the few items that remained. It was best just to hang in there, until, you had to hope, the tide would turn and reality would begin to reassert itself. Should that ever happen.

Jay glanced left and right. He was less taciturn than the others, yet he could feel the pressure to be the same. He knew there would be people queuing who didn't know what they were queuing for. For some of them it would simply be something to do, some no doubt did hope for chat. There was a comfort in queuing that Jay couldn't deny. He wondered if it were so orderly in other countries. The television portrayed them as worse than Britain, but then he couldn't quite believe it. They had all seen the propaganda before the austerity hit, and even further back they all knew the campaigns that had occurred during the Second World War. Nowadays you couldn't pull the wool over a population's eyes, but you could damn them all the same.

His ears pricked up at the unfamiliar sound of a car engine. As one, the queue turned its head. A green army vehicle curved over the horizon behind them like a beetle. As it reached the end of the queue it slowed and the queue's eyes returned to the ground. Jay, though, kept his head high. The driver looked him square in the eye as he drew level and for a moment there was the shock of recognition without understanding. Then the vehicle pulled to a halt and the driver removed his hat. Jay saw Christopher, one of his old buddies from college.

Something had to be totally fucked up for Christopher to be driving an army vehicle. He had been adamantly anti-government and all the accoutrements which came with it. Quickly, almost unseen, Christopher nodded at Jay. Jay thought for about five seconds with his head and two seconds with his stomach. Leaving the queue behind he found himself climbing into the vehicle beside Christopher. If the queue saw it, they didn't acknowledge it. Within moments Christopher had driven a square through the less visited streets and Jay found himself being taken towards the wood which flanked the town. It was only as they reached the outskirts that Christopher spoke a couple of words.

"I know. Say nothing."

Jay held back on all the questions. His tongue swelled in his mouth with the anticipation of food. He could only imagine this was why Christopher had picked him up.

They bumped off-road and headed down the barest of tracks towards the lake where Jay had gone fishing as a kid. He'd thought about returning there, but the catch had only ever been sticklebacks and he didn't want to soil his memories by eating such tiny fish. Recent rain had rutted the soil, they rattled over what might as well have been a ploughed field gone hard. After a few moments Christopher pulled up beside a collection of tents. Jay's stomach tensed, not with the thought of food now, but with other fears. The tents, however, seemed to be empty.

"I thought you might be out this way," Christopher said as he switched off the engine. "I couldn't see you leaving like everyone else."

Jay forced words up from his dry throat. "I stuck to my principles."

"No good worrying about those now," Christopher said; then, almost abstractedly, "You hungry?"

He watched as Jay ate the remains of half a tin of Spam. The meat was salty, but it tasted better than Jay could ever remember; or imagine.

"Before all this happened," Christopher said, "I remember reading Spam is a luxury food in South Korea. Something to do with the US army introducing it during the Korean War. They're almost reverent towards it. I laughed when I read it at the time, but I understand it now. I guess you do too."

Jay wiped his mouth with the back of his hand, then licked it. "What happened to you Christopher?"

He shrugged. "I ate more than one tin of Spam, that's all it is. *You* would *now*, wouldn't you?"

Jay wondered if Christopher had something as wild as a cigarette, but the food in his stomach had fired his conscience. Immediately he felt guilty.

"Maybe you should drive me back to the queue."

Christopher shrugged again. "Whatever. Try to help a buddy out." Then he sighed. "This won't last either. Our supplies are no more than yours were a week ago. Won't be long before we're eating each other."

Some thoughts flitted through Jay's head. "What happened to Laura?"

Christopher blinked once, then looked away. It was enough.

"Madeleine got Cotard delusion," said Jay. "You know what that is, right? When all this shit happened she couldn't believe it, wouldn't understand it. The sensation of reality being unpicked unhinged her. She withdrew from me,

208

neglected her personal hygiene and well-being. After a while she began to deny that she existed. She was prone to depression, we both know that – we remember those times at college – but this was different. She would describe herself as a dead body. Then one morning she left."

Christopher looked up. "Where did she go?"

Jay didn't know. But he said: "I imagine she's out there somewhere, with all the rest of them. Queuing."

Christopher picked up a stone and threw it at the side of the vehicle. Where it hit, there was a tiny dent. "You were always one for metaphor."

"When you've got nothing, maybe that's all that's left."

They sat in silence for a moment. Jay knew Christopher would have to drive him back. That the meal had been for old times sake and he could offer nothing more. Yet there was something else there, something Christopher wasn't sure about telling him. Jay knew it, but couldn't prompt it. It would either come or it wouldn't. So he picked up a stick and peeled the bark away from it whilst he waited. Eventually, Christopher said:

"I've heard things."

"Things? What things?"

"Things that are probably rumour, possibly truth."

"We've all heard rumour: The austerity measures will be over by Christmas. There will *be* a Christmas. The international monetary fund will be re-booted by the banks clearing world debt by wiping it off their spreadsheets. And it'll turn out that on paper they have the same amount of money they have in the vaults and that they did so all along. We've all heard those rumours before."

Christopher stood. "I've heard there's somewhere, somewhere close, where none of this is happening."

Jay sighed. "Take me back," he said. "Take me back to the queue."

A few days later when Jay woke the queue had started much earlier in the morning and was already further back from the High Street than his front door.

He couldn't risk the glow of his portable stove being seen from outside the building so he forwent his usual cup of tea. Instead, he stood and stretched, his bones clicking as though he had rickets; as though he were a wooden animal that hadn't been used for some time.

Jay hadn't seen Christopher since the Spam meal. His last words had been, "We've all got to be going somewhere." He'd even forced out a smile. Jay knew the reference and nodded his head in acknowledgement. It was a nice touch, but other than that it was meaningless. The meal he had had falsely indicated to his stomach that more might follow, and in the days which then passed he was hungrier than ever; waking in the night clutched in pain.

Jay left his apartment without bothering to lock it and joined the queue.

It was a misty morning, the sun but a smudge in the sky. He wrapped his arms around himself. Breath hovered at the point of departure from his mouth, and then dissipated to join the haze. The previous evening the television had finally blinked off. That probably explained the length of the queue.

As one, they moved a step forward, then stopped. Jay counted under his breath and it was a full two minutes before they took another step, and by then a dozen new people stood behind him in the queue.

Hours passed. He reached the fork between the soup kitchen and the government stores, between charity and officialdom. For a moment he was held there, as though the two strands of queues were like chopsticks and he were pinched between them. Then he took a step to the left towards the soup kitchen. It wasn't until another twenty minutes had passed before he saw that it also split in two. One strand led to the kitchen and the other headed up Turner Street. Destination unknown.

210

By the time he reached that choice, the pain in his stomach was exploding stars in his head. He dropped to his knees and slumped to the side, but the person behind didn't take his place. They just waited. Slowly, he closed and then opened his eyes; then pushed himself to his knees and then into a sitting position. Finally, he was back on his feet. In another two steps he saw the mural.

He remembered it, of course. It had been there for as long as he could remember. The entire side of an end terraced house had been painted so beautifully that the scene looked real. There was a door, and a ladder to the side of it. At the top of the ladder a man was painting the sky. Another stood with a bucket beside the ladder, looking up. The shadowing was rendered so that it looked three-dimensional. When Jay had first arrived in the town he had in fact believed it was so; it had only been close-up that the subtleties were revealed, the fabrication complete. Today though, there seemed something different. The door at the foot of the painting was ajar.

Jay moved one step further in the queue. It was shadowing, could be nothing else. Either it was always like that and he had never seen it before, or some joker had painted a thin line of black down the unhinged side of the door. But who would have done that? Did such people still exist when all that existed were the queues?

Almost unwillingly, Jay found himself leaving the queue and heading towards the door. The air was still. Mist which had clung to the queue all morning seemed to have evaporated here. He looked back at the queue but could no longer see his place, could no longer remember the back of the person he had stood behind for the past three hours. There was nothing else for it. He reached out and gripped the side of the door.

And it opened.

It was like peeling back a surface layer of the world. As though there were a curtain separating what he knew from what he didn't. The enormity of this reality threatened to overwhelm him, yet he had to keep going. Closing his eyes, he stepped through.

Once he had realised he hadn't simply walked into the wall, he opened his eyes.

Everything was different, yet everything was the same.

It was as though the High Street had not been decimated. Everything he remembered was there, filtered by the frequency of light. The view before him was neither transparent nor translucent. It was opaque. His closest approximation was the thin layer of paper which covered photos in an album. If you lifted the paper you saw the photos as they were, yet with the sheen in place the photos were still visible but protected. He had stepped within that protection, yet viewed it as if from outside. For what he saw was protected, yet not quite how it should be.

The streets were empty even if the shops were full. He walked with awe, his hunger not quite forgotten but relegated to a dull ache in his soul. Overhead, birds flew. He saw with a start that they seemed to be following a chem trail, but he couldn't see the plane. Then he returned his gaze to the ground and wandered amongst the places that he knew so well. Although this was a memory he then questioned. Had he come here as a child, and gone fishing in the lake, or had he arrived as a college student and spent all his time in the pub? Something cold crept up the back of his spine as if he were suddenly aware of being watched. But when he turned he only saw the back of the building he had walked through. His legs goosebumped all the same.

Closer to the pub he could hear chatter. He rubbed his cheek in puzzlement, then realised he was clean shaven and the beard he had sported for the past few weeks – initially in protest at the austerity measures – had gone. His pockets also felt full. Instead of a handful of coins he found his wallet stuffed with notes. Looking up, the occupants of the pub had spilled out onto the street. In fact, the shops were busy and cars sped by either side. The further he walked from his entrance point, the more the world was with him.

It was then that he saw her: Madeleine. It was then that she saw him.

212

Smiles broke out.

She spoke first: "Isn't it wonderful here?"

The words felt wrong. She knew too much. She knew more than he did. There was a knowingness to her expression, a glint in her eye which terrified him.

She pulled him over towards the beer garden at the back of the pub where he had often spouted about world affairs when they were no more than abstracts and not harsh realities. On a table, his beer waited, with a perfect head. Hers was half-finished.

"I've been waiting for you. But I knew you would come, I knew you would find it."

He sat down. The seat, the cold sides of the glass, the taste of the beer: all these seemed real enough.

"We shouldn't have been frightened of it," he found her saying. "We should have embraced it all along. The New World Order. Look at it, it's here!"

Jay found himself following her gaze. Through the opacity everything was as it should be, as it *had* been no more than a few months ago. Yet it was still viewed as though beneath a layer. And it was that layer, he realised, that he found unpalatable.

Madeline was talking at her usual speed showing none of the signs of the decline that he had witnessed. Her disintegration of herself as a person had obviously been superseded. But at what cost?

"There are literally hundreds of ancient architectural sites," she said, "such as labyrinths composed of cobblestones in the northern countries, to some of the most audacious town planning here in Britain that you'd never have believed, all based on models of the intestines of sacrificial animals; like the colons of goats. It's incredible, isn't it? Don't you find that incredible? This is one here."

Jay downed half the beer in the hope that it might offer some understanding.

213

When he looked at Madeline's face it appeared to have been plastered with tracing paper. He could see that thin lines, almost cracks, followed the indentations in her skin.

"There's an entirely new world within this one," she said. "Divined. And when this is gone, there'll be another. And another. Only those of us who have that understanding have been chosen to enter. Don't you see? You won't have to queue here. In here there are no queues."

Jay felt himself shrinking back in his own skin, as though there were another one of himself inside who just got smaller, and another in that which got smaller still. The surface was but a façade.

Suddenly he remembered Disney's *Pinocchio* and the promise of Pleasure Island. How everything the boys could ever want was there. And how this desire transformed them into donkeys. Was it too much to imagine that Pinocchio would have become a puppet of the state if he hadn't realised what was happening and tried to escape?

Madeline laughed. *Had he said something funny?* There was almost a bray to it.

Jay was up and running. He tore back along the High Street pushing past pedestrians and weaving in and out of cars; Madeline's laughter in his ears. He burst through the painted door and slewed his way across the queue which appeared to have remained motionless in his absence. But he didn't stop there, he kept on running. He kept on running and running and running in the hope that there would be another door, a further door into a further layer where the austerity didn't exist and never had done. A layer where Christopher had believed none of this was happening. A layer where in fact he was correct, and where fear was something unknown.

He's running still. The queue can see him. That dot on the horizon. If they wait long enough he'll have run around the world.

No History of Violence
By Thana Niveau

It was time to go. Sara zipped up her coat and turned towards her husband. Robin was looking out of the window, his eyes empty.

"Are you ready?" she asked softly.

He didn't answer. She hadn't really expected him to. He stood like a statue, gazing at nothing for several seconds. Silent, but not at peace. After a while he swiped at his face. "Eating, eating," he whispered. "Inside me."

"I know, sweetie," she said. "They'll be gone soon, I promise."

He stared at her, his face a mask of misery and pain. "They're all I am now."

Sara's eyes filled with tears. Sometimes she was convinced she could see the bugs herself, hear their hellish chewing.

Then, as quickly as it had come, Robin's lucidity faded and he was gone again. He gazed blankly out of the window, seeing nothing of the world outside.

Most people took their sanity for granted, never knowing how awful it could be to have to fight for it, gaining ground inch by torturous inch. Now it seemed like a wish denied. Had she dreamt it all? Robin was the one with the hallucinations but Sara suffered alongside him. It was no picnic being 'normal' when your partner lived in a world you couldn't even see.

The bugs had been there since childhood, he'd told her. Kids in school had made fun of him, teasing him relentlessly about the voices he was so obviously hearing. Robin had been confused, never realising that he was the only one who saw and heard certain things, who talked of parasites devouring him from within. Finally, a teacher

215

realised what was happening and Robin was referred to a psychiatrist. Now, more than thirty years later, he had finally reached something like stability. For the past ten years they had lived like other people did, like *normal* people did.

Robin had been free of the nightmare for so long Sara had almost forgotten how terrible things had once been. She'd done her best to forget the bad times, the times when her husband had seemed like another person entirely. One moment he would be perfectly fine and then the next his expression would turn flat and empty, his eyes looking through her, *beyond* her. Sometimes he would mumble words that sounded like another language. More than once she'd heard the word 'kill'.

And then there were the truly black days. Those were the times when Robin seemed to disappear completely. He would sit staring into the middle distance, focused intently on nothing. Calling his name or shaking him had no effect. He was simply *not there*. Except for the slow rise and fall of his chest she could almost believe he was dead.

Sara wasn't immune. Like an infection, Robin's darkness spread to her, poisoned her optimism and destroyed her sense of hope. At times like that she could see nothing but shadows and storm clouds. She could feel nothing but despair. Fantasies of death began to intrude into her thoughts and she found it harder and harder to push them away. Her own voices began to whisper insidious thoughts.

Wouldn't it be easier if...

Wouldn't it be kinder if...

Every time it happened she tapped a hidden well of strength and pulled herself out of the pit. It was like climbing up out of a deep well where they had both been left to drown. Getting herself out was hard enough; once out, she then had to pull Robin up after her. It got harder every time.

And then those terrible days became a thing of the past. At last, all the delicate juggling of pills and counselors and psychotherapy paid off and Robin began to come back to her. He stopped hearing voices. He stopped obsessing about parasites. He stopped getting lost inside his mind. Finally, he began to recognise reality. Like a miracle, Robin was whole again. And they had been so happy.

Oh, but now. The bugs. The blackness. Sara felt it pressing on her like a weight. There was the terrible sense of sliding back through time, as though down the slimy walls of the bottomless well they had spent so many years climbing out of.

Sara licked the envelope, sealed it and laid it on the kitchen table where it could easily be found. Robin watched her without really seeing. He was scratching at his face and she could see he had already drawn blood.

"Cut me open," he moaned, "they'll spill out."

Sara's heart twisted. She couldn't even imagine what he was going through but she was determined to stop it.

"Just hold on a little longer," she said. Even though at times Robin seemed far away she always treated him as though he were right there with her. Maybe deep down inside, in some lost little place, he could hear her. "We'll make them go."

When the local hospital began to shrink under the budget cuts, one of the first things to go had been the mental health treatment program. Naturally, the support group for partners went along with it. Sara had the luxury of finding her own support group online but of course Robin needed so much more than that. They'd both searched for alternative solutions but they were told the resources simply weren't there.

"It's a death sentence," Sara had said to more than one administrator, but her words fell on deaf ears. Each person had spread his hands and made sympathetic noises but to them Robin was just another casualty of a failing system. One of many. There was the implication that they shouldn't think they were special.

217

It was like being at the mercy of a killer. The police couldn't do anything until a crime had been committed and by then it would be too late. With no more access to the treatment that kept Robin in touch with the real world, their only option was to wait until he lost it completely.

"Then, of course," said a nurse who was probably ten years younger than she looked, "you would have the option of coercive care."

Sara felt her skin crawl. "Is that the PC term for 'sectioned'?"

"Well, yes." At Sara's look of horror she added, "Only if he turns violent."

"My husband has never been violent in his life."

The nurse shrugged helplessly. She had the bloodshot eyes of someone who never got enough sleep and Sara could practically read the girl's mind. She was a victim of the whole mess too. Overworked, underpaid, terrified of being cut loose herself, however thankless and gruelling her job was. Like a volunteer at an animal shelter, she simply couldn't afford to get attached to every sad stray that was brought in. All she could do was offer hollow reassurances and move on to the next distraught family member, the next hopeless case.

Robin had only been hospitalised once before. When he was a teenager his parents had him committed and the experience had traumatised him. The bullying he'd suffered at school was nothing compared to the bullying he suffered from his fellow inmates. There weren't enough staff to keep an eye on everyone and Robin had been too weak, frightened and sedated to fight back. His supposed 'carers' were no help either. They told him he'd imagined it.

Robin had made Sara promise never to lock him up again. He'd told her he'd rather die.

Sara had promised without hesitation.

Now they had run out of options. Medication alone wasn't enough to keep Robin from the creeping madness that overwhelmed him and he was slowly slipping away from her. Bewilderingly, Robin had been passed fit for work by the 'expert' who'd glanced at him for five minutes.

So Robin had stayed in his job, working alongside Sara. It wasn't terribly demanding. Just general catering duties, although he wasn't allowed to prepare food without supervision. Presumably someone had the sense to realise that thwarted benefits scroungers like her husband might have access to poison. Or that their wives might.

"Kill them," Robin said, a note of desperation in his voice now. He looked confused and frightened as he clawed at his skin. "Please."

"We will," Sara said, wrapping her arms around him. He shuddered, swatting at the air around them both as he mumbled other random words and sounds that meant nothing.

Even in his worst hallucinatory states, Robin had never been dangerous. Not intentionally. He hadn't meant to hurt her that time. He'd been lashing out at what he thought was a bug. He hadn't even known Sara was there. Afterwards he had no memory of it and of course he believed her story about tripping over the cat. She wasn't sure anyone else bought it and she deeply resented the stares of her colleagues over the next week as the bruise on her cheek turned blue, then yellow, then finally faded. She just as deeply resented the fact that, suspecting domestic abuse, no one had expressed the slightest concern.

No one cared.

And that was what it all boiled down to, wasn't it? No one cared. In a society full of victims, empathy was yet another luxury beyond their means.

'Quality of life' was a phrase that kept ringing in Sara's mind. What kind of quality was this? The slow downward spiral to inevitable hospitalisation, out of Sara's control. Robin would be too doped up to know who she was when she tried to explain. Too doped up to fight back if he were mistreated as he had been before.

In his fractured mind, would he hate her for the betrayal? She knew the answer to that and it chilled her. Yes. He would. That strange, alien part of Robin would hate her. The stranger who talked about parasites wasn't the Robin she had met and married all those years ago but he was the one increasingly in control now. He was a person she didn't know at all. A person she feared.

But it wasn't his fault. The *state* had made him into something to fear. And now it was time for them to pay.

Sara swallowed her tears as she tucked the gun into her bag. "Come on, we have to go to work."

He stared at the bag for almost a minute. Maybe the sight of the weapon had shocked him back into himself, had momentarily returned him to her, however briefly. He stopped clawing at his eyes and looked at her, as though he understood what she was about to do. As though he were almost there with her.

"Work?"

"Yes, sweetie. For the last time."

He was calmer as he followed her out to the car, as though he had managed to fight his way through the fog to be with her. He didn't ask where they were going and Sara sensed that he knew.

They'd picketed outside Parliament once, with other casualties of the system. They were the helpless prey of the men and women inside who had sworn to protect their constituents. The ones who had then voted to cut that very protection while aligning themselves with the powerful companies who had quite literally ruined the lives of thousands of people.

Tonight some of those men and women would be dining in luxury at the five-star hotel that Sara's company was catering for. The dinner would be lavish and extravagant, just the sort that men who made life and death decisions for others felt they deserved. It was probably a good way to escape the horror of their consciences, the reminder of all those broken promises. They could numb themselves with

220

exquisite food and drink and tune out the shouting from the streets below.

Robin hesitated when they reached the service door. He turned to Sara, a look of confusion crossing his features as he scratched absently at his scalp. "I can still feel them," he said. "What if I...?"

"You won't," Sara said. She withdrew the gun and checked that it was ready for action. "*I* will."

For a split second Robin looked frightened. Then his expression softened into one of complete understanding. And gratitude. He pulled her towards him and kissed her, hard, one final time.

"I love you so much," he said. "Even though I'm crazy, I've never lost sight of that."

Sara clung to him, savouring the moment for as long as she dared.

"You're not crazy," she said fiercely. "The parasites are real. They always have been."

Afterword
By Tom Johnstone

This book is dedicated to the people struggling against cut-backs and privatisation: striking fire-fighters, striking refuse-collectors, striking teachers, striking oil refinery workers, striking civil servants, striking tube workers, striking university cleaners and lecturers and the students standing (or rather sitting in) alongside them, claimants and workers fighting against benefit cuts. The list could go on. Some of the stories in this book suggest a very bleak future, and it's the efforts of the people fighting these austerity measures, I believe, that could help to prevent such a future coming about.

Well, make it a little less bleak perhaps…

It's also dedicated to someone without whom this book wouldn't have been possible. I only met Joel Lane once, very briefly during the 2012 Fantasy Con in Brighton. Aware of his work as co-editor (with Allyson Bird) on the anti-fascist anthology *Never Again* (2010), I plucked up courage and approached him. I was a little daunted. His owlish physical presence was impressive, though not over-bearing or intimidating. Remembering his NHS privatisation-themed stories like 'For Their Own Ends' and 'A Cry for Help', I asked if he'd thought of following up *Never Again* with another 'political' anthology, this time show-casing horror and weird fiction around the austerity measures that were then beginning to bite. Though his reaction was muted at the time, it was clear that this idea had struck a chord with him.

We only spoke again once after that, a mobile phone conversation. Our subsequent contact was entirely via email, but his sudden death in late November 2013 was a terrible blow. His experience of publishing had helped me to avoid various pitfalls in the early stages of this anthology. Many writers and others have expressed their disbelief at his passing. I for one still find it hard to believe that he won't be around to see this book in print. But in the wake of this loss, both Gary Fry of Gray Friar Press and I were all the more determined to see this project through, not least as a memorial to Joel and all he stood for. I'm all too aware in completing this anthology, I'm standing on the shoulders of a giant. That's one of the reasons why this volume opens with one of his stories, a typically short, bleak, and savagely sardonic tale suggesting how, in a society where money has the loudest voice, *everything* has a price.

Now I'd like to say a little about the background to the project.

The Road to Austerity

The meeting that heralded the genesis of *Horror Uncut* took place two years into a Conservative-led Coalition government committed to a programme of cuts and other austerity measures. But the drive to privatise key public services such as health and education didn't start then: New Labour's application of the Private Finance Initiative in hospitals helped pave the way for the present government's wholesale privatisation of the NHS, while Tony Blair was a champion of the privately-backed Academies. The financial crisis and deficit used as justification for the cuts isn't new either. As Joel Lane and Allyson Bird pointed out in the introduction to *Never Again*, capitalism is prone to crisis.

But the origins of more recent global crises can be traced back to the USA's abandonment in 1971 of the Bretton Woods agreement, which had provided for a system of fixed exchange rates, a decision widely seen as ushering in a period of increasing instability in the global financial system, leading to a whole series of crises (including the Asian financial crisis in 1998), of which the recent one was merely the latest and most severe. On the plus side (for the bosses, at any rate), the increasing autonomy of global finance capital made it easier to undermine wages and working conditions in the UK and more advanced capitalist countries, where decades of struggle had secured relatively high wages and living standards. Capital could shift to places where labour power was cheaper, and the workers more compliant, not protected by troublesome unions, pesky labour laws, and so on.

However, while the 1980s saw crushing defeats for key sections of the organised working class in this country under Thatcher, this capital flight failed to drive down wages across the board. On the contrary, this period saw rising real wages for many, helping to keep the Conservatives in power. With up to three million unemployed, it might be expected that employers could drastically reduce wages. Something was wrong. The reserve army of labour wasn't doing its job properly! Why did these people refuse to slave for peanuts? The answer, as far as the Right was concerned, was that unemployment benefits were too generous and didn't have enough strings attached. This is of course a continuing theme now, with the Tory press full of headlines about 'scroungers', 'benefit cheats', 'benefit tourists', etc.

Though the Thatcher government may have been eager for confrontation with the miners and other entrenched, unionised workers, and keen to privatise public utilities such as telecoms and gas, it stopped short of a full-frontal assault on the 'Welfare State'. Tory election campaigns were always keen to stress that that sacred cow the NHS was 'safe' in their hands, and when the Thatcher government tried to add insult to injury with its regressive Poll Tax, it met mass opposition in the form of wide-spread non-payment and civil disorder.

A weakened Tory government under John Major struggled to use high unemployment to discipline the working class, tightening up the benefit regime to force the unemployed to compete for the few jobs available. The Tories had taken a body blow from the 1992 collapse of the

Exchange Rate Mechanism, and were busy tearing themselves apart over Europe. The door was open for a reinvigorated Labour Party under Tony Blair to sweep into power in 1997. It was his government that first coined the term 'Welfare Reform', a phrase still very much part of the lexicon of ministers such as Ian Duncan Smith. With its 'neo-liberal' ideology, it consolidated the legacy of 'Thatcherism', enthusiastically adopting the Tory Private Finance Initiative. Despite Capita's disastrous handling of their contract to administer Housing Benefit in Lambeth under the PFI, and the fiasco over the 'public private partnership' on the London Underground, New Labour pressed on with a massive hospital building programme under the scheme, which allows companies to profit from public funds. Capita itself is now a key player in the privatisation of Birmingham public services, with predictably catastrophic results. Capita wasn't the only private company to make private profit from managing aspects of social security either. French IT firm ATOS took over the running of the already-controversial Medical Examination Service, which tests sick and disabled people for Incapacity Benefit (later renamed Employment Support Allowance): payment by results now meant that passing sick or disabled people as fit for work had a financial incentive, a profit motive, and since the payments came from the Department of Work and Pensions, it was the 'taxpayer' who paid.

As with the Tories, New Labour ran into trouble from its own internal divisions and contradictions. There were also external forces at work. Having enthusiastically supported the US 'War on Terror', the government now had heavy and expensive military commitments by the middle of the new century's first decade. For its part, in 2008 the US economy ran into serious trouble over 'sub-prime' mortgages, and Europe was to experience the shock waves from this for years to come. In Britain, the Chancellor (and by-now PM) Gordon Brown had continued successive governments' encouragement of financial deregulation and easy credit, fuelling a housing bubble that now burst.

With the collapse of Brown's embattled premiership and the revival of the Conservatives, albeit propped up by the opportunistic Liberal Democrats, incoming Chancellor George Osborne quickly established a consensus that the main problem facing the country was the deficit, and the only way to restore the confidence of the international markets servicing the UK's massive debt was by means of swingeing public sector cuts and other austerity measures. It was difficult not to imagine him rubbing his hands with glee as he announced this, but once this orthodoxy was in place, those with opposing viewpoints could be dismissed as 'deficit deniers'. And there have been opposing viewpoints. Many economists on the Left, and some on the Right, have argued that New Labour inherited a larger budget deficit in 1997 than the Coalition did, or that the post-war Labour Government set up the NHS that the government's now dismantling in worse economic circumstances. For those with Keynesian views, working class prosperity and 'purchasing power' through higher wages and job creation schemes are the key to economic growth.

The truth is, George Osborne isn't as worried about the public deficit as he claims. It's true that in order to borrow more money from the international markets to service the debt, the government has to show them that it is being efficient in disciplining the working class, or its creditors may refuse to cough up the funds. We shouldn't of course allow the Coalition to claim powerlessness in the face of inscrutable global movements though. Undoubtedly, the Tory Right saw in the crisis an opportunity to revive and complete the 'Thatcherite' project. And significant sections of their capitalist backers saw it as an opportunity too, to make a killing: both from allowing their firms access to hitherto untapped markets in the public sector, and from holding down or further reducing the wages of an increasingly fragmented working class. However, the

Conservatives knew that employers couldn't make full use of rising unemployment without a more determined structural assault on the social security system than had previously been attempted.

This is the true meaning of Conservatives' speeches about 'dependency culture', and George Osborne's notorious phrase about the benefit-claiming 'lifestyle'. It was something of a *faux pas* for this heir to a wallpapering firm's fortune to go on about this, and he really didn't need to. The Conservative press, alongside dole porn TV shows like *The Jeremy Kyle Show* and *Benefit Street*, can make the point much more effectively from the apparently neutral stand-point of popular culture. Work and Pensions Secretary Ian Duncan Smith has attempted to draw political gains from the public controversy over Channel 4's show, claiming that his policies will put an end to the supposed abuses depicted on *Benefit Street*. In fact, the episode I saw seemed to draw more attention to the area's sanitary problems, over-crowding and fractious mix of ethnic groups than to its population's alleged reliance on social security payments. Moreover, the Eastern European migrant workers interviewed were not claiming anything, ineligible for state assistance, thanks to government restrictions to deter so-called 'benefit tourists'. As the episode showed, this made them more vulnerable to ruthless exploitation by gangster bosses, as they struggled to send pitiful amounts of money back to their families while dwelling several to a room in a small terraced house, then finding that they had to give most of their wages back to their shyster employer as payment for some dodgy 'contract', ending up destitute, sleeping rough, apparently on the run from their boss's hired thugs!

But this is exactly the situation Duncan Smith and his colleagues want to promote, and not only for migrant workers. The restrictions on foreigners claiming social security payments are the thin end of the wedge, similarly with moves to charge foreigners for NHS treatment. Again the government justified these charges as a clamp-down on 'health tourists', a despicable phrase that obscures the NHS's historical reliance on migrant labour power. It's a measure that may well serve to soften up the 'British' public for the more widespread introduction of health charges.

Before I move on to proposing what role (if any!) horror fiction can play in challenging the drive towards austerity, I'd like to put these cuts in context by taking a brief look at the origins of the 'welfare state' in this country, and the ideology that underpins it: social democracy (which shouldn't be confused with the SDP, the off-shoot of the Labour Party that went on to form part of today's Liberal Democrats). In fact, the British variant of social democracy is Labourism, i.e., the Labour Party, together with the 'Labour Movement' of Labour Party-affiliated trade unions. Speaking more generally, social democracy is the integration of the working class into the state, represented economically by trades unions and politically by political parties such as Labour in the UK, the Socialists in France, the SPD in West Germany, or the Democrats in the USA. The introduction to *Never Again* commented on how fascism emerged in the Thirties as a counterweight to communism. Social democracy represented a different response to the threat of communism, offering concessions rather than confrontation. To put it crudely, if fascism was the stick, social democracy was the carrot.

While fascism may have had the support of many industrialists during its period of influence, 1945 saw it defeated and discredited in Europe. However, the redrawing of the post-war map left Eastern Europe vulnerable to the advance of Stalinism. Also, the ruling classes of the USA and Europe didn't want a repeat of the revolutions that had erupted at the end of the First World War. Hence the emergence of social democracy, which incorporated some of the features of Stalinism, such as full employment, public ownership of key services and industries, etc., within the framework of liberal democracy and a Keynesian 'mixed economy'. On the continent, this was underpinned by the

228

Marshall Plan, a seventeen billion dollar US-sponsored aid programme, which aimed to contain or even reverse the spread of 'Communism' by assisting post-war reconstruction. In Britain, the establishment of the NHS was a key cornerstone of the post-war settlement, a class compromise that extended into peace-time the war-time co-operation between government and the unions. At first, successive Labour and Conservative governments both broadly supported this, the so-called 'Butskellite Consensus', named after key moderates in both parties. This class truce didn't last however, and the crisis in the late Seventies ushered in Thatcher, as we have seen, at the head of a government aggressively committed to renegotiating the post-war settlement in favour of capital, though thanks in part to popular resistance to policies like the Poll Tax, she didn't go quite as far as she might have: certainly not far enough it seems, as far as the new generation of Conservatives now holding office are concerned...

Initially the government justified the cuts by invoking the terrifying Spectre of the Deficit, but despite (or perhaps more likely feeling vindicated by) signs of supposed economic recovery such as the IMF's up-grading of the UK's growth forecast, the Tories have proclaimed austerity as a permanent, even a desirable state of affairs. For Labour, Ed Miliband has professed himself in agreement with the indefinite continuation of austerity. The government is weak, propped up by its miserable Liberal partners, perhaps hated even more than the Tories for its role in the Coalition. However, the architects of austerity have been emboldened by the relative weakness in the opposition to their policies. What resistance there is has slowed down their advance, with small victories against the introduction of 'Workfare' schemes, legal challenges against the 'Bedroom Tax', the near collapse of the Universal Credit Scheme, the successful campaign against the closure of Lewisham Hospital. At the time of writing ATOS is trying to wriggle out of its contract with the DWP early, after a wave of country-wide demonstrations against its 'work capability assessments'; during one of these protests, some of its own staff walked out in support.

Why *Horror Uncut*?

The obscene spectacle of the government openly pursuing class warfare on behalf of the rich certainly is horrifying. But it's often assumed that horror as a genre is inherently backward-looking and reactionary, portraying Injustice and Evil as an inevitable, unchangeable fact of 'human nature', rather like the Catholic 'Original Sin'. However, it's also a very extreme literary form. By showing us the worst case scenario, maybe horror can show us what can happen when we don't put up a fight. Perhaps it can even terrify us into resisting.

Some might object that we need action, not more words, and point out the irrelevance of a small press horror anthology! I can't pretend that this book will change things, certainly not by itself. It simply seeks to ask: what private nightmares, what ghosts, what madness, what after-life does 'austerity' force on us?

As may be becoming clear, the stories in this book won't necessarily cheer its readers up, though they may find them diverting, even entertaining. However, I hope they might provide a counterweight to the relentless denigration of the poor in the popular press, in 'reality' TV and popular culture generally. Channel 4's *Benefit Street* may not be quite as sympathetic to the Conservatives' agenda on 'Welfare Reform' as its reputation suggests. Nevertheless, its arrival reflects and possibly feeds into a new approach to the government's war on the poor. Where before cuts in social security were presented more in practical terms, as a necessary evil arising from a temporary crisis, now that the immediate threat of the deficit seems to have passed, the emphasis has moved onto the moral plain: stoking resentment among 'hard working families' against those the government and its allies in the media present as enjoying the dole 'lifestyle', via headlines such as *The Daily Star*'s interview with prominent *Benefits Street* figure Deirdre Kelly, a.k.a. 'White Dee', where it sneeringly suggests that she believes she 'deserves' to live on benefits. This Victorian-style division of the poor into deserving and undeserving poor obscures the fact that many of the government's austerity measures impoverish low-paid workers relying on in-work benefits such as Housing and Council Tax Benefits, as well as Tax Credits, to top up their meagre wages. I hope that many of the stories in this book may redress the balance.

Fiction can't actually change society, can it? It's just a mirror held up to nature, isn't it? But when did you last see a poster or leaflet campaigning for civil liberties that *didn't* reference George Orwell's *Nineteen Eighty Four* to warn against the dangers of excessive surveillance? This is not the only example of the language or imagery of popular genre fiction at the very least influencing public debate. What of the campaign literature that seeks to shame low-paying or exploitative employers by comparing them to Ebenezer Scrooge...?

Fictitious Capital: Horror Literature and Economic Unease

> *"Dark times lead to powerful writing – just think of what the Depression and the war brought to American horror fiction."*
>
> Joel Lane

If science fiction is widely held to be the 'literature of ideas', the best horror fiction, whether supernatural or physical, depends for its effect on the emotions and the senses. Unlike SF and its more misty-eyed cousin, pure fantasy, it often has a mundane, contemporary setting. While the early gothic novels, such as *Otranto* and *Vathek*, may have favoured outlandish and even exotic scenarios,

231

the Victorian and Edwardian 'Golden Age' of the ghost story changed the emphasis to a situation of everyday normality into which the uncanny gradually intrudes. This was certainly the approach suggested by M. R. James, though his idea of the everyday may seem somewhat rarefied by many people's standards.

However, this era offers numerous instances of what Stephen King identified as a key theme in *Danse Macabre* (1981), his survey of horror in popular culture: 'economic unease'. One classic premise for a ghost story is the hard-up family moving into a shunned house that's going for a song. King himself used a variant of this in *The Shining* (1977). The Victorian and Edwardian era, a time of rapid industrialisation and intense hardship for workers, with the first stirrings of the revolutionary wave that swept through Europe in the wake of the First World War, is the period most strongly associated with the growth of supernatural fiction as we know it today. In part, the rise of the ghost story represented a reaction against the rationalism and materialism of emergent capitalism, much as the Romanticism that had fed the rise of the gothic novel had been a rejection of the Enlightenment. On the other hand, the supernatural literature of the time wasn't simply an escape from the material problems faced by ordinary people. It often reflected them. Dickens is an instance of this, whether showing the dreadful burden of responsibility endured by 'The Signal-Man' (1866), or in the supernatural morality tale *A Christmas Carol* (1843), in which the first ghostly manifestation is Marley's ghost clanking not the traditional chains, but cash boxes, ledgers and other trappings of financial servitude. While M. R. James specialised in cloistered academics, L. T. C. Rolt set his ghost stories in coal mines and other industrial settings, where the supernatural adds to the more mundane dangers faced by his characters from their working environments. One of horror fiction's most memorable and dreadful industrial accidents occurs via the decidedly mixed blessing of 'The Monkey's Paw' in W. W. Jacobs's 1902 story, where the two hundred pounds wished for by the old man arrives shortly afterwards as compensation for his son's death, caught in factory machinery.

There is no shortage of stories from this era about destitute young women finding employment that at first seems too good to be true. Miss Lally's desperate circumstances in Arthur Machen's 'Novel of the Black Seal' propel her into a weird tale that's one of the influences on Lovecraft's 'Cthulhu Mythos'. The story turns out to be a hoax on the part of its narrator, one of *The Three Imposters* in the title of the bizarre, decadent and gruesome 1895 novel that frames this tale; an elaborate literary practical joke on the part of the author, which only serves to confirm that this is a familiar device of the time, a staple of mystery and suspense fiction, such as Conan Doyle's Sherlock Holmes tales of distressed governesses like 'The Solitary Cyclist'.

It's also the premise of Edith Wharton's classic ghost story 'The Lady's Maid's Bell' (1904). Recovering from typhoid and struggling to find work in service, Miss Hartley bumps into an acquaintance of her former employer, who directs her to a new situation, working for the lonely Mrs Brympton. She also encounters the boorishly sensual Mr Brympton, and in a bitter aside that suggests the vulnerability of young women in service to sexually predatory employers, the narrator observes:

"The typhoid had served me well enough in one way: it kept that kind of gentleman at arm's-length."

What Mr Brympton's exact role in the death of Miss Hartley's predecessor Emma Saxon is left for the reader to guess.

In Wharton's most celebrated tale of economic unease 'Afterward' (1910), she introduces us to the Boynes, an American ex-pat couple with no apparent financial worries, who would welcome a ghost to liven up their taking up residence in an English country house. The story is told from the point-of-view of Mary Boyne. While her husband Ned settles down to write a book about the 'economic basis of culture', Mary is but dimly aware of "the material foundation on which her happiness was built", her husband's unscrupulous business practices in exploiting the Blue Star Mine, the human consequences of which come back to haunt them.

When we first began discussing our approach to this anthology, Joel Lane mentioned the literary and wider cultural response to the Depression of the Thirties, such as the novels of Steinbeck and Woody Guthrie's *Dustbowl Ballads*. The supernatural fiction of the time may on the surface far seem removed from day-to-day economic realities, with the English ghost story tradition generally fairly upper middle class in outlook, and the weird tales of H. P. Lovecraft and others leaving the planet entirely! On the other hand, while his racial paranoia is often seen as an example of horror fantasy's reactionary nature, Lovecraft's chaotic vision of the universe also seems a fitting metaphor for the economic instability and political turmoil at large at the time. In Gary Fry's 2012 novella *The Respectable Face of Tyranny*, this possibly unintended metaphor becomes more explicit and intentional, with the present-day financial crisis providing the background for a memorably harrowing tale of cosmic and psychological terror.

Returning to the Depression era, in Britain D. H. Lawrence's classic psychological ghost story 'The Rocking Horse Winner' (1930) shows us the torment of the young son of a debt-ridden middle class couple, haunted by the sound of the house whispering for more money, another example of supernatural fiction responding metaphysically to themes of economic crisis in the material, physical world.

I hope these examples convey a sense that there is a tradition of supernatural literature examining the effects of hardship and financial stress on the human psyche. Late twentieth century examples include Nicholas Royle's previously mentioned story 'Archway' (1990), about the mental disintegration of a recently sacked woman living alone in a grim London flat, and Paul J. McCauley's 'Negative Equity' (1998), in which the collapse of the late Eighties housing bubble is given the Faustian bargain treatment.

But how has the world of UK horror and supernatural fiction responded to the most recent crisis: the 'credit crunch' and the ensuing austerity measures?

As well as a deeply disturbing study of psychological and cosmic terror, Gary Fry's *The Respectable Face of Tyranny* (Spectral Press, 2012) challenges the current economic orthodoxy that endless cuts in living standards for future generations are the only answer to the country's economic problems. It concerns a lone father struggling to bring up his recalcitrant teenage daughter in a seaside town. Dwelling in a static caravan in the wake of the failure of his financial dealings, he becomes increasingly obsessed with the strange symbols he finds on the beach, and begins making connections in his mind between them and the world banking crisis. The way in which these signs and wonders come back to haunt the troubled central character leads to an unforgettable climax.

The Paul Finch-edited *Terror Tales* anthology series published by Fry's own Gray Friar Press has yielded its fair share of tales exploring the psychological effects of cut-backs, austerity and general financial insecurity. Perhaps this is most in evidence in *Terror Tales of London* (2013), aptly enough given the capital's status as a densely-populated global financial hub. Roger Johnson's 'The Soldier', a haunting blend of Ackroydian psychogeography with the structure and mysticism of Machen's 'The White People', suggests the existence of a cult-like militia set up to defend the financial interests of the City of London. Successful horror author Adam Nevill's memories of his time as a struggling writer surviving by precarious security work feed into 'The Angels of London', in which we learn of the supernatural forces behind a latter-day Rachmanite landlord. As its punning title suggests, Fry's bizarre and disturbing contribution 'Capital Growth' is as much about capitalism as it is about the city. It echoes *Tyranny*, with its central male character whose preoccupation with financial matters makes him detached from the emotional needs of his family. On the other hand, it also echoes 'Afterward'. Whether by coincidence or by design, its main viewpoint character shares her first name with Mary Boyne, and this Mary is similarly detached from her husband's dodgy deals, the 'fictitious capital' that underpins her comfortable existence:

"Maybe it was ignorance of the source of their plentiful income that scared her..."

Horror Uncut contributor Gary McMahon's *Concrete Grove* trilogy (Solaris Press, 2010-12), also juxtaposes fantastic horror with the mundane life of an economically deprived and debt-mired housing estate surrounding the eponymous condemned tower block. While residents fight for their very lives against the local loan shark, they also face the more supernatural terrors of flesh-eating humming birds, the nursery rhyme horror 'Humpty fucking Dumpty', local bogeyman 'Captain Clickety', a gang of scarecrows wearing the faces of missing locals, and, er, the Angel of the North...

Exploring the links between economic and ecological crises, Carole Johnstone's novelette 'Signs of the Times' (2013) takes place in a near-future Scotland, beset by catastrophic floods and endless cut-backs. The narrator Vince charts his unlikely friendship with a strange new underclass of dog-headed bipeds, harbingers of the End of Days, interned at first in compounds as scape-goats, later released to become the attack-dogs of a police state as the crisis and associated unrest deepens. The story is a mixture of apocalyptic and dystopian themes, two areas where SF and horror meet, in a future that seems unnervingly close to being overtaken by the present, something it has in common with some of the tales printed herein.

*

'Signs of the Times' appeared in *Black Static*, a magazine that originally published one of the stories in *this* volume, Priya Sharma's 'The Ballad of Boomtown'. So perhaps this is an opportune moment to turn to what this book has to offer.

Priya Sharma's story takes place in the Republic of Ireland in the aftermath of the world financial crisis, with the central characters' relationship mirroring the wider economic troubles and social unrest. This is a theme that echoes through many of the stories in *Horror Uncut*, from the father-son relationship poisoned by greed and debt in Stephen Hampton's story, to the troubling cycle of sickness and addiction depicted in Gary McMahon's 'Only Bleeding' that reflects the self-defeating, self-perpetuating logic of the 'boom and bust' business cycle; another example is the mental and physical disturbance experienced by the librarian Richard in Rosanne Rabinowitz's 'Pieces of Ourselves' in the wake of a chaotic demonstration that brings buried memories and unresolved issues to the surface.

Following on from the inset in 'Boomtown' of a folk tale about standing stones, another cursed stone appears in Simon Bestwick's story. 'The Battering Stone' suggests that, though capitalism is a relatively new phenomenon, poverty and inequality are of far older provenance, though not immune to change and intervention for all that. Those who enjoyed Simon's 2007 tale 'Hushabye', published in Ellen Datlow's Tor anthology *Inferno*, may be interested to find out that this is another in the same series featuring down-at-heel investigator Paul Hearn; though he's not named as such in this story, there's no mistaking the bickering, wise-cracking banter between the local police-force's 'weird stuff' go-to-guy and his handler, D S Dougie Poole.

Hearn comes from a long line of occult detectives, such as Algernon Blackwood's John Silence, J. Sheridan LeFanu's Hesselius, William Hope Hodgson's Carnacki, even Dyson in some of the Arthur Machen tales, though Hearn's a more hard-boiled version of course. The other precedent is of course Joel Lane's unnamed police officer narrator who comes up against the *outré* in his 'weird detective' cycle of stories. Like certain of these, such as 'The Receivers' (2001), Simon's tale also has a strong political and social dimension.

John Howard's contribution is another tale in which stone comes to signify the hard realities that apparently only the poor must face in these difficult times of 'tough choices'. 'Falling into Stone' also calls into question the aesthetic mantra, 'less is more', by imagining it applied to economic affairs. I found this story disconcerting reading, when I realised that in my role as editor, trying to secure shorter and sharper stories made me an advocate of literary austerity according to this logic! I can only hope that my insistence on writers tightening their verbal belts has helped to make their tales more sharply honed weapons against austerity in the real world.

One story that benefits particularly from a brevity that was nothing to do with my editorial role was Joel's story, 'A Cry for Help', a reprint of a story that originally appeared in the *Fourth Black Book of Horror* (Mortbury Press, 2009), some time before the Coalition was even a twinkle in David Cameron's gimlet eye. In fact, this anthology series has a history of publishing stories about economic insecurity, from *Horror Uncut* contributor John Llewellyn Probert's urbane *conte cruelle* 'It Begins at Home' (2010), to historically-based pieces in volume Ten of the series (2013) that draw parallels between the hardships and hypocrisies of the past and those of the present, David Surface's 'The Last Testament of Jacob Tyler', a fine weird western about bitter class warfare, and Carl Thompson's 'The War Effort', exploring class tensions around war-time rationing.

'A Cry for Help', whose protagonist Carl is on his way to a conference in Harrogate on private healthcare, is not the only story Joel Lane wrote about the increasing privatisation of the NHS. His tale 'For Their own Ends', published a year or two later in *Black Static*, was written in response to Andrew Lansley's Health and Social Care Bill (still just a white paper at the time. It shows us the effects of the machinations depicted in 'Cry' through the eyes of a patient, though in a similar weird, dream-like way to 'Cry'. Three other stories in this volume explore different facets of the health carve-up pushed by the government. David Williamson's 'The Procedure' imagines the horrific implications of a health system run for profit, even for routine operations. Thana Niveau's 'No History of Violence' looks at the psychological effects of NHS cut-backs on mental health patients and their carers, and is no less shocking for that. Laura Mauro's '*Ptichka*' shows us what the government's measures against so-called 'health tourists' actually mean for people like the pregnant Russian woman in the story, and I should add that this part of the story is not fiction. Anyone who believes that the NHS is still free at the point of delivery take note: for migrants, it's no longer so.

Other stories, such as David Turnbull's 'The Privilege Card', Anna Taborska's 'The Lemmy / Trump Test', Andrew Hook's 'The Opaque District' and Alison Littlewood's 'The Ghost at the Feast' take place in a near-future Britain blighted by austerity. 'The Privilege Card' and 'The Ghost at the Feast' respond to the demonization of marginalised elements in society by the government and its supporters in the media, which have turned austerity from an expedient measure driven by temporary fiscal imperatives into a punitive moral crusade. This move to a state of permanent austerity seeks (and regrettably to some extent secures) the support of those it praises as 'hard-

239

working'. The protagonist of Alison Littlewood's story finds to his cost that his work ethic won't save him from the 'Square Footage Tax'. We also meet a hypocritical MP who styles himself a friend of the 'working man', particularly prescient in the light of the Tories' absurd and infuriating attempt to rebrand themselves as 'the Workers' Party'.

The 'SFT' is of course something of a parody of the 'Bedroom Tax'. Stephen Bacon's bleak and eerie ghost story, and John Forth's more visceral horror tale both tackle the subject by name. All three stories though deal with the way capitalist austerity measures turn the human need for shelter into a scarce commodity, something to be callously rationed and fought over. Other contributions like Anna Taborska's and Andrew Hook's show a similar thing happening to another basic human necessity: food, with more and more people becoming desperate enough to need food banks.

Andrew's 'The Opaque District' is particularly vivid in its description of the relentless war of all against all that characterises the kind of absolute 'free market' sought by the Conservative Right. The title is one that Joel Lane would have loved, and its treatment of the theme of a lost, mythical 'other' place put me in mind of Joel's renowned story 'The Country of Glass' (1998), as well as Peter Ackroyd's *The House of Doctor Dee* (1993).

While this story and many others use weird or supernatural elements to make their point, those of John Probert, Anna Taborska and Dave Williamson put the *conte cruelle* at the service of political satire. Anna's harrowing tale of survival 'Little Pig' presented us with the ultimate cruel choice. There is something of the trial by ordeal in 'The Lemmy / Trump Test', suggested by the horrifying exploits of Eighteenth Century gentlemen's clubs as well as the witch-hunts of the century before that. The result is something like *Saw* or *Hostel* meets the Bullingdon Club: grimly entertaining. Another cruel choice is the basis of John Probert's 'The Lucky Ones', suggesting what might happen if a kinky version of Roald Dahl's 'Man of the South' were left in charge of *Who Wants to be a Millionaire?*

Can horror change the way things are going?

The simple answer is of course, no. Only people can. But I'd like to think that some of these stories might be able to offer questions, if not answers. What happens if we get angry and fight back? If we restrict ourselves to passive protest, will the politicians ignore us or just laugh at us, like the MP in Alison Littlewood's story? If we resist more violently, will this just lead to madness, as in John Howard's or Thana Niveau's tales? But is this madness just the madness of futile, isolated gestures, when perhaps what's needed is collective action and self-organisation? And the other alternative? The madness of silent quiescence, or of trying to escape into a fantasy alternative reality where austerity never happened, as in the contributions of Andrew Hook and Stephen Bacon.

Perhaps, given that for infinitely sad reasons, Joel Lane is unable to help steer this book to its conclusion, he should have the last word, or rather words, from his 2011 story 'For Their Own Ends':

"They were pressed together like torn sheets of paper, crammed against the windows, unable to get through or be heard. At that moment, he realised it didn't matter how many of you there were. Without a voice, you were lost."

Contacts

If you have been affected by any of the issues raised in this book, here is short list of organisations campaigning against austerity (but not comprehensive!):

General Cuts and Austerity

Coalition of Resistance
Housman's Bookshop
5 Caledonian Road
London N1 9DX
Mob.: 07872 481769
Email: office@coalitionofresistance.org.uk

UK Uncut
Direct action group campaigning against cuts and corporate tax avoidance.
Tel: 07415 063 231
Email: ukuncut@gmail.com
Twitter: @ukuncut

Housing

Defend Council Housing
PO Box 33519
London
E2 9WW
http://www.defendcouncilhousing.org.uk/
Email: info@defendcouncilhousing.org.uk
0207 987 9899

No Bedroom Tax
Grass-roots campaign group organising against evictions arising from the 'bedroom tax'.
http://nobedroomtax.co.uk/
Mobile: 07765122829
Email: info@nobedroomtax.co.uk

Health

Keep Our NHS Public
Organisation campaigning against privatisation of the health service: http://www.keepournhspublic.com/

Social Security

Benefit Claimants Fight Back
Campaigns against ATOS 'work capability assessments' and other attacks on benefits.
http://benefitclaimantsfightback.wordpress.com/

Boycott Workfare
Campaign group consisting of various grass-roots local organisations, dedicated to stopping work-for-dole schemes, naming and shaming workfare providers and offering help and support to those forced onto such schemes:
http://www.boycottworkfare.org/
Tel: 07840 381195
Email: info@boycottworkfare.org

243

Education

University Anti-Privatisation Campaigns
Sussex: http://sussexagainstprivatization.wordpress.com/
Birmingham: http://www.defendeducationbrum.org/
Lancaster: http://nouclanprivatisation.wordpress.com/
Falmouth and Exeter:
http://falmouthexeterprotest.wordpress.com/

Migrant Support

National Coalition of Anti-Deportation Campaigns
http://www.ncadc.org.uk/
Registered office:
NCADC
Praxis Community Projects
Pott Street
London, E2 0EF
http://www.ncadc.org.uk/
Telephone: 0207 749 7616

No One Is Illegal
C/o Bolton Socialist Club
16 Wood Street
Bolton
http://www.noii.org.uk/
BL1 1DY
info@noii.org.uk

Acknowledgements

'A Cry for Help': © Joel Lane, 2009. Originally published in *The Fourth Black Book of Horror*, ed. Charles Black (Mortbury Press, 2009). Reprinted with kind permission of Ella Lane.

'The Battering Stone': © Simon Bestwick, 2006.

'The Ballad of Boom Town': © Priya Sharma, 2012. Originally appeared in *Black Static*, #28 (TTA Press, May-April 2012), and *The Best Horror of the Year*, Vol. 4, ed. Ellen Datlow (Night Shade Books, 2013). Reprinted with kind of permission of the author.

'The Lucky Ones': © John Llewellyn Probert, 2014.

'The Sun Trap': © Stephen Hampton, 2014.

'Only Bleeding': © Gary McMahon, 2014.

'The Lemmy / Trump Test': © Anna Taborska, 2014.

'Falling into Stone': © John Howard, 2014.

'Ptichka': © Laura Mauro, 2014.

'The Devil's Only Friend': © Stephen Bacon, 2014.

'The Procedure': © David Williamson, 2014.

'Pieces of Ourselves': © Rosanne Rabinowitz, 2014.

'A Simple Matter of Space': © John Forth, 2014.

'The Privilege Card': © David Turnbull, 2014.

'The Ghost at the Feast': © Alison Littlewood, 2014.

'The Opaque District': © Andrew Hook, 2014.

'No History of Violence': © Thana Niveau, 2014.

Thanks also to Ella Lane for permission to reprint an extract from 'For Their Own Ends', originally printed in *Black Static*, # 23 (TTA Press, June-July 2011), and for her help and support at what must have been a very difficult time.

Thanks to Gary McMahon for permission to quote Joel Lane's words from email correspondence between them.

Thanks also to Charles Black, Michael Kelly, Anna Schwarz, Andy Cox, and of course, Gary Fry for his support and help, as well as permission to quote from his story 'Capital Growth' (printed in *Terror Tales of London*, Gray Friar Press, 2013).